"You are the first woman—the first *lady*— who has looked at me like this in many years."

⌒⌒⌒∞⌒⌒⌒

"Like what?" Was that her voice, so soft, so husky?

"Like I am a man." He raised her hand to his cheek, pressed her palm there. "A man a lady would want for a lover."

"You're very much a man." She needed no guidance now, and let her fingers drift down the dusky flesh of his face, pausing at his mouth. "I can't imagine a woman alive who wouldn't want you."

His eyes flared at that, and he turned his head, catching one of her fingers between his lips. She let out a squeak of surprise and yanked her hand from his grasp. Was she mad, to be carrying on so in private with a man like Rathmore? Another moment, and she might end up beneath him on the sofa.

Might beg him to take her there.

Other **AVON ROMANCES**

Debra Mullins

A Necessary Bride

AVON BOOKS

An Imprint of HarperCollinsPublishers

This is a work of fiction. Names, characters, places, and incidents are products of the author's imagination or are used fictitiously and are not to be construed as real. Any resemblance to actual events, locales, organizations, or persons, living or dead, is entirely coincidental.

AVON BOOKS
An Imprint of HarperCollins*Publishers*
10 East 53rd Street
New York, New York 10022-5299

Copyright © 2003 by Debra Mullins
ISBN: 0-380-81909-0
www.avonromance.com

First Avon Books paperback printing: March 2003

Avon Trademark Reg. U.S. Pat. Off. and in Other Countries, Marca Registrada, Hecho en U.S.A.
HarperCollins® is a registered trademark of HarperCollins Publishers Inc.

Printed in the U.S.A.

10 9 8 7 6 5 4 3 2 1

For my sister,
Christine Mullins Logue,
who understands about deadlines:
Thanks for being there.

Chapter 1

Knightsbridge Chase, Devon
Late June 1816

The Earl of Rathmore came to the wedding.

No one noticed him at first. After all, the man wore black, and with his coal-black hair and the dark skin inherited from his French mother, he all but blended into the shadows at the rear of the Knightsbridge family chapel. Still, one would think that such a tall, handsome man would be noticed anywhere, but Rathmore had a way of standing very still, so still that one almost forgot he was there, except when those dark, dark eyes focused so intently on whatever drew his attention.

Or whomever.

Needless to say, Rathmore was all but invisible as he stood silently watching his childhood friend, the Earl of Knightsbridge, wed the lovely Lady Penelope Albright. Lady Farvendale, Lady Penelope's grandmother, was the first to notice him, and then only by the veriest chance when the long, curling feather from her hat happened to tickle her eye. She turned her head to blow the offending feather back into place and noticed the dark shadow that was Rathmore against the rear wall of the chapel.

A peculiar choking sound escaped her lips, drawing the attention of those around her. With a weak smile, she feigned a cough and returned her attention to the wedding. But moments later, her gaze once more strayed to the back of the chapel.

Lady Agatha Strathwaite, grandmother to the groom, noticed Lady Farvendale's preoccupation and followed her gaze. She frowned as she saw Rathmore, not in anger but more in puzzlement. Whatever was he doing here? What did he think to accomplish by coming to the wedding?

One by one, like ripples on a pond, heads turned. One would hardly know a wedding was going on with all the attention being paid to the far wall.

But then again, it was very rare that a murderer was invited to a wedding.

Miss Margaret Stanton-Lynch, granddaughter of the Duke of Raynewood and cousin to the groom, knew something was amiss when Reverend Starks stumbled over the vows. The vicar prided himself on the precision of his elocution, and he had no doubt practiced for the earl's marriage ceremony so many times that she was sure he murmured the words in his sleep. But stumble he did, substituting the word "life" for "wife," and then staring so intensely at the rear of the chapel that Meg was certain Lucifer himself must have arrived at the wedding.

But when she glanced behind her, she saw nothing to cause the reverend such consternation. All she saw was a tall, dark-haired man dressed impeccably in black, who gazed rather fiercely at the couple standing before the vicar. The man had the face of a fallen angel, long and lean with high cheekbones and a sensual mouth, so no doubt the reverend could be forgiven for imagining the devil had indeed attended the ceremony. But no, this was just a man, a wealthy one from the cut of his clothing, and while he was certainly a handsome specimen, she wasn't impressed. She'd learned the hard way that a kind heart did not necessarily accompany such good looks.

Though his *was* an attractive face. She pondered the matter for a moment, studying the stranger's aristocratic visage as if he were some majestic work of art. Perhaps sensing her scrutiny, he looked over, locking his dark gaze on her with the same ferocity with which he had regarded the bridal couple. She didn't look away, not even when a shiver of attraction rippled through her. Instead she smiled at him and nodded politely.

She turned back to the ceremony, but out of the

corner of her eye, she glimpsed the incredulity that flashed across his face before his perfect features tightened into a scowl.

She paid him no mind. She had seen his like before, men so handsome and so charismatic that they attracted women like flies to honey. Well, she wouldn't be dazzled. No doubt the fellow had expected her to blush and stammer in response to being noticed by a man of his magnificence. It wasn't going to happen.

No, the man who turned Meg Lynch's head would have to prove himself more than good-looking and well bred. He would have to be a man of sound moral stamp who cared more for other people than he did for his wardrobe.

Except for her cousin Knightsbridge, she had yet to meet such a man in England.

But as people continued to glance back at the stranger against the far wall, as they continued to whisper, she wondered if she would see him at the wedding breakfast.

Justin St. James, Earl of Rathmore, ignored the stares of the congregation. Let them stare. Let them whisper. He had expected it.

The whispering grew slowly, like a stirring in the leaves of a tree. Clothing rustled as people turned to glance back at him. He looked back impassively. Let them think what they would. He knew why he was there.

He tried to focus on the bride and groom, but a

movement drew his attention to a dark-haired young woman sitting at the front of the chapel. The gel was studying him as if he were a butterfly on a pin. It unsettled him, the way she contemplated him so analytically. He gave her his fiercest stare, the one that had caused Miss Prudence Gunn to swoon at the one and only soirée he had attended since he had returned to England. But this girl did not swoon. Nor did she blush, titter, or flirt.

She smiled at him.

He couldn't have been more stunned if she'd pulled out a pistol and shot him. And then after she smiled at him, she had the audacity to turn back to the wedding as if she had forgotten his existence.

His brows snapped together, and he found himself growing unreasonably annoyed. Was the girl mad? Or was she simply foolish? There had to be something wrong with her, some defect that made her smile at him in front of an entire church of people. Had she no care for her reputation? Didn't she realize who he *was*?

He kept an eye on the intriguing brunette, so caught up in his thoughts that he almost didn't realize that the murmuring of the congregation had slowly risen to the level of a lively hive of bees. When the disturbance became so loud as to be noticeable, the reverend frowned and raised his voice as he said the words that would seal the union of the couple before him.

Suddenly the wedding was over, and Knightsbridge turned to proudly present his lovely bride to the congregation. Rathmore knew the exact moment the groom spotted him. A smile of pure pleasure transformed Knightsbridge's features.

Damn it all. He was trapped.

He couldn't leave now. He would have to follow through and make an appearance at the wedding breakfast. Only then could he slip quietly away to obscurity—which was where society preferred him anyway—and attempt to continue his impossible quest.

Blasted gossips, he thought with a glare at the busybodies cramming the pews. And damn that black-haired chit for distracting him until it was too late to take his leave.

Champagne and good wishes flowed in equal plenty at the wedding breakfast. Lady Knightsbridge blushed and looked adoringly at her new husband. Knightsbridge appeared proud enough to pop the fastenings of his coat. Rathmore stood alone in the corner of the room, his face remote, a glass of champagne forgotten in his hand.

Not a soul spoke to him.

He hadn't expected anything different. He would stay only long enough to satisfy convention, and then he would take his leave. Not that a man with his reputation should give a fig about convention, but he would not have it said that the Devil Earl, as society called him now, had ruined Knightsbridge's wedding. So conventional he would be, at least for today.

He scanned the crowd, noting that the usual overly plump country gentry and their equally well-fed wives had all attended the affair. Fashionably dressed young bloods, some of whom he had once counted among his friends, ignored his existence. Stone-faced matrons looked past him when he chanced to gaze on them, and the delicate flowers they guarded, this year's crop of marriageable virgins, all blushed and giggled and pretended not to see him.

All but one.

There she was, the dark-haired girl from the chapel. And she was staring at him again, a slight frown between her slim black brows, her lush bottom lip caught between her teeth. She tapped her glass of lemonade with one finger and didn't seem at all disconcerted to discover him looking at her. Instead, she nodded at him, and her expression changed from concentration to determination. She began to make her way toward him.

She was daft. She had to be. Only a madwoman would approach the Earl of Rathmore in full view of all of society.

But if she was a madwoman, she was a beautiful one.

She moved through the crowd like a swan across a lake, all grace and slender beauty. Her skin was the palest white, making a sharp contrast to her ink-black hair, though the gentle rose of good health graced her cheeks. Her pale blue morning dress emphasized her unusual coloring as well as her sweetly curved body. Rathmore found his gaze drifting to her breasts—just a bit more ample than one would expect for so slender a girl—before he jerked his attention back up to her face. As she reached his side, he noticed that her eyes were the same shade of blue as a lake on a clear summer day, and when she smiled, adorable dimples creased her cheeks.

His own romantic thoughts shocked him. Dear God, had solitude turned him into some maudlin poet? She was just a girl, and a bold one at that.

"Hello," she said when she had reached his side. "I'm Meg, the groom's cousin. And you are . . . ?"

Her accent gave her away. Not daft, then. Just American.

"Rathmore," he replied after a moment. Then he waited.

She didn't freeze in terror. She didn't run screaming from the room. She smiled at him. Again.

"Is that your title?" she asked. "I've noticed that most English gentlemen prefer to be called by their titles."

"It is." He peered at her curiously. Intelligence lurked in those guileless blue eyes, but she obviously had the survival instincts of an infant. Still, at least she was talking to him. Standing abandoned like a bloody pariah was not a way to keep wagging tongues from tainting Knightsbridge's wedding day.

He sipped champagne, biding his time. No doubt someone would come fetch the girl at any moment, once they realized to whom she was speaking. "You're American, aren't you?"

"I suppose my accent gave me away," she said with a laugh.

"You'd be right." Her laugh was lower than he expected, huskier. Sensual. "How long have you been in England?"

"Since the beginning of the Season." She blinked those lovely blue eyes and smiled with a crease of dimples. "I don't recall seeing you about."

"I've been out of the country."

"How exciting! I love to travel, though so far I've only been here to England, and of course, to America."

"Of course." He glanced around. No rampaging mama in sight. No irate husband or furious brother. "And you say you are Knightsbridge's cousin?"

"Second cousin. Or is it third?" She shrugged, sending her dark curls shifting over her shoulders. "I can never keep such things straight, but every Englishman I've ever met can recite his family tree back to the Conqueror." She paused, pursing her lips as she regarded him thoughtfully. "May I ask you a very rude question?"

"Certainly," he replied, fascinated despite himself.

"Who are you? I've noticed that no one but me has come forward to speak to you. Have you been gone so long that no one remembers you?"

He gave a grim smile. "Oh, they remember me."

"It must be your looks," she mused, once more tapping her finger against her lemonade glass. "You're very fierce-looking, you know."

"Am I?" He sipped his champagne, surreptitiously scanning the room. Still, no one came to fetch her.

"I'm certain you know it. Your eyes are so dark they're almost black."

As was his heart, if society was to be believed. "My mother was French," was all he said.

"My mother was Irish," she said. "I wonder if I win."

He glanced at her, and her impish grin encouraged his lips to curl in response. "Win what?"

"Win the prize for being the most disreputable. I've often been told by gentlemen that they would be willing to overlook my unfortunate Irish heritage should I do them the great honor of marrying them. No doubt the dowry my grandfather has settled on me would cancel out such a blemish on my acceptability. But given the recent war, perhaps being half French is even worse than being half Irish. What do you think?"

He stared at her for a long moment, and then he burst out laughing, drawing the attention of everyone in the room.

No irate papa rushed forward to rip her from his clutches. No incensed suitors threatened him with dawn appointments. He saw Knightsbridge glance over and smile at them, but that was all.

And he was glad for it.

He glanced back at Meg. Who was this girl? How was it she could stand and talk to a man society had condemned without damaging her own reputation? She was either a paragon of society or else had committed some sin far worse than his.

He leaned toward the former.

Captivated, he asked, "Where does a woman like you come from?"

"America." Her blue eyes twinkled with mirth.

And he laughed again.

Meg smiled as Rathmore's booming laugh echoed throughout the room. It sounded as if he hadn't had much laughter in his life, and she was glad she had amused him. There was something about him that called to her, a loneliness that she knew all too well.

She saw the way he kept looking around, as if he expected someone to come and drag her away from him. Obviously he was not a favorite in the Polite World. She wondered if he was new to society. Or poor. Or, God help him, in trade.

When he looked behind her again, she couldn't take it anymore.

"If you are looking for my chaperone," she announced, "look no further than the bridegroom."

His brows arched in surprise. "Knightsbridge is your duenna?"

"For the moment." She looked down at her glass, a pang of worry going through her. "My grandfather is quite ill, so he did not attend. And Lady Agatha, who usually accompanies me, has suffered a dizzy spell and gone upstairs to rest. She's not as young as she thinks she is."

"I'm sorry to hear your grandfather is unwell. And your chaperone." The sympathy in his voice smoothed over the ache in her heart.

She sighed. "Grandfather seemed fine at the beginning of the Season, when Garrett came, but after Garrett married Lucinda and went back to America, Grandfather grew very ill and has not left Raynewood Abbey since."

Rathmore grew very still. "And who is your grandfather, Meg?"

"The Duke of Raynewood," she replied. "Lady Agatha, his sister, is—"

"—Knightsbridge's grandmother," Rathmore finished for her.

"Which is why we're cousins."

"And who is Garrett?"

"My brother. He married Lucinda Devering, and they went back to America. They're coming back in March for the Season."

Rathmore set his glass down on a nearby table. "Meg, you should not be talking to me."

"Nonsense," she said with a wave of her hand. "I know that under most circumstances, unmarried girls do not talk to gentlemen alone, but we are hardly alone in front of an entire room of people."

"You don't understand." He hesitated. "I am not the sort of man your grandfather would want you to be talking to."

"If you are so terrible, how did you get invited to the wedding?" she challenged.

"Knightsbridge and I were boyhood friends. My estate adjoins his."

"Are you a rake?" she demanded. "A fortune hunter?"

"Of course not." Irritation edged his tone. "Miss . . . Meg, please trust me when I tell you that you risk your good name by being seen with me."

"My name is Miss Stanton-Lynch," she said, "but Meg is just fine. And as long as you do not intend to break my heart or steal my fortune, then Grandfather would have no objection to my talking to you."

"You might be surprised."

Before she could reply, a servant approached them with a note in hand. "Your pardon, Lord Rathmore, but this just arrived for you." With a bow, the servant withdrew.

Rathmore ripped open the note. A ripple of concern crossed his face, and Meg had to force herself not to peek at the missive over his shoulder. Then he looked up, and his face was shuttered and polite.

"Is it bad news?"

"Emily—my ward—has run away." He crumpled the note in his hand. "If you will excuse me, I must take my leave of the bride and groom."

His distress was a palpable thing, for all that he tried to hide it. She laid a hand on his arm. "I hope you find her quickly."

"So do I." He sketched a bow, then left her to bid

farewell to Knightsbridge and Penelope. His duty done, he didn't look at her again as he left the room.

She nibbled her lower lip as she watched him leave. What a fascinating man. And those dark eyes. Goodness, but her heart still fluttered in her breast, even though he had already quit the room. Who exactly was he? And why was such a handsome and charming gentleman so obviously shunned by society?

"My word, Miss Stanton-Lynch, are you all right?" Lady Farvendale, clad head-to-toe in her favorite shade of purple, hurried to her side. "Did that man say anything to upset you?"

"Of course not." Meg sipped her lemonade to hide her annoyance at the woman's assumption. "Lord Rathmore was most pleasant."

"He'd better have behaved himself." The dowager clasped a jewel-beringed hand to her ample bosom. "I don't know what possessed Lord Knightsbridge to invite such a person to my dear Penelope's wedding. It's all I could do not to swoon when I saw him in the chapel."

"Why?" Meg asked flippantly. "Is he in trade?"

"No, dear." Lady Farvendale fixed serious gray eyes on Meg's face. "He's a murderer."

"Oh." Meg blinked. "Well, I guess he wins after all."

Chapter 2

Rathmore Hall, Devon
Two weeks later

Emily St. James slouched in her chair, her posture the very picture of misunderstood youth. Her light brown hair was tousled, the ribbon hung askew, and the hem of her dress was ripped and soiled. Her lovely shoes were covered in mud. And had they been pistols, her blue eyes would have shot him dead on the spot.

Rathmore dared show no weakness in the face of her defiance. He remembered Emily as a sweet child with ringlets in her hair whose laughter had warmed the cold rooms of Rathmore Hall. Much had changed in the six years of his exile. Somehow his adorable godchild had metamorphosed into the rebellious half woman before him.

15

And her mission in life seemed to be to drive him to madness.

"Emily, I have told you before that it is forbidden for you to leave the hall without proper escort," he scolded, keeping his features impassive. Lord knew, the child had a way of twisting his every word and expression. "Something could happen to you, and no one would know until it's too late."

"Nothing's going to happen to me," Emily retorted. "I've been running around the estate since I was a baby."

"I'm aware of that." Rathmore forced himself to speak reasonably, though he longed to throttle her when she used that snobbish tone of voice. "But things have changed. You're a young lady now, not a little girl. And you need to act like a young lady."

"Why, so you can marry me off and get rid of me?" She jumped to her feet. "I'm never getting married! You can't make me!"

He winced as her voice hit a particularly shrill note. "Sit down, young lady."

She crossed her arms across her muddy frock. "I choose to stand."

"Fine. Then I will stand, too." Rathmore rose, his full height of just over six feet making him tower over his ward. "From now on, if you wish to ride, you will take a groom with you."

"Or what?" She tilted her chin in challenge.

"Or you will not be allowed to ride anymore."

Her mouth fell open. "You can't do that! Guinevere is *my* horse, and I can ride her whenever I like!"

He raised his eyebrows. "Actually, Rathmore Hall and everything on its lands belongs to *me*."

She narrowed her eyes at him. "I hate you."

"You're not the first." He heard the weariness in his voice, and apparently Emily did as well. Her mutinous expression softened for an instant, and he could swear that he saw a glint of affection in her eyes. He wanted to reach out to her, to touch the heart of the joyous child she had once been. But he didn't dare. All he had to recommend him these days was his ability to raise Emily well and teach her to become the lady she had been born to be. Nothing could interfere with that. It was all he had left.

"Now go to your room until it's time for dinner," he said, and watched the glimmer of warmth disappear from her expression.

She glared at him for a long moment, her blue eyes slits of malevolence above her adorably freckled nose. Then she pointed that nose in the air, spun on her heel, and marched from the room with an outraged dignity any martyr would envy.

As soon as the door closed behind her, Rathmore sank into his chair and wearily rubbed a hand over his face. He would rather face the scorn of a thousand society matrons than deal with the emotional ups and downs of this female creature who resembled the beloved godchild he remembered.

Two weeks ago she had scared him to death when she had run away from home. He had left

Knightsbridge's wedding and managed to intercept her just before she caught the mail coach to London. She had scared off five governesses in the past several weeks with her wild antics, and now she thought she could ride anywhere on the estate without a word to anyone. And if anybody corrected her behavior—especially him—she responded by doing something even more outrageous.

Once she had adored him. Once she had wanted nothing more than to spend all her time with him. How he longed for those days.

His relationship with Emily was just one more casualty of Ophelia's murder.

He sat in his chair, letting his head fall back in weariness. Sometimes he was just sick of all of it. How long did a man have to pay for a crime, especially one he hadn't committed in the first place? Due to lack of evidence, he hadn't been charged with Ophelia's murder, but his family had banished him from England nonetheless to hush up the scandal. Whether he was innocent or not mattered little. Society believed he had indeed murdered his cousin's fiancée, and therefore it must be so.

For six years he had roamed the world, never able to come home to the green hills of England. And with the war going on, he couldn't even seek refuge in his mother's native land. So he had gone elsewhere: India, Africa, the West Indies, America. And he had prospered. But always he had longed to come home to England.

He glanced up at the portrait of the previous earl hanging above the mantel. His uncle, Alfred St. James, had truly believed him guilty of the crime. As had Alfred's son and heir, Desmond. After the death of his fiancée, Desmond had been only too happy to see him banished from England. At the time, Rathmore used to wonder how spiteful Desmond had managed to father a child as sweet as Emily—but lately he had started to notice a family resemblance.

Just over a year ago, when his uncle and cousin had both died in a tavern fire on the way back from grouse hunting in Scotland, he had inherited the title, as well as guardianship of young Emily. Eagerly had he returned to England and Rathmore Hall, only to discover that sweet, six-year-old Emily had changed into a moody and intractable twelve-year-old, and that society had forgotten nothing.

Oh, he had tried to dismiss the rumors. When the first invitation had arrived, he had eagerly attended, hoping that his hosts had decided to ignore the talk and believe in his innocence.

Foolish.

He had been invited as a curiosity, to be stared at and whispered about. Young ladies swooned at the sight of him, matrons glared as if he were the devil incarnate, and men watched him warily, as if he would reach out and choke the life out of the nearest of them merely for entertainment. He had not accepted any more invitations until Knightsbridge had begged him to come to his wedding. And he had attended that function only because of his friend's loyalty during the scandal. Algie had never believed him guilty, bless his cheerful soul.

But the Polite World *did* believe him a murderer. And his own family—Desmond and Uncle Alfred—had gone to their graves believing him guilty. He fisted his hands. *How could you think such a thing?* he railed silently. Had his French blood been such an anathema to his own family that they would so easily believe speculation over his own word? *Uncle Alfred . . . Desmond, surely you knew me better than that?*

With effort, he pushed the hurt aside. He had Emily to think about now. What sort of future would the girl have as the ward of a murderer? No one but the hungriest of fortune hunters would pursue her hand, and she deserved better than that. While she made his life a living hell right now, he knew that somewhere inside the sulky young girl was the sweet child he had so adored. And he would do right by her.

But first he had to prove his innocence.

Raynewood Abbey, Hampshire
The same day

Meg stared at her grandfather in dismay. "But I want to come with you."

The old duke shook his head slowly, and Meg despaired at the feebleness of the movement. Only months ago, her grandfather had been striding through the halls of Raynewood Abbey, barking orders at the servants and going head-to-head in verbal battles with her brother, Garrett. But in a few short weeks, the duke's illness, which he had managed to conceal from all of them for so long, became so consuming that he now looked every day of his eighty-five years.

"You're young, Margaret," he rasped. "And you have done nothing but care for me since the Season ended. You should be out in society. You should be dancing and mixing with people your own age."

"I went to Algie's wedding," she pointed out. "I mixed with plenty of young people. Now I want to go to Bath with you and Aunt Agatha. There are people my age there."

Again the duke shook his head. "You have turned down many invitations in favor of caring for an old man, Margaret, and while my heart appreciates your attention, I cannot be selfish." He coughed, then remained still, wheezing for a moment, before continuing. "I am going to Bath to take the waters for my health, not to socialize. You will stay in Devon at Knightsbridge Chase and visit with your cousin and his new bride, now that they are back from their wedding trip. Lady Penelope will look after you."

"But what about you?"

"Agatha can see to my needs."

"But—"

"I don't want you to see me like this, child!" he roared. His near-black eyes glittered with some of his former arrogance in his pale, thin face. "Please do as I ask. Go to Knightsbridge Chase. Spend a month or so attending house parties and local fêtes with Lady Penelope. It will lift my spirits to know that you are enjoying your youth instead of locking yourself away with an old, sick man like me." He leaned forward. "Do this for me, Margaret."

She couldn't resist the plea. "Are you certain, Grandfather?"

"You're a dear child to want to help," he answered, "but my mind is settled on this."

"Then I will do as you ask." She came to him and pressed a kiss to his frail cheek. "But I will miss you."

He patted her hand. "And I you, my dear. But this is for the best. Now off with you. I'm certain you have much to do to prepare for your holiday."

Since she could see he was tiring, Meg obeyed her grandfather and left the study, but she paused just outside the doors. Tears stung her eyes. She was losing him. Every day the Duke of Raynewood grew weaker. She feared that one day she would come seeking him, only to find that he had faded completely away. She had only just gotten to know her grandfather in recent months; she didn't want to lose him so soon.

One of the footmen walked by, and Meg quickly swiped away the tears with the back of her hand. Keeping her face averted from the staff, she walked swiftly down the hall and slipped into the library.

The room smelled of books and beeswax. Wandering over to the window that overlooked Raynewood's spectacular rose garden, she stared blindly out at the sunny summer day. The beauty of England never ceased to amaze her, and yet sometimes she ached so much to see the familiar wharves of Boston again. She missed her brother, Garrett, and she missed her new sister-in-law, Lucinda. Even though her life back on Boston had been far from perfect, it was still home.

And at least there she wouldn't be forced to sit by helplessly and watch her grandfather die.

Living as the debutante granddaughter of the Duke of Raynewood was much more restrictive than living as the sister of Captain Garrett Lynch. The beautiful clothes and grand balls had seemed exciting at first, but the thrill had quickly begun to wane. Sometimes she thought if one more gentleman complimented her on the shade of her eyes, she would scream.

Though her grandfather had once claimed that he loved the color of her eyes.

She had to get past this. Ruthlessly suppressing her grief, she forced herself to think of something else—anything else. But everything that came into her mind seemed trivial in comparison.

If she could only help . . .

With a sigh, she sat down on a nearby settee and idly watched a sparrow hop through the branches of the shrubbery just outside the window. Everyone around her seemed to have a place or a purpose. Her grandfather the duke had his title. Her brother, Garrett, had his shipping business, as well as the courtesy title bestowed on him as the duke's heir. Lucinda had her place as Garrett's wife. Knights-bridge, Penelope, even Lady Agatha all had a place or a purpose.

But Meg had none.

She had thought to contribute to the family by helping her grandfather, but it seemed that when-ever she tried to help, someone was shooing her off. Now they were shipping her off to Devon to stay with Algie and Penelope instead of letting her do her part to care for her grandfather. Balls? Fêtes? How was she supposed to go off and be merry while her grandfather was dying? Did they really think her so shallow? Did they really see her as nothing more than a decoration? Just a pretty young woman who served no useful purpose?

Unacceptable. There had to be something mean-ingful she could do with her life. Something that was purely Meg. Something she could turn to when life became too restrictive.

She had liked the city of Boston, but if she went back there, her brother would oversee her life as if she were a babe all over again. She would be noth-ing more than Garrett Lynch's sister. She would have nothing of her own, standing on the outside of Garrett and Lucinda's happy marriage.

She liked living in England, but if she stayed here, her grandfather would expect her to marry some English peer. And because she loved him so, she would do it.

Though she longed to someday have a husband and children, she had always intended to fall in love with her mate. And the *last* thing she wanted was an English husband, one who was no doubt unaccustomed to freethinking American women. By law, an English husband would control her money and her body, and no one could stop him from abusing either. She had seen it time and again throughout her stay here. An English husband would leave her to wither on some country estate while he entertained his mistresses in London. Again she would have nothing of her own, except the loneliness that would smother her.

Somehow she needed to find her own path.

"Margaret, are you in here?" The door clicked open, and Meg hastily wiped the last vestiges of her distress from her cheeks as her great-aunt, Lady Agatha Strathwaite, entered the room. A plump, diminutive woman with snow-white hair, Lady Agatha had a propensity for odd-colored clothing, a lamentable habit that nonetheless did nothing to detract from her impressive social eminence. To-day's morning dress was a peculiar shade of mustard yellow that was accented by three ropes of pink pearls, a combination that made Meg think of a bowl of fruit, all pears and grapes.

"There you are, child," Lady Agatha said. "Whatever are you doing in this stuffy library on such a lovely day?"

"I was just thinking." Meg wanted to believe that she had hidden her worry rather well, but Lady Agatha had very sharp eyes for a woman of her eighty-seven years. She sat beside Meg on the settee and patted her hand.

"There now, my dear. You've been to see my brother, haven't you?"

Meg nodded, the tears once more welling up despite her will. "I just hate to see him like this," she whispered.

"Old age isn't a pretty sight," Lady Agatha agreed with a resigned sigh. "And heaven knows, it doesn't feel that wonderful, either. But it's a fact of life, my dear. Just like birth. Just like death."

"Don't even mention death! I don't want Grandfather to die, not when I've just found him!"

Lady Agatha chuckled. "Don't plan the funeral just yet, Margaret. My brother is as stubborn as they come. It's a Stanton family trait. If there's a way to cheat death, Erasmus will find it."

"I just wish he would let me come with you to Bath. I hate being left behind."

"You know your grandfather hates you seeing him so ill. It's better that you spend these next few weeks with my grandson and his new bride."

"I just want to help!" Meg stood and paced to the window. "Aunt Agatha, I couldn't do anything for my mother when she was dying except watch her drift away. And now I've just gotten to know Grandfather, and he is so ill . . . I'm a grown woman now. I just feel that if I could *do* something, make some sort of difference—" Her words trailed off as emotion choked her into silence.

"There's nothing you can do," Lady Agatha said gently, "except what he asks of you."

Meg shook her head. "I can hardly go gaily about my life, attending parties and the like, when I know how ill he is. Even if I stay with Algie and Penelope, I'll still worry about him."

"Margaret, listen to me." Lady Agatha's stern tone drew a surprised look from Meg. "You cannot let him see how worried you are. He is a proud man. He wants the best for you. If you want to make him happy, then marry well and settle here in England to raise your children."

"Marry!" Meg gaped at her aunt. "As if I can think of love at a time like this!"

Lady Agatha chuckled. "No one said anything about love, dear."

"I can't even think of marrying a man I don't love. That's not how things are done in America."

"But that's often how things are done in England," Lady Agatha pointed out. "A young girl's duty to her family is to marry well."

"What about a girl's duty to herself? Aunt Agatha, if I marry, Meg Lynch will cease to exist. She will disappear into the identity of one more society wife."

Agatha shook her head. "Not necessarily. There is power in marriage, dear girl. And more freedom than you know."

Meg shrugged away the words. "I want to do

something with my life, something that only I can do and no one else."

"Marriage can be a very satisfying thing for both parties involved. A man needs a wife to bear his children. A woman needs a husband to provide for her. Everyone gets what they want."

"That's not what *I* want." Meg clenched her fists. "I want to be more than the extension of a man. More than a possession. There must be something else I can do, something more to my existence."

"Think on marriage," Lady Agatha said, rising from the settee. "In the end, that's what most girls choose."

Meg watched the elderly lady exit the room. "But I'm not most girls," she whispered. "That's what no one understands."

Chapter 3

Devon
One week later

Lady Denniston's Midsummer Ball was one of the most popular events in Devon. She always held the affair in mid-July in an effort to alleviate the tedium of summer with a bit of sophistication. Anyone who was anyone was invited to the event, which promised to be a terrible crush. But no one ever thought to refuse the invitation.

Meg had been at the ball merely an hour, and already she was bored. She had danced with several eligible gentlemen, none of whom wanted to have a conversation of more depth than the exact shade of her eyes or whether the temperature would climb higher the following day. When she considered that she could have been in Bath helping her grandfather, she wanted to scream with frustration.

Instead she stood in an overcrowded ballroom that was so hot that two young ladies had already fainted, and she watched the dancers take their places for yet another set. Among them were Knightsbridge and his bride, Lady Penelope.

During her come-out, Penelope had been dubbed Perfect Penelope because of her flawless blond beauty and faultless manners. The fact that she was the daughter of an earl and possessed a substantial dowry had only added to the image of the perfect English debutante.

Knightsbridge was also blond, though his hair was much darker than Penelope's. He had inherited the slashing dark brows and bold nose shared by Meg's grandfather and brother, but his green eyes and cheerful personality came from his father's side of the family.

As newlyweds, Algie and Penelope were completely besotted with each other. Very often—as now—they would stare into each other's eyes and forget anyone else was in the room. Meg had almost gotten used to it, but she had to admit, she had felt rather like a fifth wheel on a four-wheeled carriage ever since arriving at Knightsbridge Chase two days ago.

Oh, the newlyweds never meant to exclude her. But sometimes they would get lost in each other and forget Meg was even present. Other times they would disappear together for long periods of time, leaving Meg to her own devices. Even tonight, as they had made their way down the receiving line to greet their host and hostess, the Knightsbridges had momentarily forgotten that Meg was with them and had started into the ballroom without her. Luckily they had remembered her existence at the last minute and waited, thus allowing the three of them to enter together.

Meg didn't resent Algie and Penelope their preoccupation with each other. After all, since they were so newly married—and a love match to boot—it was to be expected. But the whole experience made her only more determined to find something to fill her time. She couldn't go through life hanging on the fringes of her family like a loose thread on a favorite shirt.

"Miss Stanton-Lynch!" a young male voice called.

She winced. She had been so caught up in her musings that Mr. Edward Barrington, her partner for this set, had come upon her without her noticing. Barrington was a harmless sort. Indeed, as he executed his bow with a flourish, she fancied that his big ears and bushy hair reminded her of a large, overly eager puppy.

"Good evening, Mr. Barrington," she said, forcing a smile.

"This is our dance, Miss Stanton-Lynch," he told her with enthusiasm. "And might I say, that dress certainly brings out your eyes. Like sapphires they are."

She resisted rolling those sapphire eyes with great effort. His reddened complexion and overly bright gaze made her wonder if he had been sampling a bit too much champagne. And suddenly she just couldn't dance with him. Couldn't listen to another vapid social conversation while smiling until her face hurt.

Not without going insane.

"Please do forgive me, Mr. Barrington," she said as sweetly as she could, "but it is so frightfully hot in here that I'm afraid I might swoon if I try to dance. Would you be so kind as to fetch me a glass of punch?"

Mr. Barrington's brown eyes widened. "You want me to fetch you some punch? Of course, I shall do so at once! And then I shall sit with you while you drink it!" After another sweeping bow, the boy bounded toward the punch bowl.

And Meg headed toward the terrace and slipped through the French doors with a sigh of relief.

He probably shouldn't have come.

Rathmore entered the ballroom, ignoring the momentary hush that had followed the announcement of his name. He skillfully lifted a glass of champagne from the tray of a passing servant and then made his way to the sidelines so he could scan the crowd for the man he had come to seek. Originally he had not intended to attend Lady Denniston's ball, but then he had learned that Lord and Lady Aggerly would be in attendance.

Both of them had been present at the house party six years ago when Ophelia had died.

He knew a great deal about the Aggerlys. He had spent the years of his exile collecting information about the other guests present at that long-ago house party, and his intelligence had revealed a very interesting fact. Of all the guests, only three had no solid proof of their whereabouts at the time of Ophelia's death.

One of these was Lord Aggerly.

Rathmore had some questions for the blustering lord, which was his only reason for attending Lady Denniston's affair.

His hostess had all but had the vapors when Rathmore had darkened her door. She *had* invited him; she just clearly hadn't expected him to come. But the lady had kept her wits about her and welcomed him, leaving him to prowl the sidelines, trying to find old Aggerly and his lady in the sea of bodies jamming the ballroom.

Fifteen minutes later he had discovered two things: Aggerly had not yet arrived, and no one wanted to associate with the Devil Earl.

Weary of the stares and the whispered conversations that stopped abruptly when he came near, he turned and stalked toward the terrace. Maybe he could wait for Aggerly there in peace.

As he stepped outside, he lifted his face in appreciation of the coolness that was such a contrast to the overheated ballroom. The night was beautifully clear. Stars dotted the ink-dark heavens, and a crescent moon hung like a pendant in the sky.

A scraping sound from farther down on the terrace drew his attention. "Who's there?" he asked softly.

"I am." Following the quiet words, a young lady stepped out of the shadows. Dark hair fell in graceful curls over ivory shoulders, and he caught a glimpse of light-colored eyes before she ducked her head. "Forgive me, my lord. I will just go back inside."

"Wait a moment," he said when she would have rushed past him. "I know you. We met at Knightsbridge's wedding."

"Yes, we did." For some reason she would not look him in the eye. She folded her hands in front of her, twisting her fingers together. "Now if you will excuse me . . ."

"I don't remember you being so meek," he said with a frown. "Miss Stanton-Lynch, isn't it?"

She stiffened. "Yes, that's my name, my lord."

He scowled. He remembered the lovely brunette as a friendly prattlebox with a wicked sense of humor. Why was she acting like a wet goose now? "Come over here," he said, his bemusement making his voice rougher than he intended.

She hesitated for an instant, then took one tentative step toward him. Her diffidence added to his already frayed temper. "For pity's sake, girl, I'm not going to eat you!"

Her head shot up, and he got a clear look at her eyes.

Fear.

It was like a punch in the gut. This girl, who three weeks ago had been the only one brave enough to walk up to him at Knightsbridge's wedding and talk to him, was afraid of him.

Something broke inside him. How much was a man supposed to take? Society's ostracism, Emily's rebellion, the frustration of not being able to prove his honor—he had weathered them all with stoicism. But this one thing, the fact that this girl who had been so bright and beautiful in his presence only three weeks ago now feared him, all but broke his heart.

What made him think he could do this, any of it? Solve a six-year-old murder? Raise a girl to become a young lady? Was he daft?

He couldn't look at her, at those beautiful blue eyes that had laughed at him only weeks before and now held a wariness he could barely stand.

Turning his back, he muttered, "Never mind. You had better go back inside." And he braced himself for the sound of her retreating footsteps.

Meg had recognized the Earl of Rathmore the instant he had stepped out onto the terrace. He looked fearsome in the moonlight, his sensual features seemingly carved from cold marble, his eyes dark and searching. When she had first seen him at Knightsbridge's wedding, she had ignored his formidable appearance because she had fancied that he needed a friend. But now she couldn't help but admit that he did look like Lucifer unleashed, savagely beautiful yet with an edge to him that seemed to defy basic goodness.

His dark coloring, chiseled bone structure, and black evening clothes fed her lurid imagination, especially when she remembered what was being said about him.

A murderer. Never proven, but considered dangerous. And she was out on the terrace alone with him.

She had thought if she acted the mouse, then he would let her pass. And her plan had worked. He had just told her to go back inside . . . yet the pain in his voice held her where she was.

Could he be a murderer? No one had ever proven anything. And Meg couldn't forget the concern on his face the day she had met him, when he had received word that his ward had run away. Surely a murderer wouldn't feel such love for a child?

She stared at his stiff back. Despite his reputation, she really had no reason to fear him. There was no evidence that he had killed anyone, only gossip. And he was still invited to events, which meant that he wasn't totally ostracized. And Algie had asked him to attend the wedding.

Good Lord, what had she done? Had she insulted an innocent man?

She cleared her throat, took a step toward him. "How is your ward, my lord?"

He spun to face her, astonishment clear on his face. "What did you say?"

"I asked about your ward." She swallowed hard, her heart thundering in her chest. "The last time we met, you had to leave rather suddenly because your ward had run away."

"Yes." The word hung in the air between them. He tilted his head to look at her curiously, his eyes fathomless. "My ward. Yes, we found her. She's safe at home."

"That's good news. I had wondered." Meg placed a hand over her racing heart and took another step closer.

"Is something the matter?" The deep tones of his voice vibrated over her, sending a shiver through her body. He really was a beautiful man, and his presence—especially the aura of danger about him—had a seductive effect on her.

"I'm simply overheated from the dancing." She smiled politely despite her pounding pulse, and when he smiled back, her heart leaped again.

Control, Meg.

"It is revoltingly hot inside, isn't it, Miss Stanton-Lynch? Much cooler out here."

"Quite so. But my lord, must we talk about the weather?"

She could tell she'd startled him. "Not at all. What would you like to talk about?"

She took a deep breath. "I've heard the rumors about you, my lord. Are they true?"

He froze. Not a muscle moved, not so much as an eyelash. His dark eyes bored into hers, fierce emotion churning in their depths.

"That," he said softly, "is a very bold question, Miss Stanton-Lynch."

"Perhaps." She swallowed. What if the rumors *were* true? What if he tossed her over the railing right now and then went back inside to dance without a second thought? Still, she held her ground. "But I do not like to give heed to gossip, my lord. I am told you killed someone. Did you?"

He remained quiet for a long time.

Insects chirped in the garden below them, and inside the ballroom, the orchestra started a country dance. Still she waited, her pulse racing from her own daring. She wasn't certain what had possessed her to ask him such an audacious question. Or why she was suddenly so certain that he would not harm her.

"No," he said finally. "I killed no one. And do you know, Miss Stanton-Lynch, I believe you are the first member of society to even ask me if I am innocent or guilty."

"How can that be? Surely there was an inquiry?"

"Of course," he bit out. He turned to face the night. Staring up at the sky, he continued, "The magistrate was called, but there was no proof. The lady appeared to have fallen down the stairs in the middle of the night."

"A woman?" she gasped. Drawn by the pain that radiated from him, she joined him at the balustrade. "It was a woman who died?"

He glanced at her. "I thought you had heard the stories."

She shook her head. "No, I only heard tell that

you . . . that someone had died. I thought perhaps it was a duel of honor or some such thing."

He laughed, a deep booming sound that seemed suited to the darkness around them. "My, you have such an imagination, Miss Stanton-Lynch."

"Oh, do stop calling me that," she snapped. "My name is Meg."

He raised his brows. "It would not be at all proper for me to address you by your Christian name."

"It's not proper for me to be out here alone with you," Meg replied, "but here I am. Please, this is the most interesting conversation I have had all evening."

"I'm flattered."

"You're interesting," she corrected. "And you haven't mentioned the color of my eyes once. I'm eternally grateful."

He laughed again, and his shoulders seemed to lose some of their stiffness. "This is the intrepid girl I remember from the wedding," he said. "Who was that timid creature who tried to slip past me a few moments ago?"

She rolled her eyes with exasperation. "My lord, I had been told that you were a murderer, and I found myself alone with you on a dark terrace. What would you have me do?"

"I see your point." He turned to face her and leaned one elbow on the railing. "However, you are still alone with me on a dark terrace."

"True." She shrugged, leaning back against the railing as well. "But I already know that you respect me, sir. I remember how you tried to preserve my reputation at Algie's wedding."

He was quiet again, then said softly, "Don't mistake me for a lapdog, my sweet. I'm as much a man as any other, and you are a very lovely woman."

She heard the warning in his voice and recklessly ignored it. The air had become charged with an energy that made her flesh tingle. She felt *alive*. Letting her head fall back, she gazed up at the night sky. "Isn't it a beautiful night?"

"Are you listening to me?"

She glanced at him out of the corner of her eye. "Of course. I'll go back inside in a minute."

"You're not listening at all," he murmured. "You think me defanged, my dear, simply because I said I was innocent?"

He moved, and suddenly he was looming over her, pressing her body into the railing, his hands closing around her waist. His dark eyes bored into hers from inches away.

"What are you doing?" She meant the words to be a demand, but they came out a plea.

"Sweet Meg," he whispered, nuzzling her neck. His breath swept across the tops of her breasts bared by the neckline of her ball dress. Instantly her nipples hardened, and she let out a small sound of surprise as something raw and primitive clenched deep in her belly. "Sweet Meg," he said again.

"Don't you know that all accused murderers claim to be innocent?"

Before she could speak another word, his mouth found hers.

This was nothing like the chaste kisses she had received from her suitors back in Boston! *This* was a man's kiss.

His lips coaxed hers apart, and he tangled his tongue with hers. Another jolt shot through her, warming her insides and making her ache. When his tongue stroked the roof of her mouth, a whimper escaped her throat. Her knees weakened, and she clenched her fingers in his jacket.

As kisses went, this one was way, way out of her realm of experience.

He lifted his mouth from hers so slowly that their lips clung an instant before parting. Still he didn't move away.

"You trust too easily," he said, staring into her eyes. "If I wanted, I could do anything to you, and no one would ever know. Remember that the next time you ask a man bold questions in the dark."

He pushed away from her and stalked into the ballroom, leaving her trembling and aching and alone in the night.

As he reentered the ballroom, Rathmore wasn't sure which one of them deserved his anger more, himself or the trusting girl he had left out on the terrace.

What had possessed her to ask a man known as a murderer if he had indeed committed the crime? And to ask him that while they were alone in the dark was the height of foolishness.

And yet no one else had even thought to ask. He found it extraordinary that it took a slip of a girl to challenge the rumors that everyone else had accepted as truth.

But then she had taken him at his word and dismissed him as a potential threat, and for some reason that had irritated him more than being thought a murderer did.

He was a man, damn it, not a trained pet, and he was as susceptible to the charms of a beautiful young girl as any other man. Miss Margaret Stanton-Lynch had best learn to be on her guard around a man—*any* man—lest she find herself compromised by the first horny fool to trap her alone in the moonlight.

But she was not the only one at fault here.

Why had he gone and kissed her? Oh, he could justify it by telling himself that he was only trying to teach her a lesson, but the truth was that he had wanted to kiss her. Had ached to. She was beautiful and bright and charming and reminded him of things he could no longer have. Her lovely body and quick mind appealed to him, aroused needs he'd been able to push aside in the months since he had returned to England. He wanted her. It was as simple as that. As impossible as that. She was an innocent girl.

And he was the Devil Earl.

He scowled at a young fellow who was gaping at him, then sneered as that same young man gasped and scurried from his path. He could see Lord Aggerly across the way, talking with another gentleman. Aggerly's wife stood beside him, looking bored. It was obvious they had just arrived.

People moved out of Rathmore's path as he cut a swath toward his target. The gentleman Aggerly was talking to moved away, and Aggerly happened to look up and see Rathmore approaching. The portly gentleman turned pale. Aggerly's wife followed her husband's gaze just as Rathmore reached the couple. For an instant she looked right into his eyes.

Then she pointedly turned her back and tugged her husband along with her in the opposite direction.

Gasps came from the bystanders, and Rathmore stood frozen in his tracks. Lady Aggerly had just *cut* him!

Rage shuddered through him. He gazed at Lady Aggerly's retreating back, her ample figure in blue silk blurring his vision as he struggled to control his temper. Titters of laughter reached his ears. He glanced toward the sound, and several onlookers quickly averted their eyes. Humiliation burned like a ball of fire in his gut, but he refused to allow any evidence of it to show. Once, when he was no more than the impoverished nephew of the Earl of Rathmore, he would have retreated from the room in disgrace. But now . . .

Now he was the Devil Earl.

He swept a glacial glare over the assembled spectators, many of whom quickly dipped their heads and slunk away into the crowd. Dismissing the observers by arrogantly turning his back, he lengthened his stride and in three steps managed to intercept the Aggerlys.

"Lord Aggerly," he said, smoothly moving into the couple's path. "A word, if you please."

Aggerly's iron-gray brows lowered in a frown of confusion. "Rathmore," he blustered. "Didn't see you there."

"I'm certain."

Lady Aggerly's plump cheeks reddened at his mocking tone. She gaped at him, wide-eyed, clearly at a loss as to what to do at such a breach of etiquette.

Aggerly cleared his throat. "Apologies, Rathmore, but there are some acquaintances who await our presence at another affair—"

Rathmore clapped a steely hand on Aggerly's shoulder. The portly man flinched. "I believe you can spare me a moment before you take your leave."

Lady Aggerly came to life. Straightening her spine, she looked down her pudgy nose at him. "Lord Rathmore, we are *very* late."

He raised his brows. "Too late to exercise good manners? Why, my dear Lady Aggerly, had I not stopped you, the entire assemblage might have misinterpreted your . . . ah . . . *hurry* . . . for a cut directed at me."

"How unfortunate that would have been," she replied, thrusting out her chin in challenge.

Rathmore bared his teeth in a smile. Lady Aggerly's hostile expression faltered, then faded to uncertainty. She took a step back.

"My business with your husband won't take a moment, my lady," Rathmore said in a tone that held only a hint of menace. "Perhaps you might like to take your leave of our hostess while I converse with Lord Aggerly."

Lady Aggerly's mouth opened and closed, but no sound ever emerged.

Lord Aggerly puffed out his chest in obvious indignation. "Now see here, Rathmore—"

"Or," Rathmore continued smoothly, "we can discuss Presque-à-Mer right now, Aggerly, with your lovely wife."

Aggerly's bluster deflated like the sails of a becalmed ship. "Do as His Lordship says, Eloisa."

"But—"

"*Go*," Aggerly snapped. "Take our leave of Lady Denniston. My conversation with Lord Rathmore should take but a moment."

"Fine." Nose clearly out of joint, Lady Aggerly marched away.

Lord Aggerly gave Rathmore a hard stare. "What do you want from me, Rathmore?"

"Walk outside with me." Well satisfied with the

way things had evolved, Rathmore headed out the terrace doors, Aggerly following reluctantly behind.

Meg had come back inside and rejoined Knightsbridge and Penelope just in time to see Lady Aggerly give Rathmore the cut direct.

Meg and Penelope gasped along with the rest of the crowd at the incident, and Knightsbridge spat an oath. Anger twisted his features. "That evil-minded harridan," he snarled. "What does she think she's doing?"

"She's cut him, Algernon," Penelope whispered, distress in her lovely blue eyes.

"Damn it all," he muttered, watching Rathmore step forward to confront the Aggerlys. "Why do people put so much store in gossip?"

"He is innocent, then?" Meg asked.

Knightsbridge gave a short nod. "On my life, he is. I've known Justin since we were in short pants. He's no more a murderer than I am."

"You're certain?"

Algie gave her a hard look. "As certain as I'm standing here. Justin St. James is no murderer, and someday the people who so accuse him will know it, too. And they'll be sorry for the way they've treated him."

Meg watched curiously as Rathmore exchanged words with the couple. Then Lady Aggerly stormed away, while Rathmore and Lord Aggerly made their way outside.

She hoped no one got hurt.

Penelope tugged at Knightsbridge's sleeve. "Let's do go home, Algernon. I've the headache."

"Of course, my dear. I've lost my taste for this place, anyway." Knightsbridge led Penelope toward the ballroom doors, Meg trailing behind, her thoughts awhirl.

She couldn't discount Algie's opinion of Rathmore, despite the earl's scandalous behavior out on the terrace. On Algie's say-so alone, she was tempted to believe Rathmore innocent.

But why had he kissed her?

She continued to ponder the matter and so didn't notice that Lady Aggerly was standing beside their hostess near the door until they were almost upon her.

"Lord Knightsbridge!" Lady Aggerly cried with delight. "Do let me congratulate you on your recent nuptials."

Knightsbridge sailed right past the woman as if she didn't exist. "Come, my dear," he said to Penelope in an overly loud voice. "I believe we are to meet my good friend Lord Rathmore at the Hattersley affair."

Titters rippled through the crowd as it became evident that Lady Aggerly had been given the cut sublime by the powerful Lord and Lady Knightsbridge. Meg hurried behind her cousin and his bride, but took a moment to savor the shocked expression on Lady Aggerly's face.

She only wished Rathmore had been around to see it.

* * *

No one else had taken refuge in the cool darkness of the terrace. Aggerly turned belligerently on Rathmore as soon as they stepped outside. "Now, what do you want from me?"

"The truth."

"You should know the truth better than anyone," Aggerly sneered.

"Perhaps." Rathmore smiled thinly. "I know the truth about your mistress, a Bonapartist spy. And about the two children you sired on her. I understand you gave her a choice, be your mistress or die as a traitor. She chose the little house where you keep her in the south of France." He tapped his chin thoughtfully. "I wonder what society would make of that?"

"Keep your voice down." Face flushed, Aggerly glanced back furtively at the crowded ballroom. "How did you find out?"

"I had a lot of time during my exile to travel. Miss Rondelle is most charming." Rathmore gave him a taunting smile. "Thankfully, your sons resemble their mother and not their poor excuse for a father."

"I'll kill you if you speak a word of this to anyone," Aggerly hissed.

"Is that what you said to Ophelia?"

Aggerly's features relaxed. "So that's your game. You think to blame me for that girl's death. Well, it won't work Rathmore. I didn't do it."

"Then where were you that night? You certainly weren't sound asleep in your bed as you claimed."

"What? What did you say?"

Rathmore's lips curled as he heard the panic in the man's voice. "Your valet came into your chamber that night. Your bed was empty."

Aggerly backed away. "Stay away from me, Rathmore. I want nothing to do with your wild theories."

"Oh, it's a fact," Rathmore murmured, arrested by the worry creeping into Aggerly's eyes. "I found your old valet, and he signed a document stating exactly what happened. You really should pension off your servants better, Aggerly."

"Bugger you," Aggerly snarled. "I'll not play your game. And if I hear one word about the town of Presque-à-Mer, then you will be sorry, Rathmore." His angry words still ringing in the night, Aggerly spun and stormed back to the ballroom.

"One of us will be sorry," Rathmore whispered into the night, "but I doubt 'twill be me."

With a small smile of satisfaction, he turned and walked down the terrace toward one of the lesser-used doorways. He'd accomplished his mission; there was no reason to put up with the sneers of society any longer. Without a word to anyone, he left Lady Denniston's home, a glimmer of hope waking within him.

Lord Aggerly had something to hide.

Perhaps it was murder.

Chapter 4

Why couldn't she get that kiss out of her mind? Meg sat on a stone bench in the garden the day after Lady Denniston's ball, playing with Penelope's little white dog, Pudding, and trying desperately to forget her encounter with Lord Rathmore last night. That kiss on the terrace had completely slipped through her careful defenses. It was a little too exciting, a little too tempting, for her peace of mind.

Algie and Penelope sat across from her on another bench, completely wrapped up in each other as usual. Their soft murmurings and adoring looks made it extremely difficult for Meg to banish Lord Rathmore from her thoughts. What would it be like to have someone look at her as if she held his world in her hands?

What would it be like to have Lord Rathmore look at her that way?

She steered away from that dangerous path. The last thing she needed right now was a romance with an Englishman—any Englishman—much less one who was suspected of murder. Rathmore was a man with dark secrets about him, even with Algie's word that he was innocent.

But he kissed like sin.

In an instant her memory brought her back to the terrace, back into his arms. Dear Lord, his touch had melted away all her defenses as if they had never been. She was tempted to turn her back on her upbringing and stay in his arms forever, to discover the sweet delights and dark sensuality to be found there.

Yes indeed, Lord Rathmore was a very dangerous man, and not because of his reputation.

Before she could get lost in fantasy, Pudding nudged her hand, the scrap of material that he liked to play with dangling from his mouth. Glad of the distraction, she obligingly grabbed hold of the toy and watched with amusement as the tiny dog began tugging at the material, throwing his entire body behind the effort and growling and snarling as if she were trying to steal his possession from him.

Knightsbridge and his lady never looked up, not even when the little dog pulled so hard at the scrap of material that it tore in two, sending his little body tumbling backward. Meg giggled at the puppy's antics and looked over at the couple, expecting them to share in her mirth, but they were lost in their own world.

Knightsbridge rose suddenly from the bench,

holding out his hand to his bride. Penelope accepted Algie's assistance, and the two started toward the house, gazes locked adoringly. Then Knightsbridge happened to glance over and see Meg. He stopped abruptly, causing Penelope to bump into him.

"Cousin," he said—a bit too loudly, Meg thought. "Cousin, my lady and I are going inside to . . . ah . . . view the orangery. Yes, that's exactly where we are going. I trust you will be fine enough out here in the gardens by yourself?"

"Of course," Meg replied. She noted Penelope's blush and the furtive, heated look Knightsbridge sent to his wife. Orangery, indeed! Smothering her smile, she gave in to a mischievous impulse and said, "Perhaps I should accompany you. I have always wanted to see an orangery."

"No!" Penelope replied hastily. "That is . . . dear Pudding needs his exercise. You would be bored silly in the orchard—"

"Orangery," Algie muttered.

"—in the orangery," Penelope continued with a smoothness that Meg had to admire. "Do stay out here in the sunshine with Pudding while Algernon and I attend to our tedious duties."

Meg bit the inside of her lip to keep from laughing. "If you're certain you don't need assistance," she said solemnly.

"Not at all!" Knightsbridge hastened to assure her. "Lady Penelope and I have everything well in hand."

"Or we will soon," Penelope murmured near her husband's ear.

He flushed, sending her an ardent look, and Meg pretended she hadn't overheard the whispered remark. "Very well then. Shall I see you at this afternoon?"

"Yes!" Knightsbridge gave Meg his most charming smile, but she knew his thoughts were far away. In the orangery, perhaps. "This afternoon. Exactly. See you then." Knightsbridge grabbed Penelope's hand and headed for the house at a speedy clip.

"Enjoy your morning," Penelope called back, nearly running to keep up with her husband's impatient stride.

Once they were gone, Meg burst out laughing. "The orangery!" she said to Pudding. "Can you imagine? They just want to be alone together, but of course they don't expect me to know why. No English girl would, that's for certain!"

The little dog yipped and wagged his stub of a tail as if in agreement. He picked up the small scrap of material that was left from their game and brought it to her, nudging her hand.

"I suppose you're all the company I will have today," Meg said. "I bet you could do with a walk."

She rose and began to stroll along the path, pleased when the animal followed her. She had to laugh at his antics as they strolled along, watching him sniff at various shrubbery and bark at butterflies. At one point, he scared the dickens out of a flock of birds, sending them into panicked flight with his excited yapping.

Even the darned dog knew his place, she thought wistfully. But where was hers?

She had a unique opportunity right now, one she hadn't considered in her distress over her grandfather's illness. With Garrett home in America and Grandfather and Aunt Agatha away in Bath, there was no one to watch her every move. Algie and Penelope were certainly too caught up in each other to pay much attention to what Meg was doing, leaving her free to explore her options to her heart's content.

She wasn't a fool. She knew she had to marry someday; it was the way things were done, the way women survived in the world. But before she did, she would use this time to find something of her own, some cause or hobby that she could turn to in order to rediscover herself when her other obligations began to overwhelm her.

Perhaps gardening. She'd always liked flowers, roses in particular. Or better yet, botany. Once her grandfather returned, she would be restricted to a "lady's" pursuit anyway. Might as well begin her search there.

Her grandfather loved her and wanted her to marry and stay in England. While she was tired of playing the debutante, she didn't want the duke to realize that. He was ill enough without worrying about her. And so she continued to entertain suitors, though none of them really interested her. Thus far the only man who made her heart race was considered a murderer by the Polite World. Of course, Algie vouched for his innocence.

But what if Algie was wrong?

Algie had known Rathmore since they were boys, and he was exceedingly loyal to those he called friend. What if Algie was blinded by his long friendship with Rathmore and didn't see him for what he really was?

Her heart pounded as she considered the possibility. Her instincts told her that Lord Rathmore was no killer, but her instincts had been wrong before. She had been wrong about Malcolm, and that had nearly ruined her life.

Even now she had to shudder at how close she had come to lifelong misery. Last Season, Malcolm, Viscount Arndale, had charmed her into running away with him to Gretna Green, but before she could meet him, he had abducted her friend, Lucinda, and revealed his true colors. He had only been using Meg to get to Lucinda.

All had turned out well, as Meg's brother, Garrett, was in love with Lucinda and had rescued her. They later married, and Garrett showed the world how dishonorable Arndale was when the viscount tried to cheat in a duel of honor.

Everyone had recognized Lord Arndale for the liar he was, except Meg. How could she trust her instincts now when she had been so wrong before?

Her fate with Arndale would have been marriage, though she would have been miserable as his wife. If she was wrong about Lord Rathmore, then the cost could be her very life.

Everything was such a muddle.

She reached the iron gate that led out of the garden. The Knightsbridge estate stretched as far as she could see. A vast field of green spread before her, topped by blue sky and accented by the dark shadow of the woods at the other side of the grassy expanse.

"It is gorgeous here," she said to the dog, "but somehow it still doesn't feel like home."

He barked at her and wagged his tail, his dark eyes bright in his fuzzy face. He poked his head through the gate, looking out toward the field, and then suddenly he squeezed his entire body through the bars to the other side.

"Pudding!" Meg cried. "Come back here at once!"

On the other side of the gate, the animal turned completely around and yapped at her once more, as if encouraging her to come and join him.

"No, I will not come out there. Do come back in before you get lost."

The dog cocked his head to the side.

"Don't you act like you don't know what I'm talking about," she warned. Slowly she unlatched the gate and swung it open. "Come, Pudding," she called, patting her leg in invitation. "Come on now."

The dog barked, tail wagging, but didn't budge. He watched her expectantly, tongue hanging out the side of his mouth.

"Pudding, come *here*!"

He took a step backward, barked.

Meg blew a sigh of frustration and came through the gate. "I shall pick you up and carry you back then, you silly animal."

Pudding yipped at her twice, waiting as she approached. Just when she would have reached for him, he turned tail and sped off across the field toward the woods.

"Pudding! Come back here!" Grabbing up her skirts, she rushed after him, certain she would be able to catch him easily. After all, he was just a small dog.

A small, *fast* dog, she amended a few minutes later, huffing with exertion as the white streak that was Pudding reached the woods lengths ahead of her. Heavens, Penelope loved that dog, and she would be most upset if anything happened to him. Meg paused to catch her breath and glanced back at the house. Perhaps she should go fetch someone to help her catch the animal.

But just then Pudding paused at the edge of the trees, barking at her and running in circles, as if this was all some demented doggy game that he was playing with her. If she went back to the house for help, there was every chance she would lose the dog, and then Penelope would be heartbroken.

Fate smiled on her in the form of the gardener's boy, who suddenly appeared near the gate.

"You there!" she called. The boy jerked with surprise, then shaded his eyes to look at her.

"Would you fetch a footman?" she called. "Lady Penelope's dog has run away!"

He hesitated, then nodded and dropped his garden tools as he took off at a run toward the house.

"There," Meg said with satisfaction. "I'll just wait here for the footman."

Then Pudding suddenly darted into the trees and disappeared from sight.

"Dratted dog," she muttered. "All right then, into the woods we go. You should be able to handle one small dog, Meg. And the footman will be just behind you."

Lifting her skirts to her ankles, she plunged through the trees after the escaped canine.

Rathmore didn't know which disturbed him more, the fact that Lady Aggerly had gotten up the nerve to cut him socially last night or the fact that he couldn't get Meg out of his mind.

Seated at his desk in his study, he watched the patterns the sunlight made on the floor, ignoring the pages of notes in front of him. Lady Aggerly's public rejection had demonstrated to him how daunting the task of proving his innocence would be.

It seemed the more he appeared in society, the more comfortable society seemed to feel about insulting him. But in order to prove his innocence, he needed them to respect him. Perhaps even fear him.

He needed to be the Devil Earl at his worst.

He had nothing to lose. His honor was already tarnished, and from the way minor nobility like

Lady Aggerly reacted to him, there was nothing he could do to make his reputation any worse. He would find the truth, damn them all. He *would* find some way to prevail.

If he could get Miss Margaret Stanton-Lynch out of his mind.

The kiss from last night still haunted him. He was so close now, he really couldn't afford to be distracted from his pursuit of the truth. But every time he tried to focus on the business at hand, he would see Meg's face in his mind. Her inquisitive blue eyes. Her dark hair and ivory skin. Her luscious mouth.

Her delicious, luscious mouth.

He had given in to temptation and kissed those sweet pink lips, and he had liked it, too. It had been way too long since he'd enjoyed the softness of a woman. But he shouldn't have done it. No matter that he felt she had provoked him. He was a gentleman, by God, even if he was the only one who knew it, and gentlemen did not steal kisses from innocent maidens in the moonlight.

But despite lamenting his lapse in honor, he couldn't regret the kiss. It had been too sweet, too innocently passionate. Nectar to a man who had been starving. But it was over now, and it should be relegated to a place of lesser importance in his mind, merely a pleasant memory to review when he was lonely and in his cups. It could be nothing more.

She could be nothing more. Just a delicious interlude on a summer's evening.

Resolutely he turned to the pages of notes before him. During the years of his exile, he had taken the funds given to him by his uncle and invested them. His investments had prospered, leaving him financially comfortable and more than capable of investigating the fourteen people who had attended the house party that fateful summer when Ophelia had died. Since he knew *he* wasn't the murderer, it stood to reason that one of them must know something about what happened.

Looking at the names of the men in attendance, he noted himself, as well as Uncle Alfred and Desmond, both deceased. Sir Charles Wraxton was a bachelor and had been a favorite hunting partner of Uncle Alfred's. Lord Tilton and Lord Aggerly were neighbors and had been friends of Uncle Alfred's. Laertes, Lord Fenton, was Ophelia's brother and an old school chum of Desmond's.

As for the ladies, Lady Tilton and Lady Aggerly had both attended with their husbands, and Lady Tilton had brought her daughter, Catherine, with her. Catherine had since married Lord Nussburton. There was Mrs. Imogene Pelton, Uncle Alfred's amour of the moment. Lady Alston, a widow with whom Sir Charles had been enamored. Miss Eugenia Minor was the maiden aunt of Lord Fenton and had been chaperone to Ophelia.

And of course there was Ophelia herself.

Beautiful, grasping Ophelia. Sister to Lord Fenton and fiancée to Desmond. Dark-haired and dark-eyed, she had not been very tall, but what there was of her had been lushly curved. Every step she took and every word she spoke whispered of seduction. He couldn't blame Desmond for wanting her.

Early that fateful Tuesday morning, Ophelia had been found by a maid at the foot of the stairs, her neck broken. The whole thing should have been dismissed as a tragic accident.

If she hadn't been found dead so close to his own bedchamber. If Desmond hadn't been so jealous. So suspicious.

Rathmore sighed and rubbed his hands over his face. Ophelia had made no secret of the fact that she was attracted to him, and Desmond had believed the worst. He had tried to reassure Desmond that he was not interested in stealing away his fiancée, but his cousin would not listen. Desmond had ever been envious of Justin's good looks and easy way with women, despite the fact that Desmond was heir to the title and Justin was little more than a poor relation. His cousin was proud to have won Ophelia as his bride, and it drove him mad that she seemed to prefer Justin over him.

Not that she would have ever broken off the engagement. Oh, no. Ophelia had every intention of becoming a countess. She just thought to enjoy her title more by dallying with her husband's cousin.

After the incident Desmond had been the most vocal of his accusers, Rathmore remembered. It was his certainty that Justin had had something to do with Ophelia's death that had started the rumors and turned the St. James family against him.

It was Desmond's distress that had prompted Uncle Alfred to banish Justin from England, an embarrassment to the family name.

Who could have known he would return to inherit the title of the very man who had sent him away? Somewhere, Fate was laughing.

With effort, he turned his attention back to his notes. During the inquiry, all of the servants had been accounted for, but three of the fourteen guests had provided information about their whereabouts that could not be validated: Lord Aggerly, Lord Fenton, and Mrs. Pelton.

During his exile, he had taken the time to investigate everyone's excuses. Through a complex network of contacts, he had interviewed servants and relatives, business relations and old lovers.

On the night in question, Lord Aggerly had claimed to be asleep in his chamber. This excuse was proven false by Aggerly's ex-valet, who had come into the room in the middle of the night and found his master gone. Subsequent investigation had turned up Aggerly's Bonapartist mistress and children living quietly in southern France, a weapon Rathmore did not hesitate to use in his quest for truth.

Lord Fenton said he had been on the terrace, smoking a cigar, at the time of his sister's death. Since he suffered from sleeplessness, this was not unusual behavior for him. The investigations that followed had turned up nothing of note about Lord Fenton. His family had had some financial troubles, true, but that was not unusual. Money was the reason Ophelia was marrying Desmond, and it had never been a secret.

Even if Fenton were the type to do away with his own sister—something Rathmore found hard to contemplate—Fenton would never do anything to ruin the alliance with the St. James family. In fact, after Ophelia's death, Fenton had suffered severe financial setbacks until Uncle Alfred had settled money on him out of regret for the marriage that had never taken place.

That left Mrs. Imogene Pelton. Rathmore knew her well, as she had tried more than once to lure him to her bed. In the six years since Ophelia's death, the late earl's paramour had married and buried her fourth husband. Her name was now Mrs. Imogene Warington, and she had claimed to be with the earl when Ophelia had died. However, Uncle Alfred had been prone to the megrims, and Rathmore had gotten it from his valet that the earl had taken his tonic that evening, a concoction that habitually rendered Uncle Alfred unconscious. While it was true Mrs. Warington had been in the earl's company initially, the manservant had entered his master's room just before the murder to find his master snoring and the lady nowhere to be seen.

Both Aggerly and Mrs. Warington had reasons for hating Ophelia—she had rejected Aggerly and earned Mrs. Warington's wrath by flirting with the old earl. Ophelia and Mrs. Warington had even entered into a physical fight that had to be broken up by the earl and Desmond. Either Aggerly or Mrs. Warington could have done it, Rathmore mused. And the man-hungry widow Warington was next on his list of suspects.

A knock on the door pulled him back to the present.

"Come," he snapped, irritated that he had yet to fully concentrate on his task.

Grimm, his butler, peered into the room. The elderly man had a long face like a donkey, thinning gray hair, and pale blue eyes that missed nothing. "Your pardon, my lord," the aging servant said. "I have come to report that Miss Emily has run off."

"Again?" Exasperated, Rathmore sat back in his chair and regarded the solemn-faced butler. "What was it this time?"

"I believe Miss Emily discovered that she was no longer allowed to ride her horse. Those were your instructions, were they not, my lord?" Grimm arched his bushy eyebrows.

"No need to look at me like that, Grimm," Rathmore said. Having known the butler since he was in short pants, he felt more like he was addressing an eccentric uncle rather than a servant. "Emily needs to understand that she can no longer run wild across the estate. She needs to start becoming a young lady."

"Indeed, my lord. However, the 'young lady' has run off into the woods. Would you have me send a footman after her?"

Rathmore sighed and rose. "Of course not, Grimm. I'll go after her myself."

The merest softening crossed the butler's face before he regained his stoic demeanor. "Very good, my lord."

Surrounded by trees and with no sign of Pudding, Meg started to get discouraged.

Her pale blue afternoon dress was definitely not the correct outfit to be wearing for tramping in the woods. Her skirts kept getting snagged on branches, and once or twice a stone bruised the soles of her feet through the soft material of her slippers. Nonetheless, she pushed on, calling for the dog and listening for either the sounds of the animal's progress through the brush or the more welcome indications that a footman was following close behind. But all she heard was the wind in the trees and the occasional birdsong. As she made her way deeper into the woods, the gentle babbling of a stream reached her ears. And over that soft trickle came the sound of someone sobbing.

"Hello," Meg called as she followed the sound.

There was a rustling of branches and then an excited yip. Pudding! Meg broke through the brush to find the little white dog licking tears off the face of a young girl sitting beside the stream. The girl giggled between her sobs and hugged the puppy tightly.

"Hello there," Meg said. The girl's head shot up,

and she stared at Meg in suspicious silence. "My name is Meg. Are you all right?"

"Go away," the girl muttered, burying her face in the dog's fur again.

"I can't just leave you alone in the woods," Meg said. "Though you aren't really alone, are you? Pudding is keeping you company."

At the sound of his name, the dog barked and tilted his head to look at Meg, his tongue hanging out of his mouth as if to say, "Were you talking to me?"

The girl tightened her arms around Pudding and narrowed her eyes at Meg. "Is he your dog?"

"He belongs to my friend." Meg cautiously sat on a nearby rock, wary of staining her dress but even more concerned with scaring the child away. "She'll be dreadfully upset when she finds out that he's missing. But I can wait until you're done with him before I take him home."

"I'm not done with him yet."

Meg shrugged. "As I said, I'll wait."

"It could be a long time," the child warned. "Maybe hours."

"I hope not," Meg replied evenly. "I imagine we'd get hungry. You're going to want to go home for dinner eventually."

"I'm never going home again!"

The vehemence of the statement took Meg aback, but she didn't let the child see it. Instead she said calmly, "I'm certain your parents would miss you."

"I don't have any parents." The little girl hugged

Pudding closer, a single tear sliding down her cheek. "They died."

Dear Lord. Meg closed her eyes for a moment as sympathy washed over her. She knew how much it had hurt to lose her own parents, and she had been an adult when her mother had died. The poor child! "What's your name?" she asked.

"Emily."

"Emily, who takes care of you now?"

"My godfather. I hate him." Emily bent her head and seemed intensely interested in scratching Pudding's ears. "He never lets me do anything."

"Surely it can't be that bad."

The child's head came back up, and she glared at Meg with tear-filled blue eyes. "He used to like me, but then he went away for a long time, and now he's come back and keeps telling me what to do like he's my father!"

"I'm sure he's trying his best to take care of you."

"You don't know anything about it," the girl retorted. "He's so mean. Do you know he wouldn't even let me ride my horse? *My* horse!"

"I remember how angry I used to get at my brother," Meg said, nodding sympathetically. "My father died when I was just three years old, and my brother decided that he was going to act like my father, just because he was eight years older."

"Did he tell you what to do all the time?" Emily swiped a hand across her tearstained cheek.

"All the time," Meg replied. "And do you know what made it worse? He was always going off to sea and leaving mother and me alone. He never understood that we wanted him to stay home with us."

"I remember when Cousin Justin—that's my godfather—used to be around all the time. He used to play with me and carry me on his shoulders." Her young face grew troubled. "Then he went away for years and years and never came home again until Papa died."

"Was he in the army perhaps?"

The girl shook her head. "No. I remember there was something bad that happened, and then one day he was gone."

"And now that he's come home, he's different?"

The youngster gave an emphatic nod. "He never wants to play with me anymore. He's always locked up in his study working."

"Well, he can't exactly carry you on his shoulders anymore."

Emily giggled. "No, I'm too big."

"And it would be most unseemly," Meg said. "Perhaps your cousin is simply overwhelmed with business matters. There's usually quite a bit of fuss involved with inheritances."

"Well, he doesn't have to be so mean about it." The girl played with Pudding's ear, her expression thoughtful.

"Maybe he just needs some time to get his business matters concluded," Meg said. "I'm certain he cares for you very much."

Emily didn't answer, but her troubled frown revealed her opinion of *that* statement.

They settled into silence, Emily petting the dog and Meg studying Emily. The girl was dressed in fine clothing, and from the way she spoke, Meg assumed that she must be from a good family. Her light brown hair had been arranged into fat curls with a ribbon threaded through it, though her tramp through the woods had left it somewhat snarled. Mud streaked her cheek, dust mixed with tears.

Since she didn't want to leave the girl alone, and Pudding was safe, Meg decided to simply sit still and wait until the footman from Knightsbridge Chase found them. Besides, Emily seemed to need the serenity of the forest and the comfort Pudding could provide. She didn't want to take the dog away from the child so soon.

So they both sat beside the stream, watching the birds hop from branch to bush. The sunlight sparkled off the water and the soft babble of the brook soothed away their troubles. As the minutes passed, Emily stopped crying, her sobs settling into mere sniffles as she held on tight to Pudding.

Finally the sound of footsteps tramping through the brush broke the serenity. Meg gave a sigh of relief even as Emily's head jerked toward the sound. "Never fear, Emily," Meg said with a smile. "I'm certain that's just a footman coming after Pudding and me."

Emily slid her a sidelong look. "Maybe," she said, doubt heavy in her voice.

"We're over here!" Meg called. The footsteps

hesitated, then continued, this time in their direction.

"Why did you do that?" Emily gasped. "I don't want them to find me!"

Meg rose to her feet and brushed off the back of her dress as she approached the girl. "Nonsense. I've already found you. The footman can escort us back to my cousin's house, and once we've restored Pudding to his owner, I'll see that you get home safely."

Emily scowled. "I thought you liked me."

"I do like you, but no one ever solved a problem by running away from it." Meg bent down and brushed a stray lock from the child's forehead. "Would you like me to speak to your guardian? Explain what happened?"

Emily hesitated, then nodded. "But he probably won't listen," she said. "He'll probably yell."

"I doubt he will yell at *me*."

"He yells at everybody," the girl replied glumly. "You'll see."

The crunching of footsteps stopped abruptly, and a man stepped into the grassy clearing. But it wasn't the footman Meg had been expecting. Slowly she rose to her feet as Lord Rathmore appeared.

He, apparently, was Emily's "Cousin Justin."

He met her gaze for one, heated moment. The memory of their kiss flared between them, and her lips parted in response. For an instant he looked as if he might step toward her, but then he glanced at Emily. His expression hardened.

"Emily!" he barked. "Have you any idea how much trouble you've caused? Have you no common sense?"

His voice thundered throughout the clearing. Emily sent Meg a sidelong look. "I *told* you he would yell."

"So you did." Meg put her hands on her hips. "My lord, neither of us is deaf, so I will thank you to lower your tone."

Emily and Rathmore both stared at her openmouthed, and then Rathmore found his voice. "Miss Stanton-Lynch, do you make a habit of issuing orders to members of the peerage?"

"I believe I do, my lord," she shot back. "My brother is a marquess, and my grandfather is a duke, and I speak my mind to both of them constantly."

"My sympathies to them both."

"And my sympathies to your household if you bellow at them the way you have at us!"

Pudding yipped as if to punctuate her point.

Rathmore glowered at her, and even with so disagreeable an expression on his face, she couldn't help but appreciate how handsome he was. Too bad his attitude didn't match his good looks!

"Emily," he said, turning dismissively from Meg, "you know the consequences for running off unaccompanied."

Emily's chin came up. "You've already prevented me from riding Guinevere. What will you do to me now, lock me in the dungeons?"

"Rathmore has no dungeons," he snapped impatiently. "No, my girl, you are confined to your room until further notice."

"You can't *do* that!" Emily's wail quite matched her guardian's bellow in volume, and Meg winced. Pudding yapped and ran in circles.

"I can and I will. I warned you what would happen if you went off unaccompanied again."

"I hate you!" Emily clenched her fists, tears shimmering in her eyes, and then she turned away from him to stand staring off into the woods. Her slim shoulders shook with the effort to maintain control.

A look of pained helplessness flashed across Rathmore's face as he looked at his ward. Then he glanced at Meg, and he was once more the arrogant Lord Rathmore. "My apologies for this display, Miss Stanton-Lynch," he said tightly.

"Oh, for heaven's sake! Can't you unbend for one moment and see that she's confused and hurting?" Meg went to Emily and wrapped her arms around the girl. "There now, Emily. I'm certain His Lordship didn't mean to roar at you. No doubt he was worried for your safety."

"I hate him." Emily sniffed, accepting Meg's embrace.

"No, you don't," Meg said. "You just wish your father was here, don't you?"

The young girl nodded and began to sob into Meg's shoulder.

Meg met Rathmore's gaze as Emily cried out her

anguish. "I lost my father when I was three, my lord," she said quietly. "But to have lost a parent while going through this confusing age must be extremely difficult for your ward."

"She doesn't listen," he said, but the fire was gone from his voice. And in his face she saw only weariness. "How can I protect her if she doesn't listen?"

"Try talking to her, my lord. *To* her," she emphasized, "not *at* her."

"I've tried talking to her, but she refuses to be reasonable."

"So would I, if you addressed me like that."

He stared her down, arrogance etched in his face as if it had been carved there. "Miss Stanton-Lynch, I thank you for your assistance, but I will be taking charge of my ward now." He started toward Emily.

"I don't think so, my lord," Meg said, stopping him in his tracks. "You're too angry to deal compassionately with Emily right now, which is what she needs."

"I beg your pardon?"

She would have laughed at the astonishment in his voice, had the situation not been so grave. "I cannot allow you to take this girl home with you when you are in this sort of temper. I suggest you return with me to Knightsbridge Chase. We'll have some tea, and everyone will calm down, and *then* you may take Emily home with you."

"I don't want any damned tea!"

"Well, I do. And so does Emily, I'll bet."

"I would like that very much, Miss Stanton-Lynch." Emily sniffled. "May we take Pudding?"

"Of course." Meg scooped up the dog, avoiding the animal's muddy paws, and shoved Pudding into a surprised Rathmore's arms. Pudding immediately placed both filthy front paws on Rathmore's chest, smearing mud all over the fine material of his expensively tailored coat. "Do hold tight to Pudding, my lord, as he tends to run off."

Ignoring the astonishment on his face, she turned away and took Emily's hand. Pausing at the edge of the clearing, she glanced back at Rathmore. "Are you coming, my lord?"

His expression thunderous, Rathmore nonetheless fell into step behind them, wriggling canine and all.

Chapter 5

Rathmore wasn't certain how he'd gotten in-volved in this comedy of errors, but he meant to disengage himself as soon as possible.

As soon as Meg relinquished his ward.

He scowled at Meg's back as she walked before him, skirts swishing gently with every step. She and Emily kept up a lively, female dialogue that by its very nature excluded him, punctuated by the occa-sional bark from the furry canine that he carried. Once in a while Meg would glance back to be cer-tain he was still with them, but otherwise she ig-nored him completely.

Had she forgotten their kiss last night?

As Emily prattled on about something or other—who knew that the child could utter more than sullen monosyllables?—Meg glanced back at him yet again. This time he caught her gaze and held it, giving her a slow, rakish grin.

I remember exactly what your mouth feels like.

He felt the words as he thought them, his body tightening with remembered passion. And he made no attempt to hide it.

Alarm flickered across her features, and her certain strides faltered. She quickly regained her pace, but then she sent back a sharp, warning look.

Rathmore chuckled. She remembered.

Emily called Meg's attention back to her, and as she marched along, chattering like a magpie, Rathmore was struck by the brilliant smile on her face. When had he last seen the child smile like that? Her expression was animated as she regaled Meg with her tale, her blue eyes sparkling and her curls bouncing as they walked.

Emotion clutched his heart and squeezed. Right now she looked so much like the little girl he remembered, the child he had missed so much during his enforced exile. She never smiled like that at *him*. No, somehow her beloved Cousin Justin had become the devil incarnate in her young mind. But he had no choice. He was her guardian now. She needed him to be her parent and not her playmate, even if she didn't realize it.

But how could she not know how much he loved her? That he would do anything for her, even attempt the impossible task of solving a six-year-old murder so she could have the future she deserved?

Feeling bereft, he studied the way the two females interacted. Meg had such a way with Emily. The tears had dried on the young girl's face, and the hysterical child of moments before was gone as if she had never been. As eager as he was to be on his way, it was worth any inconvenience to see Emily so happy. They would stay for tea, he decided, and then he would take Emily home and attend to his business.

They reached the garden gate at Knightsbridge Chase, where they met a footman who had been wandering about in search of them. Rathmore gratefully handed the dog to the footman as Meg gave instructions to bathe the animal, and then she led Rathmore and Emily into the house.

At the foot of the great staircase, she stopped a passing maid. "Please take Miss St. James upstairs to refresh herself, Polly," she said. Turning to Emily, she indicated a nearby door. "This is the drawing room. As soon as you've washed up, come back down here with Polly, and I'll have Cook send in some tea and cakes."

"Thank you, Miss Stanton-Lynch." With a wary glance at her guardian, Emily followed the maid upstairs.

"She's not the only one who's filthy," Rathmore pointed out.

"I want to speak to you before you go upstairs." She gestured toward the drawing room. "This way, my lord."

He sketched a bow and swept his hand before him. "Oh, no, my dear. Ladies first."

She narrowed her eyes at him, then sailed into the drawing room. He followed behind her, thoroughly enjoying the view of her gently swaying hips.

Meg was very much aware of Rathmore as he followed her into the room. She closed the door behind them, and as she turned back to face him, he gave her that mocking look, both eyebrows raised.

"May I be of service, Miss Stanton-Lynch?"

The velvety purr of his voice gave the innocent words a decadence that even a virtuous woman like herself couldn't miss. Scalding heat flooded her cheeks, but she raised her chin and forged onward with her mission. "I wanted to talk to you about Emily where the servants wouldn't overhear."

"Ah, so this is about Emily then. Not about that kiss last night."

"Of course it's about Emily!"

"Are you certain?" His deep voice wrapped around her senses like a silken rope.

The man looked at her as if he could see right through her skin to the soul inside. The strength of his gaze made her tremble, but she did her best to hide it from him. Why did he have to be so accursed handsome? He was so darkly sensuous, so irresistible. Ink-black hair curling over his forehead. Dark, seductive eyes. High cheekbones, and a lean face that was saved from being too pretty by the negligible crookedness of his nose and the slightly thick eyebrows. Dusky skin inherited from his French mother. A full, sensuous mouth.

And oh, how well she knew that mouth.

"Miss Stanton-Lynch?"

The hint of humor in his voice jerked her from her schoolgirl mooning. The man was way too observant. "Yes, Lord Rathmore, I'm certain this is about Emily." Airily she added, "Last night is already forgotten."

"Is it?" He clearly didn't like that.

"It was just a kiss, my lord." She gave him a knowing little smile that hid the tremors inside her. "And hardly my first."

"Really?" He folded his arms across his chest, at once the all-powerful male. "And what does Knightsbridge have to say about that?"

"Not a thing, as it is none of his affair."

"Interesting choice of words, Miss Stanton-Lynch."

She waved a hand dismissively. "Lord Rathmore, we are here to talk about Emily, not about my suitors."

"So we are." He tilted his head, regarding her with an intensity that made her want to squirm. "Do you have many?"

"Many what?"

"Suitors."

"You are the most exasperating man!" she exclaimed. "My suitors are none of your business. I want to talk to you about Emily, about your handling of her."

He scowled at that. "What do you mean, my 'handling' of her?"

She paused, choosing her words carefully. "Emily is a young girl who is starting to bloom into a woman, my lord. A young girl who only a year ago lost her father and grandfather."

"I'm aware of that," he said tightly.

"You need to try and be more patient with her," Meg explained. "She needs understanding now."

"What she needs, Miss Stanton-Lynch, is discipline."

The implacable expression on his face did not bode well for mutual understanding. She sighed. "Yes, she does need *some* discipline," she agreed. "But girls of this age are notoriously emotional and overly sensitive. Emily tells me her mother died some years ago."

"When Emily was two," Rathmore replied. "An illness."

"She needs a female figure in her life at this important time. Is there someone you can turn to? An aunt or some other female relative? What about your own mother?"

"My mother died last year. And there are no other relatives." He smiled grimly. "Otherwise the title would certainly not have passed to me."

"Then you're all she has." She held his gaze for a long moment. "She resents you, you know. From what she told me, she adored you when she was little."

His face softened. "She was a charming little thing."

"And then you went away. You never visited, never wrote."

"I couldn't." Pain underscored his words. Pain . . . and anger. "I was banished. An embarrassment. They didn't want me to come near her."

"Well, she depends on you now." She paused. "But she does think you are too dictatorial."

"I do what I have to in order to keep her safe." His eyes, when he looked at her, held a fascinating combination of earnestness and determination. "She takes foolish chances with her safety."

"Maybe she's just trying to get your attention. She says you work all the time."

"I'm very busy, yes." The shortness of his answer did not invite further comment. "But she must learn to obey rules set in place for her safety."

"And you must learn to be more sensitive to her needs."

"I *am* sensitive!" he roared. His shout rattled the windowpanes.

"Indeed," Meg said blandly.

There was a long moment of silence.

"Miss Stanton-Lynch. Meg . . ." He sighed. "I'm doing the best I can with Emily. I'm certain a lot of what she does has to do with her grief. But I cannot let her run wild. Someone needs to keep her safe, if only from herself."

Meg couldn't help but be moved by the sincerity

of his words. She could tell he had no idea how to raise a young girl, no clue as to the merry chase Emily could lead him. But he was trying. "I wish there was someone who could help you," she said. "Some female relative who could help Emily with the coming years as she grows into a young woman."

"There is no one." He took her hand, raised it to his lips. "But I thank you for your concern."

He brushed his mouth across her fingers, and a quiver shot through her.

He glanced at her face. Helpless, she looked back, and she knew the instant he saw how his touch affected her. He squeezed the fingers he still held, a growing need in his eyes that awoke an answering longing within herself. The tugs and tingling of her own body were unmistakable.

Impossible! She wouldn't be attracted to him, couldn't get involved with him. Not only was there the question of his reputation, but she had her own goal. To find her true path. To discover the one thing that she could contribute to the world that was pure Meg Lynch. To find a purpose for her life, a place for herself.

Something that she had to discover alone.

Yet she stood there, unprotesting, lost in those dark, dangerous eyes, as the Devil Earl stroked his thumb across her knuckles. She swallowed audibly, and with a wicked lift of his brows, he turned her hand palm up and pressed a kiss to her wrist, against her racing pulse.

Sweet Lord in heaven.

Her entire body hummed with awareness as he once more glanced at her. Hunger etched his features.

God help her, but she wanted him.

She had never lain with a man, but that didn't make her ignorant of what went on. She had grown up on the docks of Boston surrounded by sailors, and she was fairly cognizant of what the act of physical loving entailed. But she had never been tempted to experience it for herself.

Until now.

"Meg." He stroked the palm of her hand, uncurling her fingers and then twining them together with his own. "You are the first woman—the first *lady*—who has looked at me like this in many years."

"Like what?" Was that her voice, so soft, so husky?

"Like I am a man." He raised her hand to his cheek, pressed her palm there. "A man a lady would want for a lover."

"You're very much a man." She needed no guidance now, and let her fingers drift down the dusky flesh of his face, pausing at his mouth. "I can't imagine a woman alive who wouldn't want you."

His eyes flared at that, and he turned his head, catching one of her fingers between his lips. She let out a squeak of surprise and yanked her hand from his grasp. Was she mad, to be carrying on so in private with a man like Rathmore? Another moment, and she might end up beneath him on the sofa.

Might beg him to take her there.

"Meg—" He reached for her, and she threw up a hand to stop him. Her palm landed splat in the mud that covered his coat.

They both stared at her begrimed fingers for a moment. She snatched her hand back, then raised her chin. "We are done here, my lord."

Finality echoed in her tone. He hesitated for a moment, then he nodded. "We are done *here*."

Meg ignored the implication and cleared the huskiness from her throat. "I'll have someone show you upstairs where you can clean up."

"My thanks."

She marched to the door, threw it open. "Remember what I said, my lord. Patience and sensitivity are the key."

"Indeed," he agreed, following her as she stepped into the hallway. "But are you talking about my ward? Or yourself?"

"My lord," she warned in a whisper, conscious of curious ears all around them.

"Have no fear, Miss Stanton-Lynch," he said with a canny glint in his eye. "I already know the answer."

When Meg returned to the drawing room some minutes later, she found Emily sitting at one end of the room, and Rathmore sitting at the other. Neither spoke.

The tea tray had arrived, and Cook had sent along some of her delectable lemon cakes. Emily

politely nibbled on one, watching Rathmore as one
would watch a wolf about to pounce. He looked
the part of a lean, dark predator, despite his decep-
tively relaxed pose, and as he sipped tea from a delicate china cup, Meg couldn't help but watch his
mouth. He turned and caught her at it, and the silence swelled with tension.

Think of the child. With effort, Meg drew her attention away from Rathmore's sensual grace and
focused on Emily.

"I see Cook has sent lemon cakes," Meg said
brightly. "She's famous for these, Emily. Algie told
me that Lady Denniston has tried many times to
steal Cook and her lemon cake recipe away from
Knightsbridge Chase. But Cook has been here
since His Lordship was a boy, and she won't
budge."

Emily smiled a bit at that but continued to eat
her cake in silence.

"Do you remember, my lord?" Meg said, turning
a bit desperately to Rathmore. She helped herself to
tea and sat down, careful to keep her expression
bland and polite. "I heard that you and Algie were
boyhood chums."

"True." A wistful smile tugged at his lips. "I
spent many a day running wild over Knightsbridge
Chase."

"That you did," came Knightsbridge's cheerful
voice as he sauntered into the room. "And now I
find you sitting in my drawing room and eating all
of Cook's lemon cakes as if the years haven't passed

by. What have you to say about that, St. James? Or actually it's Rathmore now, isn't it?"

Rathmore grinned. "I say you should learn to arrive earlier if you want us to save you any."

"Such a friend." Knightsbridge laughed heartily, then clapped Rathmore on the back hard enough to rattle his teacup in the saucer.

"Hello there, Algie," Meg said. "As you can see, Lord Rathmore and his ward have come to call." She lifted her tea and glanced at him innocently over the rim of her cup. "Have you finished inspecting the orangery?"

Knightsbridge flushed and grabbed a teacup from the tray. "The orangery is doing well, quite well, thank you."

"What's an orangery?" Emily asked.

Knightsbridge choked on his first swallow of tea. "It's . . . ah . . . a garden house where one grows orange trees."

"I should like to see that," Emily announced.

"Perhaps later," he said, hastily biting into his cake.

"Yes, no doubt His Lordship is tired of the orangery, since he and Lady Knightsbridge spent the whole morning there." Meg sent an impish grin at Rathmore. "Wouldn't you say so, Lord Rathmore?"

Amusement lit his dark eyes as he caught her meaning. "Indeed. I'm certain Lord Knightsbridge found his duties there most wearying."

They shared a conspiratorial smile, and for a

moment, the room seemed to hum with invisible energy.

Knightsbridge laughed, breaking the spell. "Enough of that, you two. Really, Meg, you should be ashamed of yourself."

"What?" Meg jerked her gaze away from Rathmore, her heart racing. Had Algie noticed the way she couldn't take her eyes off the man?

"Teasing a newly married man in such a way," Knightsbridge scolded playfully. "Shame on you."

"Is this what women do in America?" Rathmore asked, his tone casually aloof. Only the heated gleam in his eyes revealed the truth. "Tease men?"

"I should say not," Meg replied indignantly.

Knightsbridge chuckled again. "You've done it now, Rathmore. You've ignited her American temper."

"You're an American?" Emily exclaimed. "A colonist?"

"Not quite a colonist," Meg replied, more to Rathmore than to Emily. But then she softened her tone for the child. "My family is rather well off, and we lived in a city very much like London. When my mother died last year, I came to stay with my grandfather, the Duke of Raynewood, to learn about my English heritage."

"Oh. That's all right then," Emily declared, sipping her tea.

Meg chuckled. "I appreciate your friendship, Emily."

Knightsbridge reached for another lemon cake, just beating Rathmore to it. "So this is Desmond's girl? I don't believe I've been introduced. Shame on you, Rathmore."

"It is. Emily," Rathmore said, "this is Lord Knightsbridge, your host." His voice held a stern warning that made Emily's mouth firm in rebellion.

Seeing the danger signs, Meg jumped in. "Algie, did you know Emily's father?"

"That I did," Knightsbridge replied, diverting Emily's attention immediately. "And her mother, too. I was at their wedding. And at your christening," he said to Emily with a fond smile.

"You knew my mother?" Emily asked eagerly. "Would you tell me about her? Please, my lord."

"We both knew her," Knightsbridge said, indicating Rathmore. "Rathmore, surely you've told the child about her mother."

"He did when I was little," Emily said. "But he doesn't have time now."

An awkward silence descended.

"Emily," Meg said quietly, "it would be wiser to keep your battles with your guardian private. You dishonor your mother's memory by not remembering your manners."

Distress crumpled the girl's features. "I apologize, my lord," she said to Knightsbridge.

"No harm done," Algie said brightly. But the glance he sent to Rathmore was troubled.

Meg leaned closer to Emily. "You should apologize to Lord Rathmore, too," she whispered. "You have embarrassed him."

A mulish light entered the girl's eyes. "I don't want to."

Meg put down her teacup. "Miss St. James, you owe your guardian an apology." She folded her hands in her lap and waited, never taking her eyes from the girl.

Emily resisted, but finally she glanced at Rathmore. "I am sorry if I have embarrassed you, Cousin Justin," she said reluctantly.

Meg picked up her teacup, amused by the stunned look on Rathmore's face. "That's better. More tea, Lord Rathmore?"

"Uh . . . yes, thank you." Rathmore handed over his teacup so that Meg could pour.

Penelope chose that moment to enter the room, a clean and groomed Pudding in her arms.

"Here you are, Algernon," she said. "Eating all the lemon cakes again, I see."

"Not I, my love," Algie protested, after hastily swallowing. Crumbs clung to his lips as he and Rathmore got to their feet. " 'Tis Rathmore's ward, Miss St. James, who is devouring them like she hasn't eaten in weeks. I do believe Rathmore doesn't feed her."

"He does, too!" Emily exclaimed, drawing a surprised look from Rathmore at her unexpected defense.

"Very well done," Meg said approvingly. "Lord

Knightsbridge has a peculiar sense of humor. Lord
Rathmore, have you met Algie's bride?"

"Not formally," Rathmore replied, clearly still
bemused by his ward's supportive behavior. "I'm
afraid I left the wedding before I had the pleasure."

"What a clod I am," Knightsbridge said. "Rathmore, this is my beautiful wife, Lady Knightsbridge. My dear, this is my good friend, Lord
Rathmore, and his ward, Miss St. James."

"It's lovely to finally meet you, Lord Rathmore,"
Penelope said. Once she was seated on the settee,
both men sat down again. She put Pudding on the
floor and reached for a teacup. An amused smile
curved Penelope's lips as Emily called softly to the
dog, enticing him with a bit of lemon cake. "My
husband has told me much about you," Penelope
continued, gracefully pouring herself a cup of tea.

"Has he?" Rathmore sent an inquiring glance at
his friend.

"Pen knows everything," Knightsbridge said.
"And she feels as I do. We both know you had
nothing to do with that distasteful matter."

"Absolutely," Penelope agreed.

"We were at the Dennistons' when that old cat
Lady Aggerly cut you," Knightsbridge said. "Don't
trouble yourself over that sort of thing. Half of society isn't worth your time."

"Did you know Algernon cut Lady Aggerly after
you left, Lord Rathmore?" Penelope sent a beam-
ing smile at her husband.

"Did you?" Rathmore asked, brows arching in surprise.

Meg glanced at Emily, who was distracted with the dog. "Perhaps this isn't the best time to discuss this."

"You're quite right, Meg," Penelope said. "Perhaps Miss St. James would like to take Pudding out to the garden to play with him."

"Oh, that would be lovely," Emily exclaimed.

"Just have a care," Meg warned. "The little imp escaped the garden once, and I wouldn't want to have to go looking for both of you in the woods again."

"We'll send a footman with her to keep Pudding under control," Penelope decided. "I shall see to it."

A footman was summoned, and Emily skipped off happily with Pudding trotting at her heels.

"There," Penelope said, once the door had closed behind the girl. "Now we may speak of matters unfit for a child's ears. Your ward is quite lovely, Lord Rathmore. When she comes out, she will no doubt be a sensation."

"Perhaps," Rathmore said. "But I rather doubt it, with this reputation of mine hanging over her head."

"Society is full of empty-headed widgeons," Knightsbridge declared. "As if anyone could believe you murdered someone, much less an innocent woman."

"Desmond believed it. My uncle believed it."

Rathmore placed his teacup back on the tray, his expression troubled. "Ever since I've arrived back in England, I have been trying to find out the truth for Emily's sake. But no one will talk to me. No one wants to be tainted by my black reputation."

"But I don't understand," Meg said, moved more than she cared to admit by the despair behind his words. "If you didn't do it, if nothing can be proven, then why do people treat you like this?"

"As Algie said, society can be foolish," Penelope replied. "Someone decided that Lord Rathmore could have done the deed, and since society cannot resist a delightful tidbit such as having a murderer among them, they chose to believe it." Her mouth thinned. "Never mind that it cost a man his reputation."

"No one could have imagined that you would inherit," Algie said with a little smirk.

"Indeed," Rathmore replied, a bitter twist to his lips. "Calling the poor relation of the Earl of Rathmore a murderer is one thing. I was unable to do anything to defend myself, as I was completely dependent upon my uncle."

"But now you *are* the earl," Knightsbridge pointed out with a wicked grin, "and they don't know what to do with you. You're rich and powerful. No one dares insult you, given your reputation."

"And much of that wealth is my own." Rathmore smiled rather grimly. "I more than doubled the estate during my time away from England."

Knightsbridge burst out laughing. "Oh, to see

the look on the old biddies' faces were they to know that little fact! If not for this dreadful rumor, Rathmore, you would no doubt be the catch of the Season. The women never could stay away from you."

Rathmore sent Meg a sidelong glance. "Some could."

Meg busied herself pouring more tea. "In America, a man is presumed innocent until proven guilty."

"Well, in England, Miss Stanton-Lynch, society decides a man's fate with a mere flap of the tongue." Rathmore leaned back in his chair, folding his hands across his stomach. "Take a word of advice and have a care for your reputation."

"No doubt being seen with you would be enough to ruin my reputation," Meg retorted, settling back into her seat with her tea. "But I choose my own friends, Lord Rathmore."

"What ho! Well put, Meg!" Knightsbridge cried with a whoop of laughter. "Wouldn't you say, Pen?"

"Very well said," Penelope replied, a smile curving her lips as she lifted her teacup.

"As I told you, Rathmore," Knightsbridge hooted, pointing his finger at the earl. "The women love you."

"Indeed." Rathmore cast Meg a glance that made her want to squirm. Must he look at her as if she were one of the lemon cakes?

"Desmond was always jealous of that," Knightsbridge continued, oblivious to the undercurrents around him. "He had the money and the position, but Rathmore here had inherited all the good looks in the family. It was no secret that Ophelia wanted him."

"Algie!" Penelope glanced sideways at Meg. "This is not fit conversation for a lady to hear. Especially an unmarried lady."

"So right," Knightsbridge said. "Apologies, Meg."

"But—" Meg began.

"Lord Rathmore, do tell us about the improvements you have made to your estate," Penelope said.

As Rathmore began to detail the progress he had been making in repairing the estate, Meg simmered with impatience. What had Algie meant, that Ophelia had preferred Rathmore to her fiancé? Was that why society was so willing to believe that he had killed her? Had he been her lover?

The more time she spent with Lord Rathmore, the more she began to truly believe that he was the innocent victim of malicious gossip as far as killing Ophelia. But what if they *had* been lovers? What kind of a man did that make him?

Twice she had allowed him to kiss her, though perhaps the nibbling of her fingers that occurred earlier could not really be counted a true kiss. Still, she had not protested such liberties not only because she was so completely attracted to him, but also because she trusted Algie's opinion of him. But was Lord Rathmore merely another bored nobleman out to callously conquer a lady's affections? Is that what had happened to Ophelia?

Perhaps it hadn't been murder at all. Perhaps the lady had been distraught over Rathmore's rejection and ended her own life.

And what of Emily? Meg could hardly stand by silently and let an innocent girl be influenced by a rake and murderer. If she was going to form a correct opinion of the man, she would have to find out the facts. And the best place to find out information about any member of the *ton*, especially one so close to home and so infamous, would be the local Friday night assembly.

She would attend this Friday, Meg decided, nodding politely as Rathmore went on about his plans for building another school for the tenants' children. And then she would discover what kind of a man Rathmore really was—a wrongly accused bystander or an immoral killer.

And if he were the latter, she would not rest until Emily was safe from him.

Chapter 6

As always, the Friday night assembly was a terrible crush. However, Meg took comfort that, though she had been there for but half an hour, she had already accomplished the first step in her plan, in the form of Mr. Freddie Adderton, son of a local baron.

"Miss Stanton-Lynch, dare I tell you that your eyes remind me of a lake on a summer day . . . the type of day when one might catch the fattest trout?"

Meg managed a tolerant smile as she performed the steps of the country dance. "Why thank you, Mr. Adderton."

"And your hair." Freddie swallowed hard, his prominent Adam's apple bulging above his cravat. "Your hair reminds me of my favorite hunting dog, Argos. He's a splendid hound, Miss Stanton-Lynch."

"Truly the highest of compliments, Mr. Adderton," she murmured, torn between insult and amusement.

Freddie seemed to be encouraged by her subdued responses. "You have the grace of a falcon, Miss Stanton-Lynch, when it soars down for the kill. Indeed, you are a most splendid figure of a female."

"Mr. Adderton, please." She cast down her gaze in what she hoped appeared to be modesty. "You'll turn my head with all these compliments."

"So sorry." Tall and gangly with a shock of auburn hair that stood on end, Freddie turned red in the face. "Don't mean to embarrass you. Just wanted to tell you how much I admire you."

Meg gave him a dazzling smile and watched his greenish eyes widen. "Mr. Adderton, you are most kind to a lady like myself, who knows practically no one at this affair."

"Miss Stanton-Lynch, it would be my utmost delight to introduce you to anyone you care to meet." He beamed at her. "You are most beautiful for an American and charming as well."

She laughed. "Why, Mr. Adderton, you say that as if you were expecting something else."

"One hears stories, Miss Stanton-Lynch, of the savages in America and how the Americans have no culture, no refinement. I am pleased to see that there are some exceptions."

Meg barely resisted the urge to tread on his toes. "And I had heard that England was ripe with overbearing windbags full of their own consequence," she said with a sweet smile.

He laughed. "Silly rumor."

"Indeed." Meg controlled her annoyance with the oblivious young man and focused on her real objective. "Mr. Adderton, I have heard that you are a relation to Mrs. Abigail Peacham."

"I am." He puffed out his chest. "She's my sister."

"Oh, how fortunate!" Meg threw in a flutter of eyelashes. "I would so love to make her acquaintance. I have heard that Mrs. Peacham is the first stare of fashion here in Devon."

Not to mention the biggest gossip in the area.

"Indeed she is. And do you know what else?" Freddie lowered his voice. "I have heard that she may even be approached to become a patroness for the Friday assemblies."

Meg widened her eyes. "No! Really? How wonderful!"

Freddie nodded. "Quite so. And if you consider that in the past, a patroness has always been at the very least a titled lady, then you will understand how rare and amazing it is that my sister, a mere missus, might be considered for such an auspicious position."

"She must truly be a paragon," Meg agreed, though she had no doubt the entire story was a fiction devised by Mrs. Peacham herself. She bit her lower lip and then flashed her best dimpled smile. "Mr. Adderton, would it be too rude of me to ask for an introduction?"

"Of course not, Miss Stanton-Lynch." He stood a bit taller and smiled somewhat condescendingly. "After all, despite being an American, you are the granddaughter of a duke and therefore the social equal of my sister. I shall elect to introduce you once the set is over."

"Oh, thank you, Mr. Adderton!"

Meg prayed for the end of the set to come soon, before the laughter that she had contained for so long burst free and ruined everything.

The Friday night assembly had to be the most boring affair on Earth, Rathmore decided as his carriage approached the assembly hall where the event was held. But since he was finding it difficult to corner his prey at the more private functions, he hoped to have better luck here.

The weekly affairs were governed by a committee of three local ladies: Lady Denniston, Lady Ellworth, and Lady Presting. They did their best to imitate the patronesses of Almacks, insisting on rigid propriety at the assemblies and serving the most insipid refreshments imaginable. The only thing they did not insist upon was knee breeches for the men, and a good thing, else the upper reaches of the aristocracy would never attend the assemblies.

Since it was a less exclusive event than the local balls and house parties, the lower orders of the gentry were invited, and Rathmore had hope that he might run into Mrs. Warington at the affair. His contacts had informed him that she was expected to attend.

Too bad he had to wade through the shark-infested waters of society to achieve his goal.

As a man who had always been widely received socially, even pursued in some cases, his current status frustrated him to the point of fury. He hadn't done anything wrong, but society needed the proof of it shoved under its collective nose before admitting the truth. And yet they were effectively shutting him out, preventing him from getting to that proof.

He hated the way men watched him warily, the way women shied away from him. The momentary hush that fell over the room when his name was announced. If he thought forward to the future and imagined that same reaction every time Emily's name was announced with his, it was more than he could stand. Why should an innocent girl suffer needlessly because the *ton* loved malicious gossip?

The assembly had to yield some answers. He was running out of options.

As he entered the assembly room, he heard several alarmed gasps, and one person hissed, "What's *he* doing here?" He cast a warning glance in the general direction of the speaker, and there were no more outbursts.

Lady Denniston flew over to him, cutting through the crowd like a frigate at full sail. "Good evening, Lord Rathmore."

He sketched a bow. "Lady Denniston. May I say you are in fine looks this evening?"

"You may say anything you like, my lord." She gave him a hard stare. "I want no trouble here this evening."

"And I intend to cause none."

"See that you don't." She turned away from him, her nose in the air. Before she could take two steps, someone hailed him.

"Justin St. James!"

Lady Denniston whirled back, mouth agape, and conversation all but died as a man made his way through the crowd toward Rathmore.

He was not a tall man, but he was sturdy with curling blond hair so fine it looked like a babe's. His round face showed no expression, but his dark eyes were fixed on Rathmore.

"Justin St. James," the man said again as he reached them. "Oh, but it's Lord Rathmore now, isn't it?"

"It is." Every muscle in his body tensed. He hadn't found the prey he sought, but someone else who had been present at the house party. Someone with whom he hoped to avoid a scene. He forced his tone to sound casual. "How are you, Lord Fenton?"

Ophelia's brother gave a sad smile. "As well as can be expected, considering the circumstances."

Lady Denniston stepped forward. "Lord Fenton, I had no idea you were visiting the area. Do tell me if there is anything I can do for you this evening."

Her implication was clear. Rathmore half expected the footmen to come drag him from the room on the spot.

Lord Fenton shook his head. "Not necessary, Lady Denniston. I have no problem with Rathmore being here."

"Are you certain?" Lady Denniston cast Rathmore a look of distaste. "It would be quite simple to persuade Lord Rathmore to leave."

"My thanks for your concern, Lady Denniston, but all is well." Fenton glanced around. "However, I do believe the orchestra has stopped."

"Heavens!" Indeed, the music had ceased, and the dancers milled about the dance floor, watching the unfolding drama. Lady Denniston caught the eye of the orchestra leader and gestured imperiously with her hand. The orchestra started up again, and a hard look from the patroness had the dancers scrambling for their places. She pushed back through the crowd, shooing the onlookers away, leaving Rathmore face-to-face with Fenton.

"Let's get out of the middle of the room," Fenton said. "We're drawing attention to ourselves."

As they moved to a secluded corner, Rathmore said, "What are you doing in the area, Laertes?"

"Visiting Lord Presting. House party. And you— you are the Earl of Rathmore." Fenton shook his head, amazement plain on his face. "Who could have known that your uncle and Desmond would be lost in that fire?"

"No one could have predicted such a thing."

"I'm sorry for it," Fenton said. "Desmond was my friend."

"And he was my cousin. I loved him, for all that he didn't believe that."

"Yes, Desmond was always jealous of you, even when we were boys." Laertes glanced up at Rathmore. "He hated that you were sent to Eton with us, you know, when he was the heir and you were just a poor relation."

"My uncle did his duty. He knew that my father wanted me to be educated as befitted my station."

"Well, you *are* a St. James."

"I am. You haven't mentioned Ophelia, Laertes."

Fenton gave a hard, brief laugh. "You cut right to the point, Justin, as you always did."

"I see no reason to dance around the issue. I'm sorry for your loss, Laertes, but please believe that I had nothing to do with it."

Lord Fenton said nothing for a moment. Then he sighed and said, "I don't know what happened with Ophelia. I know her behavior was not what our parents would have wanted. She threw herself at you, even though she was betrothed to Desmond."

"I never touched her. I would not dishonor my cousin or my friendship with you in that way."

Fenton shrugged. "I wouldn't have blamed you if you did. My sister was beautiful, but she had the morals of a cat in heat. She wanted to marry Desmond for the title, but it was you she wanted in her bed."

"It never happened."

"Of course not." Fenton's patronizing tone indicated that he believed otherwise. "But don't trouble yourself, Justin. I know my sister could be determined."

"I was never her lover," Rathmore insisted.

Laertes clapped a hand on his shoulder. "Of course you weren't. Nonetheless, Ophelia always got what she wanted."

"Not this time."

"And I know she could be opinionated and irritating in her determination. I'm sure it was just some lover's spat that caused the accident. I never doubted that Ophelia brought it all on herself."

"I didn't kill her, Laertes."

"No." Fenton's tone grew sad. "She killed herself, didn't she?"

"What do you suppose they're talking about?" Mrs. Abigail Peacham asked. A rather pretty brunette with a narrow face and almond-shaped dark eyes that reminded Meg of a ferret, the woman craned her neck, trying to see over the crowd to where Lord Fenton and Rathmore stood talking quietly in a corner.

"I rather thought they would come to blows by now," Freddie said. "But it all seems very civilized. Got Fenton to thank for that, I'm sure."

Meg glared at the two of them, though neither one noticed, distracted as they were by the two men in the far corner of the room. She, too, wondered what they were saying, but she didn't doubt that Rathmore was just as responsible for the civility of it as Lord Fenton.

Good Lord. *Ophelia's brother*. What must Rathmore be feeling, to have come face to face with that man in the middle of a crowded assembly room?

"Is Lord Fenton from this area?" she asked.

Mrs. Peacham actually pulled her gaze away from the tableau to look at Meg with a gleam in her eyes. "No, his estate is near the borders of Scotland. I believe he is here tonight because he's a guest at Lord Presting's house party."

"So his presence here was unexpected."

Mrs. Peacham gave a low chuckle. "I should say so."

"How difficult this must be for Lord Rathmore."

"Not really," Mrs. Peacham replied. "Lord Fenton and Lord Rathmore knew each other at school, as did the earl's cousin, Desmond St. James."

"So they were all friends?"

"Of a sort. Desmond and Lord Fenton were friends. The current Lord Rathmore was just the tagalong cousin." Suddenly she gasped and tapped her brother on the arm with her fan. "Freddie, Miss Corning has finished her dance with Mr. Lindsay. Do hurry and get your name on her dance card."

"Yes, Abigail." He bowed. "Miss Stanton-Lynch, it has been a pleasure to be in your company."

"I might say the same, Mr. Adderton."

Freddie took himself off, and Mrs. Peacham sighed. "That boy hasn't got a thimble's worth of social sense. I am trying to educate him, Miss Stanton-Lynch."

"I think you're doing a splendid job."

Mrs. Peacham glanced over at the far corner and gave a squeal of dismay. "Where did they go?"

Meg had noticed the two men parting ways, but she had deliberately not said anything to the notorious gossip. "I imagine they both went back to the dancing."

"Nonsense. Lord Rathmore never dances."

"You were telling me how they all used to be friends," Meg said.

Mrs. Peacham eagerly took up the conversation. "Not exactly. Desmond was his father's heir, of course, as was Lord Fenton. Justin—the current earl—was Desmond's cousin, the son of his father's younger brother. Justin's father died in a hunting accident when Justin was barely five years old. His mother married an Italian count and left England almost immediately. Justin stayed behind to be educated and raised as a St. James."

"How awful," Meg whispered. "His own mother abandoned him?"

"What could she do?" Mrs. Peacham said with a cavalier shrug that set Meg's teeth on edge. "Celeste was completely dependent on the earl for her living. If he chose not to provide for her, she had no choice but to remarry. I believe he settled a sizable dowry on her, on the condition that she leave her son in England to be raised as his father would have wished."

"The poor boy," Meg murmured.

"As they grew older, it was so hard on Desmond," Mrs. Peacham continued with a sympathetic sigh. "Justin inherited his mother's wicked French looks, which the ladies cannot seem to resist. And Desmond looked like the earl's family—short, stout, and losing his hair by the time he was nineteen. Some even say that Desmond needed spectacles, but if he did, he never wore the dreadful things in public."

"So Justin was handsome where Desmond was not."

"Indeed. But Desmond was the heir, which won him his rightful share of attention from the female population." She paused dramatically. "And then there was Ophelia Haversham."

Meg moved a step closer. "Tell me about her."

Mrs. Peacham pursed her lips. "You understand that I am not prone to gossip, Miss Stanton-Lynch."

"Of course not," Meg agreed.

"But," the woman continued without missing a beat, "Ophelia Haversham was fast, Miss Stanton-Lynch. There was a rumor at the time that she had allowed young Mr. Etheridge liberties no lady should allow."

"Really," Meg breathed, playing the part of eager audience. "Such a scandal!"

Mrs. Peacham preened. "It was hushed up, of course, and Mr. Etheridge was called home by his father and promptly affianced to an heiress who lived nearby. One still does not see him in Town all that often."

"And what happened to Miss Haversham?"

"Her brother took her in hand and betrothed her to Desmond. It was a good match, as Lord Fenton is a viscount and the earls of Rathmore go all the way back to the Conqueror." Mrs. Peacham sniffed with disdain. "Of course, Ophelia Haversham wanted to be a countess. But she also wanted her fiancé's cousin. Justin St. James was always too handsome for his own good," she added darkly. "And he finally got his comeuppance."

"What do you mean?"

"Why, everyone knows that he killed her," Mrs. Peacham said, lips trembling. "She was making trouble and endangering his living with his uncle by advertising their affair."

"What!" Meg exclaimed. The Rathmore she knew—the man who cared so much for his ward that he was attempting the impossible—would never dishonor his family in such a manner. "And do you have proof of this?" Meg demanded, rashly giving vent to her rising fury with every word. "Of their affair? Of murder? Of any of it?"

Mrs. Peacham's mouth thinned in sudden disapproval. "Miss Stanton-Lynch, I am certainly not going to discuss such matters with an unmarried lady!"

"You had no problem doing that a minute ago."

"I said I shall not discuss this with you." The woman gave Meg a scathing head-to-toe glance. "You are an American, so I suppose you have no idea how young ladies in England are expected to behave. Rest assured I will overlook your terrible propensity for gossip this one time."

"*My* propensity for gossip? I'm not the one spreading lies about someone I don't even know. *I* am not the one condemning a man for a crime no one can prove he committed!"

"Miss Stanton-Lynch, you forget yourself," Mrs. Peacham said coldly. "Do recall your manners, lest I am forced to have you ejected from the hall."

"As if you could," Meg snapped. "I may be an American, Mrs. Peacham, but I am also the grand-daughter of the Duke of Raynewood and cousin to the Earl of Knightsbridge. *And* I am a friend of Lord Rathmore's. If I ever hear you mention his name in public again, I will have *you* ejected from the hall."

Mrs. Peacham gaped, her eyes bulging in shock. Several conversations around them died down as it became obvious that the American was challenging Mrs. Peacham's social standing.

Mrs. Peacham, seeing they were the center of at-tention, lifted her haughty nose in the air. Then she deliberately turned her back.

Meg gasped. She had been *cut!*

Fury overrode her common sense, and she took a step toward the arrogant woman, fists clenching. But someone caught her arm, and she whirled to confront whoever held her back.

Rathmore's dark eyes held a warning. "What do you think you're doing?" he asked in a low voice.

"That woman just cut me dead."

He flicked a glance at the avidly watching by-standers. "Dance with me."

"I don't want to dance." She tugged at her arm, but he didn't release it. "Let me go," she hissed.

"Miss Stanton-Lynch, may I have this dance?" he said, louder this time.

Titters of laughter came from the spectators, and Meg suddenly realized that Rathmore was putting his own reputation on the line. She could accept his offer to dance and gracefully escape Mrs. Peacham's presence. Or she could reject him in front of everyone and start the rumors all over again.

Her heart melted in the face of his selfless act.

"I would love to dance with you, Lord Rathmore," she said, placing her hand on his arm.

He led her out to the floor.

Chapter 7

The next dance was a waltz.

Rathmore hesitated. "Are you sanctioned to dance the waltz by the patronesses of Almacks? If not, I had best escort you back to Lady Knightsbridge."

Meg angled her chin, her eyes glittering like gemstones with rekindled temper. "Even if I weren't, I wouldn't step away at this moment if the Prince Regent himself asked me to."

He gave her a wicked smile. "Then let's dance." He took one of her hands, marveling at the daintiness of it in his much larger one. He placed his other hand at her slim waist, then swept her into the waltz.

Rathmore couldn't remember the last time he had danced the waltz—probably sometime during his exile, but certainly not since he had returned to

England. And the woman in his arms was as light as a feather. He noted with amusement that she was a tiny thing, her head barely reaching his chest. For some reason, he had never noticed her lack of height before. Perhaps it was because her ferocity made her seem taller somehow. That and her American fearlessness.

"So," he said, "are you going to tell me what you thought you were doing, conversing with the biggest gossip in Devon?"

Guilt flickered for a moment in those guileless blue eyes. "Nothing, my lord."

"Shall I tell you my theory?" He whisked her into a quick turn that had her clinging to keep up. "I believe, Miss Stanton-Lynch, that you were meddling in my affairs."

"Now why would I do that?" Her tone seemed innocent enough, but her eyes fixed on his shoulder, his ear—everywhere but his face.

"I don't know," he mused. "Perhaps you have formed a *tendre* for me."

She jerked her gaze to his. "I should say not!"

"It's a plausible explanation," he went on. "Especially considering the way you've kissed me in the past."

"The way *I* kissed *you* . . . !" she spluttered.

"Though if you do have some other explanation, I'd be happy to listen to it." Then he whirled her around so quickly that she gave a squeak of surprise. He raised his brows. "Is there a problem, Miss Stanton-Lynch?"

"Lord Rathmore," she gasped, "if you are going to ring a peal over me, you really should call me Meg."

"My dear girl, you sound out of breath. Shall we slow down?" He immediately slowed his steps, swirling her around at a lazy pace that matched the steadiness of a heartbeat.

Looking looked down into her sweet face, he was well aware that he shouldn't be doing this, shouldn't be seducing her through the dance. But he needed to find out what she had been doing with that inveterate gossip Abigail Peacham. He knew they had been talking about him, could tell from the way Mrs. Peacham had been watching him. And this was the only way he knew to throw the formidable Meg off balance.

Though he had to admit that he did enjoy having her in his arms again.

Unable to resist temptation, he subtly moved the hand he had on her waist, briefly stroking his fingertips over the curve of her hip in a way that no one else would notice. Awareness flickered in her eyes. Her face softened, her lips parting.

And then she squeezed the hand that rested on his shoulder, returning the caress.

That easily, desire slammed through him. Damn the girl anyway, why had she done that? She was supposed to be intimidated by his seduction, not responding to it as if they were longtime lovers.

"Miss Stanton-Lynch, have a care for your reputation," he murmured. "First you attempt to pummel Mrs. Peacham, and now you seduce me on the dance floor. Shame on you, my girl."

"I wouldn't have 'pummeled' her, as you put it, though I *was* about to tear a strip off her with words." A dozen emotions simmered in those lovely blue eyes. "And as for seducing you, Lord Rathmore, you started it."

"And I can finish it, too." He pressed his thigh between hers as they turned, then in an instant returned to a more circumspect position. "So have a care, my girl."

Meg stared up at him as she searched for a clever comeback, her pulse skittering like a newborn filly attempting to stand. The light played off the sculpted features of his face, making him look more than ever like a fallen angel. But angel he wasn't, as the sensual gleam in his eyes so clearly revealed. He was attracted to her, and God help her, she was attracted to him as well.

"I should think that even you would have difficulty doing such a thing in a crowded room," she said finally. "So do not attempt your flummery on me, Lord Rathmore. I'm not one of your naïve English misses."

"That you aren't," he agreed. "You're an American with little care for her own well-being."

"I'm hardly afraid of *you*, my lord."

"Maybe you should be."

Tension thrummed between them as he watched her with that all-knowing dark gaze. What would Rathmore be like as a lover? The scandalous thought set her heart pounding as if she had run for miles. She licked her dry lips. "Maybe I like danger, my lord."

"Maybe you do." He pulled her an inch closer, and she could feel the heat emanating from his body. Could smell the scent of cologne on his skin. "But you might get more than you bargained for."

"So might you, my lord."

He laughed. "You're fearless, do you know that?"

"No, I'm American."

"You even take on society." His tone grew serious. "But don't you realize what kind of damage you would have done to your reputation if you had confronted Mrs. Peacham, as you were clearly about to do?"

"I know, but the woman was spouting lies, and I got angry." She gave him a little smile. "I'm afraid I have my mother's Irish temper."

"Scandalous," he murmured. "You certainly are a woman of strong emotion, Miss Stanton-Lynch."

"Meg," she corrected.

"Meg," he repeated, and for some reason her name sounded like sin on his lips. "Tell me what you and Mrs. Peacham were discussing."

Meg rolled her eyes. "You already know we were talking about you, my lord, so why pretend otherwise?"

"Indeed. Which raises the question, what is it about me that you felt you could not ask? That you needed to find out from a gossip?"

Heat crept into her cheeks. "I was just curious about some things I have overheard, my lord. Things no one seems willing to discuss with me."

"Meg, rest assured there is nothing you can ask me that I will not answer." He swept her into a final turn as the music came to an end. They stopped. "Nothing," he repeated, sketching a bow. "Now, allow me to escort you back to your cousin."

Rathmore navigated the way back to Knightsbridge and Penelope with the ease of long experience. The dance had shaken him more than he liked to admit. What was it about this dainty, black-haired woman that made him open himself to her so completely?

Was it the way she cared for Emily, a child she barely knew? Or the easy way she had taken his word about his innocence? The fierce loyalty she possessed that made her take on society itself?

Someone had to protect her from herself. When you were society's darling, it was difficult to imagine that anyone might not receive you, that with one little mistake you could become a social outcast. He knew how that felt, and he also knew that Meg was bound to make some powerful enemies if she went around poking into things that did not concern her.

He strongly suspected that she had been asking Mrs. Peacham about his past, which was no doubt why the woman had cut her. He'd have to put a stop to that immediately. Since he was already fallen in society's eyes, he had no problem asking uncomfortable questions, though he still took care not to force any confrontations for Emily's sake.

But Meg was different. She was an unmarried girl whose social success depended on her being free of scandal. She would never be able to make an advantageous marriage if she alienated herself by asking questions about his background. Better that she come to him with her curiosity.

Besides, he was flattered that she bothered to ask. Perhaps she considered him attractive. Certainly, she was the only woman in the Polite World who treated him like a human being and not some sort of monster. After being ostracized for so long, he found himself craving more and more of her acceptance.

"You're very quiet, my lord," Meg said.

"Just preoccupied with my own thoughts." Rathmore could see over the heads of most of the crowd, and he spotted Knightsbridge and Penelope immediately. "Looks like your cousin and his bride have taken places for the next set," he said. "I shall remain your escort until they return."

She slanted him a look of amusement. "Lord Rathmore, I am not a child."

"No, you're a beautiful young woman. Don't worry. No one will bother you while you're with me."

"Indeed," she agreed with an impish grin. "They're too afraid of what you might do to them."

He stared at her, astonished. Had she just made a *joke* about his reputation?

At his continued silence, her expression grew troubled. "Please forgive me, Lord Rathmore. I didn't mean to make light of your situation."

Her distress cut through his amazement. "No need to apologize, Meg." He grinned; the load he had been carrying for so long suddenly felt lighter. "I was just surprised. Most women speak of me in frightened whispers, yet you seem content to have the Devil Earl as your guard dog. Aren't you the least bit afraid of me?"

"Oh, I am very afraid of you, my lord," she replied, "but I don't fear for my life." She looked right at him, wet her lips, and said, "You make me think thoughts no lady should have."

Of all the things she could have said, that was the most unexpected. Before he could think of a reply—how *was* a man supposed to reply to such candor?—Lady Denniston approached them.

"Lord Rathmore, I don't believe I've seen you dance in years," she said pleasantly. "And I did see the way you rescued Miss Stanton-Lynch. Very well done of you."

"Thank you, madam," he replied, caught off balance by the matron's friendly attitude.

"And you, my dear," Lady Denniston continued, turning to Meg. "What *did* you say to Mrs. Peacham to cause her very rude conduct?"

Rathmore turned an interested look on Meg, curious to hear what she would reply.

Meg bit her lower lip, the picture of penitent innocence. Only he caught the shrewd gleam in her eye. "Please forgive me, Lady Denniston. I'm afraid I upset Mrs. Peacham by losing my temper. It's a regrettable failing of mine."

Lady Denniston's face settled into stern lines. "You must keep your emotions in check at all times, Miss Stanton-Lynch. I'm certain you need no reminder of that."

"No, my lady." Meg lowered her gaze. "I just didn't know what to do once Mrs. Peacham started filling my ears with such gossip . . ."

"What's this?" Lady Denniston snapped. "Mrs. Peacham was imparting rumors to you? An unmarried girl?"

Meg gave a hesitant nod. "I admit, I did lose my temper when she started talking about Lord Rathmore. He's a friend of the family, you see."

"Mrs. Peacham was talking to you about . . . well, this will never do." Lady Denniston's eyes bulged, and Rathmore had to stifle his laughter. In five minutes' time, Meg had turned the formidable matron against the pretentious gossip without even embellishing the story.

"I'm certain everything she said was a lie," Meg insisted, her blue eyes wide. "Why, the things she told me, something about a girl named Ophelia—"

Lady Denniston gasped with horror and sent a meaningful glance at Rathmore that seemed to ask for his support. He managed to frown in disapproval.

"You are quite correct to not listen to such things," Lady Denniston said briskly. "Especially given that Lord Rathmore is a family friend."

"I was so upset at her reaction," Meg said with a little sniff. "I have never been cut socially before. My grandfather will be so distressed when he hears. I'm afraid I was about to make a very big social blunder by confronting Mrs. Peacham, but Lord Rathmore stopped me."

"And thank the heavens he did." Lady Denniston sent Rathmore a look of approval. "I shall speak to Mrs. Peacham about her behavior. We cannot have the duke upset, and she must make allowances for your American upbringing."

"I do apologize," Meg said, all sweet eagerness. "I just want to do the right thing."

"There, there." Lady Denniston smiled maternally at Meg. "It's not your fault. Mrs. Peacham should know better."

"I do hope I haven't ruined anything for Mrs. Peacham with my impulsiveness," Meg went on. "I know she was being considered as a patroness for the Friday night assemblies, and I don't want my actions to deprive her of such an honor."

"What!" Sheer outrage flooded Lady Denniston's face with color. "Who said Mrs. Peacham—a mere missus—was to become a patroness?"

Meg looked confused. "Why, Mr. Adderton told me. Since he is Mrs. Peacham's brother, I can only imagine he heard it from the lady herself."

"We shall see about *that*. If you will excuse

me . . ." Without waiting for a reply, Lady Denniston turned away and marched over to Lady Presting and Lady Ellworth, her fellow patronesses. After a few words were exchanged, the three ladies turned as one unit and sliced through the crowd to confront Mrs. Peacham.

"That was quite bad of you, you know," Rathmore murmured to Meg as they watched the three most powerful women in Devon have Mrs. Peacham escorted from the hall.

"I only told the truth." Meg grinned up at him.

"You did indeed. And that's even more frightening."

"Are you the one who's scared now, my lord?"

Her teasing tone lightened his heart. "My dear Meg, you terrify me."

"Well, at least there was one redeeming event in the whole drama," Meg said. "Apparently Lady Denniston now sees you in the role of hero, saving the American from herself."

"You place too much importance on one moment," Rathmore said with a bitter laugh. "I guarantee you that before the evening is out, I will be the Devil Earl again."

"Only if you allow it, my lord." And with that, she was claimed by her partner for the next set. With a little wave, she stepped out onto the dance floor.

Sir Richard Ainsley had served in the war against Napoleon and was prone to mention that fact every fifth sentence. Meg smiled at appropriate moments, encouraging Sir Richard to go on talking about himself, while she remained preoccupied with her own thoughts.

Rathmore had proven to be a puzzle. She liked the man, and the more she got to know him, the less she believed that he had had anything to do with Ophelia's death. In fact, she was almost positive the man had been grievously wronged. But what could she do about it?

Her thoughts pulled her up short, so much so that she almost trod on Sir Richard's toes. Why should she do *anything*? The earl was a grown man and could handle his own problems. If her brother were there, no doubt he would advise Meg to mind her own business. But from where she stood, it certainly looked as if Lord Rathmore could use a friend.

And what of Emily? What was going to happen to that little girl if things didn't change, if the rumors didn't stop? From what she had learned about English society, Meg had no doubt that the sins of her guardian would follow Emily around like a plague.

As an American, Meg at least had a choice about her future. She could live life as the granddaughter of the Duke of Raynewood, or she could go home to Boston and live as an independent woman—at least as independent as her overprotective brother, Garrett, would allow, anyway.

But Emily had no choice. She was the ward of the wicked Earl of Rathmore, and life in England was all she knew. If there had been no scandal, Meg was sure that Emily could take society by storm and have her choice of suitors. But with her guardian considered a murderer, what would happen to her when she was ready to come out? Would she be accepted by society at all?

Someone had to discover what had really happened all those years ago. Rathmore was trying, but he was an outcast and so no one would help him. Her own foray into the world of gossip had been so distasteful that she hesitated to become involved further.

And what if her instincts were deceiving her again? What if he *had* done this terrible thing? In trying to help Lord Rathmore, she might very well be putting herself in danger.

If she were smart, she would just ignore the whole thing.

And do what? Go back to Knightsbridge Chase and watch Algie and Penelope stare into each other's eyes? Follow her grandfather to Bath only to be sent back to Devon to "enjoy her youth"? Go home to America to live under Garrett's command? And what about Emily?

For the sake of the child, she couldn't stand idly by. If Rathmore had indeed had a hand in Ophelia's death, Emily could be in grave danger. And if he hadn't, Emily could only benefit by her guardian's improved reputation.

In fact, Meg might be the *only* person capable of setting Rathmore free.

Elation shot through her, but she forced herself to calmly think the matter through. As an American, she was expected to make the occasional social gaffe, and people tended to brush it aside because they didn't want to offend her very powerful grandfather. So if she happened to ask a bold question or talk to the wrong person, society would probably forgive and forget.

In addition, she needed to form her own opinion of Rathmore. How did he run his estates? How did he treat his servants? His horses? His tenants? She knew he was inept at handling Emily, but that could be simple inexperience. The important thing was, did he love the little girl?

Society believed him unequivocally guilty. Algie and Penelope believed him completely innocent. Meg would make up her own mind.

Helping Lord Rathmore would also prove to her family that she wasn't a child to be insulated from the real world, though getting to know him better would be equivalent to cornering the lion in his den. The attraction between them was nothing to be ignored. While her life might very well be in danger if Rathmore was guilty, her heart was at risk even if he was innocent.

The Earl of Rathmore was not a man to be dismissed lightly. She would proceed with caution and not allow herself to be distracted from her purpose. Emily needed her.

And so did Emily's guardian. All Meg had to do was convince him.

* * *

Rathmore was watching Meg dance with Sir Richard when Lady Presting came to stand beside him. The red-haired matron had been a convivial beauty in her time, but now she was the highest stickler of the three assembly patronesses. He braced himself. No doubt she had come to ask him to leave.

"Lord Rathmore," she said in her cool, cultured tone. "Lady Denniston has brought to my attention the fact that you not only rescued Miss Stanton-Lynch from committing a grave social faux pas, but you have also made your peace with my houseguest Lord Fenton."

"As you say," Rathmore replied with a nod.

"Your behavior this evening makes one rethink the stories that have gone around about you, my lord. And the company you keep certainly assures that you will be received at all social gatherings." She glanced meaningfully at Meg, out on the dance floor with Sir Richard, then returned her cool green gaze to him. "Do not dismiss the advantages available to you now, Lord Rathmore."

"Madam?"

Lady Presting clucked her tongue at his obvious bewilderment. "You have not yet set up your nursery, have you, my lord? It seems to me that the proper wife could do much to help your reputation."

A wife? Thoughtfully he glanced at Meg.

"I see you take my meaning. Good evening to

you, my lord." She turned to walk away, then looked back. "Oh, and you have a ward, I believe? Your cousin's daughter?"

Startled, Rathmore nodded. "Her name is Emily."

"Perhaps she might like to come visit my Anne one day soon. I do believe they are of an age."

"Emily is twelve."

"Anne is thirteen. Yes, that would suit very well. Perhaps Thursday. Good evening, my lord."

Rathmore bowed, murmuring a suitable reply as Lady Presting walked away. As he straightened, he felt almost dizzy, though he doubted it was a physical reaction. No, it was relief that bordered on giddiness. Lady Presting, one of the most influential ladies in Devon, had just requested that Emily associate with her own daughter. Such an invitation would never have been extended had he not stepped in when Meg would have confronted Mrs. Peacham. It seemed that Meg's impulsiveness had inadvertently restored some of the respectability to his own reputation. And her family connections apparently made society think twice about shunning him when he was in her company.

Lady Presting's suggestion came back to him full force. Marry Meg? He had thought that his own black reputation would ruin a decent young lady's, but perhaps it worked the opposite way. Perhaps her sterling social standing would serve to wipe the tarnish off his, making it easier for him to prove his innocence once and for all.

But what did he have to offer her? A stained

honor, rumors and speculation, eventual ostracism. And that was *if* her grandfather even entertained the idea.

In his quest to prove his innocence, he didn't dare let himself get distracted . . . no matter how irresistibly attractive he found Meg. Courting her was tempting, yes. But courting her with a proud name and title to offer in return was even more so.

Perhaps Meg would make a proper countess for him—but until he knew he would make her a proper husband, he could not even entertain the notion.

Except in his dreams . . .

Chapter 8

"I won't go!"

Rathmore smothered his impatience as Emily set her mouth in a familiar stubborn line. He glanced down at the note in his hand. The thick, creamy stationery bore the crest of the Earl of Presting. "Emily, you must go. Lady Presting has invited you to come visit her daughter. We can't turn down such an invitation."

"*You* can't turn down such an invitation." Emily gave a very unladylike snort. "You're the one who's been going to all the social events. I've been sitting here at home."

"Watch your tone," he warned.

"I won't go." She folded her arms. "I know what girls like her are like. I met lots of them at the Flemington Academy for Young Ladies. All they talk about are dresses and parties and whom they will marry someday."

"There's nothing wrong with that."

"You're not the one who has to sit there and look interested in the conversation."

"True. But this is important, Em."

Her lower lip quivered, then firmed again. "I won't go."

He fisted his hand, crumpling the invitation. "Then go up to your room until I send for you. We'll discuss this later."

"You never listen to me!" Emily cried, then stomped out of the room.

"You're acting like an infant!" he called after her. Her only response was to slam the study door behind her.

Cursing, he tossed the mangled note on his desk, then dropped into his chair, frustration churning in his gut. Why couldn't the child ever do what she was told? He'd thought she might enjoy visiting with someone her own age. Weren't young girls supposed to like such things?

He glanced at the ruined invitation, then leaned forward and carefully peeled open the wad of paper. He slowly smoothed his hands over it, flattening it against the desk several times to try and get out the worst of the wrinkles.

Salvation. Last night Lady Presting had dangled the idea of a visit like a carrot before his nose, and now like magic, the invitation lay before him. Lady

Presting's willingness to let her daughter associate
with Emily was the first step in regaining his respectability. And Emily, curse her, had no idea that
her rebellion was ruining her best chance for a decent future.

To her credit, Emily was only twelve, and she
knew nothing about the events that had blackened
his name. Her constant insubordination was some
kind of emotional punishment intended for him, to
make him pay for some sin he had apparently committed in her world. He just wished he knew what
it was he had done.

Tapping his fingers on the desk, he considered
the situation. Somehow he had to get Emily to go to
Lady Presting's and to behave herself once she was
there. He needed advice.

He needed Meg.

Knightsbridge looked up from his ledgers, then
swiftly removed the pair of spectacles from his nose
and slipped them beneath a stack of papers as he
got to his feet. "Meg," he said a little too jovially. "I
didn't hear you come in."

From the doorway of the study, Meg stifled a
smile and tried to act as if she hadn't seen his furtive
act. "You sent for me, Algie, so I came right away.
The door was open."

"Of course. Indeed. Quite so." Clearly rattled,
Knightsbridge waved a hand at a nearby chair. "Do
sit down. I was just doing . . . well, estate business,
you know."

Meg seated herself and folded her hands primly. "Please don't let me disturb you."

"Nonsense. I called for you, didn't I? Just don't know exactly how to approach the matter."

"What matter?"

"Getting to that. Meant to address it last night, but we got in so late from the assembly, you know."

Meg clenched her fingers tighter in sudden tension. Was this about Mrs. Peacham? "Algie, I apologize. I didn't realize you'd heard about the incident."

"Of course I heard about it." He sat back down behind his desk. "I could hardly *not* hear about it."

"I didn't realize what I was getting into—"

"That much is painfully obvious, my dear."

"Well, I haven't been here all that long," Meg argued. "I was just trying to learn—"

"You could have asked, you know."

She paused in her faltering explanation. "Asked?"

"It's wise to ask before attempting something of this nature," Knightsbridge said. "After all, there are experts in this sort of thing."

"I'd forgotten." Hiring an investigator had never entered her mind, but now she weighed the idea carefully. It might be something to look into.

"You can't simply charge into things," Algie continued. "Some things need to be approached with delicacy, and I'm afraid this is one of them."

"Of course, you're right," Meg agreed.

"You could have come to me with this, you know."

"You?" Meg hesitated. "Actually, Algie, I had thought you were a little too close to the matter."

"Indeed I am," he agreed with a meaningful look. "And that's why I should have been consulted."

"Of course." For the first time, it occurred to her that Algie was an excellent source of information on Rathmore, as they had grown up together. "I apologize, Algie, and I hope you aren't angry with me."

"Not at all," he said with a dismissive wave of his hand. "The matter is of little consequence now."

"But what will Grandfather say?"

Knightsbridge frowned. "The duke won't be troubled by such a trifling thing."

"He won't?"

"Of course not." Knightsbridge chuckled. "Meg, surely you don't expect me to carry tales to the duke. These minor incidents are my domain alone."

"Because I'm your guest?" Completely puzzled, Meg began to get the feeling she had missed something. "But the cut—"

"Meg, trust me when I say that no one except the man involved cares the least bit about a cutting like that. I told him I would speak with you to assure it doesn't happen again."

"I don't intend for it to happen again." She shook her head. "I just didn't realize that he had spoken to you about it."

"Who else would he tell?"

"And it surprises me that you are so calm about

the whole thing. You certainly weren't the last time this happened."

"This has happened before?" With a sigh, Algie rubbed his temples. "I was only aware of the one incident."

"Well, I wasn't involved the first time. But you were there when it happened. And you were furious."

Algie stopped rubbing his temples and looked at her curiously. "I was?"

"Absolutely. I know how close you are to him, so I didn't want to come to you with the matter."

"Well, I suppose I have known him for some years. After all, Raines has been the gardener here at Knightsbridge since I was a boy. But I don't remember getting furious on his behalf."

"Not the gardener," Meg corrected. "Lord Rathmore."

"Rathmore? What does he have to do with you taking cuttings of my gardener's prize roses for your experiments in botany?"

"Rose cuttings? That's what this is about?"

"Of course. What did you think it was about?"

"Mrs. Peacham cutting me at the assembly last night."

"What!" Algie leaped to his feet. "Why wasn't I told of this outrage?"

"I assumed you were. You told me Lord Rathmore had told you—"

"Rathmore? What's he got to do with this? I said *Raines* had complained to me of you stealing cuttings of his precious roses. I never mentioned Rathmore."

"Oh." Meg gave him a weak smile. "I thought you had."

"Not at all." His green eyes narrowed. "Let me see if I understand. The Peacham woman *cut* you at the assembly last night? And somehow I was never told of this?"

"Well, it would have been worse," Meg rushed to assure him. "As I was about to tell that horrid woman what I thought of her, Lord Rathmore came along and stopped me from making a scene."

"Thank God." Algie sank back into his chair. Leaning his elbows on the desk, he rubbed his face with both hands. "So Rathmore saved you from social suicide. Rather ironic, don't you think? How did he do that?"

"He danced with me."

"Rathmore doesn't dance."

"He did last night."

"I don't believe it."

"And then Lady Denniston came over and seemed appalled at what Mrs. Peacham had done. Especially when I told her that woman was spreading rumors that she was to become a patroness of the Friday night assemblies."

Knightsbridge paled. "You told Lady Denniston *what*?"

"I told her exactly what Mrs. Peacham had told me. Lady Denniston and the other patronesses went over to have a few words with Mrs. Peacham."

Algie folded his arms on the desk and lowered his head upon them. "You're courting social ruin, Meg."

"Nonsense. It all worked out."

He raised his head. "You're living a charmed life," he said. "Please try not to get yourself thrown out of society while you are here. Great-uncle Erasmus would kill me."

"My grandfather will do nothing of the sort."

"You don't know the duke as well as I do."

"And as far as the roses," Meg said, "I'm sorry I didn't consult you or your gardener before I took the cuttings. It was just an experiment."

"I know," Knightsbridge said, long-suffering patience heavy in his voice. "You just want to find a hobby, something you are good at. That was also what you were about when you asked Penelope about breeding Pudding. Thought she would swoon on the spot."

Meg cleared her throat and looked down at her hands. "Well, it was just an idea. Please tell Raines his roses are safe from me in the future. I am not good at botany."

"They all died?"

Meg nodded. "Every last one."

Knightsbridge sighed. "I will placate the gardener. But in the future, do discuss these plans with me before you implement them."

"I will. Never fear, Algie, I am through with botany."

"Oh, good."

"I have decided to try singing," she announced.

"Excellent notion," Knightsbridge said. "Most English young ladies are proficient in music." A knock came at the door, and he looked up gratefully. "Enter!"

Bolton, the butler, stepped into the room. "I beg your pardon, Your Lordship, but Lord Rathmore has come to call on Miss Stanton-Lynch."

"Rathmore?" Algie glanced suspiciously at Meg, who shrugged.

"I have no idea why he's here," she said.

"Bring him to the drawing room," Algie said, "and offer him refreshments. My cousin and I will be there directly."

"Very good, my lord." Bowing, Bolton exited the room.

"What do you suppose Rathmore wants?" Knightsbridge grinned and sat back in his chair. "Perhaps he has formed an attachment for you, Meg."

"Nonsense." The mere idea made her heart trip over itself.

"Oh, I don't know. He's wealthy enough, and titled. He would make you a fine husband."

"I have no intention of marrying him."

"He's a good man, Meg," Knightsbridge said, leaning forward earnestly. "Don't believe the gossip. He was as much a victim of that incident six years ago as Ophelia."

"And what if you're wrong, Algie? What if I do become romantically involved with him, and then we discover he *did* have something to do with that woman's death?"

"That's nonsense."

"Until someone uncovers the truth, it's always a possibility." She rose. "I'll go see what he wants."

"Are you certain you want to be alone with him?" Knightsbridge taunted. "After all, he's a dangerous man."

She paused in the doorway. "If he's innocent as you claim, then I have nothing to worry about, do I?"

"Leave the door to the drawing room open," Algie said. "That way the servants can hear you scream."

She gave him a sly smile. "Or they'll hear *him* scream."

He chuckled. "Off with you. I'll be in directly."

She left the room. "Do hurry, Algie," she called back, "just in case the earl needs you to rescue him."

Rathmore paced the drawing room, too restless to sit still. He needed a woman's advice, and at the moment, just about the only decent woman willing to talk to him was Meg. That was the only reason he had raced over here as soon as the notion had hit him. *Not* because he had wanted to see her again.

Not because he had thought, even for one wild moment, that she would make a good wife.

It was an insane notion. No matter what Lady Presting thought, there was no way the granddaughter of the Duke of Raynewood would wed a man with a reputation like his.

Unless she fell in love with him.

The thought tempted him, especially if it was true that wedding Meg might help him uncover the truth. Look what her mere companionship had won him—an invitation to Lady Presting's home. What doors might open for him if she were to become his bride?

But no, he couldn't do that to her.

"Lord Rathmore, what a pleasant surprise."

He glanced toward the doorway and there she stood. Today she wore a dress of pale pink that made her complexion glow. Her dark hair was arranged in its usual tumbled curls, and her darkly lashed blue eyes sparkled with curiosity. And with every breath she took, her lush breasts shifted in a most enchanting way.

His resolve weakened.

He shifted as well, hoping his very physical reaction to *her* shifting didn't betray him. He had been fooling himself. Reputation or not, he wanted this lovely, outspoken American with a passion that stunned even him with its intensity.

Remembering his manners, he sketched a bow. "Good afternoon, Meg. Please forgive my unexpected intrusion."

She smiled, her dimples creasing her cheeks in a

way that charmed him. "So polite," she teased. "I've sent for refreshments, so why don't you make yourself comfortable?"

"I am comfortable." And he couldn't sit, not with the tight fit of his trousers, most of which was *not* the work of his tailor. "I've come to talk to you about Emily."

"Oh, dear, what's happened?" Meg sat down on the sofa and gave him her complete attention.

Rathmore tried to ignore the fact that her new position put her face right on level with his . . . tight trousers.

"Ah . . . Lady Presting has invited Meg to visit with her daughter, Anne, on Thursday."

Meg clapped her hands together. "That's wonderful!"

And so was the way her breasts pressed together with her action. Rathmore struggled to keep his mind on the conversation. "Yes, it's a marvelous opportunity," he agreed, forcing his eyes up to her face. "But Emily won't go."

"Oh, dear." Meg leaned forward, inadvertently presenting him with a new view of her succulent cleavage. "Why not?"

"Something about the girls in school and only talking about suitors and clothes. I don't know." Frustration edged his tone. "She doesn't talk to me; you know that."

"Indeed she does," Meg said with a smile. "It's just that you're a man and don't understand what she's saying."

"She's saying she won't go. I understand that well enough."

Meg laughed and shook her head, and the tantalizing flesh of her bosom rippled with the movement. He clenched his fists and repeated the word "gentleman" over and over again in his mind. Every muscle in his body tensed as he struggled *not* to pounce on her.

But her every movement seduced him, her every word lured him closer. He needed her help with Emily, but he needed her in other ways, too, ways that had nothing to do with his ward and everything to do with lust.

Lust. That sounded too crude a word to be applied to Meg. But what he felt was too basic to be called desire, too consuming to be called need. Too rough to be called love. Passion seemed too weak a word. And yet at the same time it was more than the need to satisfy a basic biological compulsion. It was more of . . . a hunger. Yes, that was a better word. A hunger that could only be sated by Meg. No other woman would do.

"Lord Rathmore, are you quite all right?"

Her soft voice vibrated over his skin, nearly unraveling his control. "Fine," he managed to say. He tried to smile, but knew from the expression on her face that he hadn't succeeded.

"What's the matter?" she asked, rising. She took a step toward him, reaching out.

He stepped back to avoid her touch, nearly tripping over a small table. "Nothing. I'm fine."

"Any fool can see that you're not." She folded her arms across her chest, and the tops of her breasts plumped above the neckline of her dress. He groaned and shut his eyes. "Lord Rathmore," she said in a no-nonsense tone. "I can see that something is wrong. Now what is it?"

"I want you."

The stark words echoed through the sudden silence of the room.

Had he really said that? Rathmore opened his eyes and looked at her. She stared at him with her eyes wide, lips parted, arms hanging limply at her sides. A flush slowly crept up into her cheeks. Fascinated, he watched the color spread across her creamy skin, even down to the tops of her breasts. Her breasts, he noticed, which were rising and falling much more rapidly than they had before.

And her nipples had hardened so much that he could clearly see the evidence of it through her dress.

"Lord Rathmore," she said finally, her voice huskier than normal, "I thought you came here to talk to me about Emily."

"I did."

"This—" She cleared her throat. "This has nothing to do with Emily."

"You're right."

He stepped toward her; she stepped back.

"This has to do with you and me," he said.

"There is no 'you and me.'" Her voice shook.

"There is."

She shook her head. "No. Impossible." She met his gaze, eyes wide and frightened like a doe's. But she lifted her chin, holding her ground.

He held her gaze, hiding nothing, intensity building between them until it was almost hard to breathe.

The rattle of a tray shattered the tension.

"The refreshments are here." Meg whirled to meet the servant who entered the room and then busied herself seeing to the placement of the tray on the table.

Rathmore stood by, hands clenched, desire gnawing at his gut, and watched Meg bend over to help adjust the tray. He doubted she realized the tempting view she offered him of her sweet derriere, and it was only the knowledge of her very real innocence that stopped him from reaching out for her.

The servant left, and Meg turned to face him, her expression uncertain. She swept a hand at the tray. "Cook has sent berry tarts. Would you care for one?"

He slowly shook his head, focused his gaze on her mouth. "That's not what I want."

"Will you hush?" She glanced at the still open door. "Algie said he would be along directly."

"I'm keeping my hands to myself, am I not?" he snapped. "You still have your clothes on. At least allow me my words."

"Even your words are scandalous." She folded her arms across her chest again, and he groaned, closing his eyes again as her breasts once more plumped invitingly.

"My words are the truth." He opened his eyes and let out a slow breath. "Meg, you might want to . . . ah . . . put your arms down."

"Why?" She glanced down, gasped, and dropped her arms.

"Thank you." He tried to smile. "That little display was making things rather uncomfortable for me."

"Lord Rathmore." Deliberately she stepped behind the table that held the tray of tarts. "Did you come here under false pretenses? I thought you wanted to talk about Emily."

"I did. I do. I was distracted. My apologies." He rubbed a hand over the back of his neck. "It's just . . . Meg, you're the first decent woman who has even spoken to me in months."

"So your reaction is the result of a . . . um . . . lack of companionship?"

"My reaction?"

She gestured at his lower body. "Your . . . you know, your *reaction*."

He chuckled at her maidenly flustering. "I didn't think you'd noticed."

"How could I miss *that*?"

"Again, you flatter me." With her every word, his spirits lifted. She wanted him. He'd bet his reputation—what was left of it, anyway—on the matter. "Most young ladies wouldn't have noticed my . . . er . . . reaction."

"I'm not most young ladies."

"Indeed you're not. You're refreshingly different."

"Different, Lord Rathmore. Not naïve." She met his gaze squarely. "I know what happens between men and women, even if I've never experienced it myself."

"And relieved I am to hear it." He stepped around the table, watched her eyes widen as he blatantly ignored the barrier she had placed between them. "A man wants a virginal wife in his marriage bed."

"I don't plan on getting married anytime soon," Meg said, tilting her chin in challenge as he loomed over her. "And you, my lord, are entirely too close."

"I haven't begun to get as close to you as I intend." He ran his finger along her flushed cheek. "I mean to have you as my wife, so you had best get used to the idea."

Chapter 9

"**Y**our wife!" She jerked back from his caressing hand. "Are you mad? We barely know each other."

"What does that have to do with anything?" A frown creased his brow. "We get along more than tolerably well. I'm an earl, and you're the granddaughter of a duke. On top of that, we want each other. It seems like a perfect match."

"There's more to marriage than lineage," she said, taking another step back.

"Not in England."

Her heart pounded so hard she was surprised it didn't echo in the room. She could barely look into those seductive brown eyes for fear that she would throw herself at him. Clearly there was some sort of attraction between them. But marriage? They were barely friends!

"I'm an American," she said. "This English custom of strangers marrying for the sake of preserving a title is completely baffling to me."

"But we're not strangers." He smiled slowly, and her heart melted in her chest. "We know the taste of each other. We like each other."

"It's not enough." She folded her hands together to stop their trembling. "I don't know your mind or your heart. I don't know your secrets. Besides, I don't want to get married."

"Every woman wants to get married."

"Not this one."

He tilted his head to the side, peering at her as if she were some oddity in a museum. "If you have no desire to get married, what do you intend to do with the rest of your life?"

Her face burned, but she refused to look away. "Why is it that men always think a woman needs a man in order for her life to be complete?"

"Women need men to provide for them."

"Why?" she challenged. "My grandfather is settling money on me that will be mine once I reach the age of thirty."

"There are other advantages to marriage, Meg." In two strides, he was so close that she had to tilt her head back to look at him. "Let me show you."

He cupped her cheek, his hand warm and firm and smelling faintly of his cologne. The scent tantalized her, making her mouth water and her body hum with awareness. And as he leaned toward her, the scent seemed to surround her, enticing her to step closer to that hard, male body, to tangle her fingers in the ink-black hair that looked so soft to the touch.

"Someone might come," she whispered.

"I don't care." His breath stirred the hair at her temple. "This may be all I ever have of you. Just one . . . sweet . . . taste."

And then he was kissing her, and she couldn't think at all.

He tasted like sin. His lips felt soft against hers, skilled, coaxing hers to part for him. It was so different from that angry kiss on the terrace at Lady Denniston's ball. This kiss seduced.

He pulled her closer with an arm around her waist, his other hand sliding from her cheek to the back of her head. A soft mew of pleasure escaped her, and she clung to him, gripping his coat as he made her head spin with pleasure.

One hand slipped lower, cupping her bottom to press her belly against the hardness of his . . . um . . . reaction. She squirmed a little at the unfamiliar feel of it, and he groaned. The gentle seduction of his mouth changed to hungry passion. He tangled his tongue with hers and pressed her harder against the ridge straining his trousers, his hands insistent, his kiss relentless.

She could barely breathe. Her blood roared through her veins like a wild thing, and her body came to life with needs and demands that jangled in her brain. Her breasts felt swollen, the nipples so hard it was almost painful. Tingles rippled along her skin, and her woman's place between her legs grew damp and achy. She suddenly wanted to know the texture of his skin, wanted to pull the clothes away from that delicious male body and explore every inch of him with her mouth.

He nipped her lower lip, and a jolt of fresh desire streaked through her. She smoothed her hands across his chest, looking for buttons, fastenings, anything that would let her feel bare male flesh.

Algie's voice addressing one of the servants in the hall doused their passion like a bucket of cold water.

With a cry of distress, she shoved him away, almost falling herself as she stumbled backward. Regaining her footing, she patted her hair, smoothed her dress, breathing as if she had run for miles and needed a long drink of water.

A drink of water named Rathmore.

She glanced over at him as Algie's footsteps drew closer. He stood where she had left him, his body absolutely rigid, hands clenched at his sides, breathing as heavily as she. And his dark eyes blazed with such naked hunger that she nearly turned back to him.

"Algie's coming," she managed to whisper.

"I know." His lips crooked in a smile. "You . . . ah . . . might want to have a berry tart. Your mouth looks like it has been thoroughly kissed."

She swallowed hard. "I *have* been thoroughly kissed."

"You certainly have," he growled, satisfaction heavy in his voice. "But you don't want Knightsbridge to know that, do you?"

"Of course not." She started toward the tray of tarts, but he stood between her and them, and she stopped. "Do you think you could move? I don't . . . that is . . . we probably shouldn't—"

"You're right. We shouldn't." His gaze touched on her mouth. "But I want to."

She opened her mouth to reply, then closed it again. Really, what was there to say?

Obligingly he moved across the room to look out the window, his back to her, and she scooted around to the sofa. She had just reached for a tart when Algie strolled into the room. Quickly she bit into the gooey treat, the purplish filling coating her kiss-swollen lips.

"Berry tarts!" Knightsbridge exclaimed. "I do hope you saved me some."

"Of course we did, Algie." Meg managed to smile. She wondered that he didn't notice the tension that swelled in the room. A glance at Rathmore confirmed that he remained staring out the window with his back to them. For some reason, that irked her. He looked completely unaffected by their encounter, whereas she had to struggle to put two coherent words together.

How could he be so unmoved by what had passed between them?

"Lord Rathmore doesn't care for berry tarts," Meg said with a bite in her voice. "There are plenty for you, Algie."

"You don't care for berry tarts, Rathmore?" Algie reached for one as he spoke. "Why not?"

"Perhaps he doesn't like the taste." She didn't bother to hide the question in her voice, and Rathmore slowly turned to face her.

The barely controlled hunger in his eyes removed all doubt. He liked the taste just fine.

"I quite enjoy berry tarts," he said, deliberately glancing at her mouth. "In fact, I believe they are my favorite."

"Then by all means, help yourself, my good man," Algie said, sweeping a hand over the tray.

"No thank you, Knightsbridge." Rathmore managed a weak imitation of his usual wicked grin. "I find that once I indulge myself in such treats, it's difficult to stop."

"I know the feeling exactly," Knightsbridge said. "Hard to resist, those berry tarts."

Rathmore's gaze honed in on Meg's mouth again. "Quite."

Meg swiftly changed the subject. "Lord Rathmore is having some difficulty with Emily and came to ask advice, Algie."

Algie chuckled. "Never thought I'd see the day that *you'd* have troubles with a female, Rathmore."

"A twelve-year-old girl is hardly the sort of female I have experience with, Knightsbridge."

"That I believe." Chuckling, Algie reached for another tart.

Meg sat frozen. How could she have forgotten Rathmore's reputation? Gossip painted him quite the rake before his exile, and after being in his arms, she certainly believed it to be true. Had she learned nothing of such scoundrels from her experience with Malcolm?

She glanced at him, so dark and handsome and in control. Every inch the Devil Earl.

Every inch a lover a woman would die for.

Had he been toying with her with his talk of marriage?

"So, what's the child done now?" Algie drawled, bringing Meg back to the conversation. "Tied up her governess?"

"No, I gave up on governesses after she ran off the last five." With a shake of his head, Rathmore seated himself in a chair across from Algie. "Grimm and the rest of the staff oversee her. If I leave the girl alone for even a moment, she finds trouble."

"No governess?" Algie exclaimed. "You can't leave things like that, Rathmore. Just isn't the proper way to bring up a young lady."

"And since when did you become an authority on raising young girls?" Rathmore snapped. "I'm doing the best I can, damn it."

Silence descended.

"Gad, man, but you are at the end of your rope, aren't you?" Algie peered closely at his friend. "Never heard you use language like that in front of a lady before."

"You're quite right. My apologies, Me—Miss Stanton-Lynch."

"Not at all," Meg said easily, hoping Algie hadn't noticed that Rathmore had almost used her given name. "You're bearing a great burden, Lord Rathmore. We all understand that you're out of your element, and I am only too happy to assist you."

"No doubt a woman's opinion would help," Algie said a little too casually. "Too bad you're not married, old friend. A wife would definitely be an asset about now."

Meg shot Algie a suspicious look, but he never even glanced her way.

"Quite so." Rathmore, on the other hand, slanted Meg a meaningful glance that made her want to squirm. "But until I do wed, Algie, I'm afraid I have no one else to turn to but your cousin. Miss Stanton-Lynch seems to understand my ward in some female way that I, as a male, am incapable of comprehending."

"It's not all that difficult," Meg said. "Emily is in a difficult position right now. She's grieving for the loss of her father and grandfather. And she is angry at you, my lord, because you abandoned her six years ago without a word and now presume to come back into her life and dictate to her as if you're her parent."

"Is *that* what it is?" The utter relief on his face humbled her. "I could tell she was angry at me, but I had no idea what I'd done."

"And then it gets more complicated because her father is dead and she resents you for taking his place." Meg paused as both men stared at her, mouths agape. "What's the matter?"

"I'm amazed," was all Algie said.

"How do you know that?" Rathmore demanded.

"It's obvious."

"Not to me."

"It's easy enough to deduce, given what Emily has told me," Meg explained. "You're too involved in the matter, so you don't see it. And besides, I remember how I felt whenever my brother would go off to sea. All I wanted was for him to stay with me, but he always left, sometimes so early in the morning that I couldn't say good-bye. I imagine Emily feels the same way about the way you left six years ago, my lord."

"I had no choice."

"But Emily doesn't know that," she reminded him gently. "She has no idea what's really going on or why it's so important that she accept Lady Presting's invitation."

"What's this?" Algie asked. "You've received an invitation from Lady Presting?"

Rathmore nodded. "She's invited Emily to come visit with her daughter."

"Outstanding!" Knightsbridge slapped his hand on the arm of his chair. "That's definitely a step in the right direction."

"And well I know it. But of course Emily won't go."

"I'll talk to her," Meg said. "You said it had something to do with the girls at school? Tell me, my lord, has Emily always been an active girl? I mean, if given a choice, would she prefer shopping for new clothes or riding her horse?"

"Riding her horse," he replied without hesitation. "And she's always more dirty than clean. She's gone through more dresses because she insists on running about like a hoyden instead of acting like a young lady."

Meg smiled. "I was much the same way. It's my guess, Lord Rathmore, that Meg doesn't fit in with most of the other girls her age. She prefers more active pursuits, whereas her peers are obsessed with things like the latest fashions and fantasies of romance."

"Yes!" Rathmore exclaimed. "She said something of the sort to me. Something about the girls at the academy and their boring conversations."

"I remember feeling much the same way," Meg said. "I didn't want to be a girl because girls got left behind. I wanted to be a sailor like my brother, and I practiced climbing so I'd be able to show him how good I was with the rigging. I climbed trees, furniture, even buildings." She laughed. "My poor mother was beside herself."

"I can't imagine it," Knightsbridge said, shaking his head. "Not seeing you as you are now."

"Believe it," Meg said. "Emily is perfectly normal, but I'll bet she's scared to visit Lady Presting's daughter because she's afraid she won't fit in. I'll talk with her. And I'll see if I can find out what sort of girl Anne is so that Emily can be prepared."

"If you can accomplish this miracle," Rathmore said, "I will owe you my life."

"No need to pledge your life, my lord," Meg

said, a bit unnerved by the gleam in his eye. "I'm more than happy to help you with your ward, for her sake as well as yours."

"And if I choose to pledge my life anyway?"

Meg cleared her throat. She would *not* let that flirtatious tone get to her. "As I told you, my lord, there is no need."

"What if I insist?"

"My lord, you're being silly."

"Am I?"

"You know you are." She cleared her throat again and glanced nervously at Algie.

Her cousin glanced speculatively from Meg to Rathmore. Tapping his chin with one berry-stained finger, he said, "Tell me, Rathmore, do you have an excitable gardener?"

"Algie!" Meg gasped. "Don't you dare say one more word!"

"What's this about the gardener?" Rathmore asked, looking from one to the other.

"Nothing, my lord," Meg said. She glared at her cousin. "*Nothing*."

Algie shrugged. "As you say." He turned to Rathmore. "And your hounds? Ever think of breeding them?"

Meg dropped the tart she was about to bite back on her plate. "Algie!"

Rathmore grinned as she grew more flustered. "Not really. Is there a reason I should?"

"Just checking." Algie chuckled.

"That does it!" Meg slapped her plate on the

table and jumped to her feet. "I am *not* marrying Lord Rathmore!"

Both men raised their brows at her. Heat crept into her cheeks. Good Lord, had she actually *said* that?

Penelope entered the room before either man could comment. "Algernon, how many of those tarts have you had?"

"Only one or two, my dear." He rose to his feet and held out a hand to his wife, who ignored it to rub at a berry stain on his chin.

"Indeed," she said.

Meg sat down on the sofa again, eager for a change of subject. "I shall come by tomorrow to speak to your ward, Lord Rathmore."

"My thanks, Miss Stanton-Lynch." Rathmore's too-smooth tone earned him Meg's narrow-eyed look of suspicion. He widened his eyes in innocence.

"What's the matter with Emily?" Penelope asked, sitting down beside Meg.

"His Lordship has received an invitation from Lady Presting for Emily to visit with her daughter," Meg explained.

"How wonderful!" Penelope exclaimed. "Lord Rathmore, this is an excellent social opportunity for you."

"I know," he said. "But Emily refuses to go."

"Oh, dear." Penelope turned a questioning look on Meg.

"Emily enjoys more active pursuits and apparently didn't fit in well with the more fashionable girls at her academy," Meg said. "She's afraid Anne might be one of those fashionable sorts."

"Poor child," Penelope said. "Shall I speak to her?"

"Meg's going to do that," Knightsbridge said. "She apparently has formed a bond with the child."

"Excellent. Do let me know if I can assist." She pursed her lips thoughtfully and turned to Rathmore. "Tell me, my lord, has she seemed moody of late? Inexplicably irrational?"

"That describes Emily most of the time," Rathmore grumbled.

"And she's twelve, you say?"

"Yes, she'll be thirteen in September."

"I see." Penelope glanced at Meg. "You might want to take that into account, Meg, when you speak to her."

"Her age?" Meg asked, reaching for her half-eaten tart.

"Her age . . . and what happens to girls her age. Physically."

"Of course!" Meg shook her head, amazed at her own lack of vision. "I should have thought of that myself." She bit into her tart.

Algie and Rathmore regarded the ladies with equally baffled expressions.

"Would you care to elaborate, my dear?" Algie asked.

Penelope reached to claim the last tart on the tray. "No."

"No?"

"No. It's not fit conversation for company." She blushed a becoming pink even as she nibbled on the tart.

"Is there something wrong with Emily?" Rathmore asked, concern spreading across his features. "Do I need to summon a physician?"

"Not at all, my lord." Somehow having managed not to get a speck of berry filling on her lips, Penelope smiled at Rathmore. "Tell me, have you tried Cook's berry tarts? They really are wonderful."

"Lady Knightsbridge, please."

Meg couldn't resist the plea in Rathmore's voice, even if Penelope could. "She means that Emily is becoming a woman, my lord, with a woman's troubles."

"What do you—" He paled. "Not that."

"Meg," Penelope chided. "Really, this is *not* a subject a lady should be discussing, especially with men present."

"She's too young, isn't she?" Rathmore asked rather desperately. "Surely she can't be . . ."

Penelope continued to eat her tart without expression, while Meg gave Rathmore an imperceptible nod. He groaned.

"You can see why I asked if there were any female relations who might assist you," Meg said. "Then you wouldn't be bothered with . . . this."

"I told you, there's no one."

Knightsbridge shuddered. "All the more reason to wed, my boy."

"Why does the conversation keep turning to marriage?" Meg asked with exasperation.

Knightsbridge shrugged. "I was talking about Rathmore, not you."

"Well, I have no desire to wed anyone," Meg announced.

"Really?" Rathmore leaned back in his chair and grinned at her. "How extraordinary for a girl your age."

"Meg, really." Penelope sighed with disappointment.

"There must be more to life than marriage," Meg said. Having finished her tart, she put down her plate and noticed a bit of filling on her thumb.

"For most young ladies, marriage is the ultimate goal in life," Rathmore said. His eyes narrowed as she lifted her thumb to her mouth and licked the sticky glob of berry filling from her flesh. The look on his face made her freeze with her thumb still poised near her mouth. The room seemed to grow smaller until it was only the two of them.

"Not for me," she whispered, slowly lowering her hand.

"There are advantages to marriage," Rathmore reminded her with a slow, knowing smile that started the fire burning all over again. "Perhaps you will change your mind."

Oh, how she wanted to give in to the seduction in his voice, to go back into his arms. But she didn't dare.

"I think not," she replied, her tone sharp from

heightened emotion. "I want to do something worthwhile with my life."

"Here we go again," Algie groaned.

"Being a wife is a worthwhile pursuit," Rathmore said. "A wife is a partner for life, the mother of a man's children. A permanent hostess. A companion."

"Exactly," Penelope murmured.

"I'm surprised to hear you say that, my lord, as that's how the Americans view marriage," Meg agreed. "But here in England, a man seems to marry for the sole purpose of furthering his social status or augmenting his fortune. And for heirs. Once he has those heirs, he ignores his wife and chases other women."

"Meg!" Penelope exclaimed. "This is—"

"—not a fitting topic of conversation for a lady, I know," Meg finished. "And I have probably insulted you and Algie, and for that I'm sorry. But it's the truth for most English marriages. And for all that I look like an English lady, *I'm not.* I'm American, and I'd rather make my own way in the world."

Algie merely stared at her, jaw hanging open in shock, but Penelope replied calmly, "I agree that many society marriages are as you have described, but not all. Algernon and I were a love match."

"Yes, you were," Meg agreed. "And I won't settle for anything less."

"I thought you said you didn't want to get married at all," Rathmore pointed out.

"If I met a man I loved with all my heart, then I would consider it."

His amiable grin turned wicked. "So you do aspire to marriage, then."

"Not so fast, my lord." She gave him an arch look. "He'd have to love me as well."

Knightsbridge chuckled. "There's the challenge."

"But would the duke be in agreement to such a match?" Penelope asked, a tiny frown forming between her brows.

"He once told me that he promised Meg she could marry whomever she liked," Algie said, "as long as the man had a title or a fortune to equal hers."

Algie didn't even glance at Rathmore after making that statement, making Meg wonder if she had imagined his matchmaking.

"Will you all please stop talking about marriage?" Meg pleaded. "Can't we change the subject?"

"As you wish," Algie said. "Though I found the conversation rather stimulating. Don't you think so, Rathmore?"

Rathmore regally inclined his head. "Indeed, Knightsbridge." He gave Meg a look that boiled with meaning. "After all, one never knows when one will crave the taste of berry tarts."

Chapter 10

What had possessed him to do such a thing?

Rathmore looked out his bedroom window at the early gray of dawn and wondered what had compelled him to bring up the subject of marriage with Meg. Hadn't he already decided that he had nothing to offer her at this time? Hadn't he determined that he dared not turn any of his attention away from his quest, to court a woman?

Yet he'd gone and declared that she would be his wife someday.

Idiot.

Meg was a distraction he could not afford. Look what had happened at the Friday night assembly. He had gone there for the express purpose of seeking out Mrs. Warington. Instead he had survived a confrontation with Ophelia's brother (which would have happened anyway, he had to admit) and then spent the rest of the evening dancing attendance on that pretty American like some sort of besotted fool.

Imogene Warington could have come and gone from the assembly, and he would never have known it. Luckily his informants had sent him a message that the lady had suffered an illness on Friday night and had therefore not attended the affair, so there was nothing lost—except his own patience with himself.

Meg was the only thing in over six years that had managed to make him forget, even temporarily, his mission to clear his name.

She was coming today to speak to Emily. Perhaps it was best if he was not at home when she arrived.

As much as Meg wanted to stay as far away from Rathmore as possible, there was still Emily to consider. So Meg arrived at Rathmore Hall the next day with her abigail in tow to speak with the child.

"I am Grimm," the butler told her when she appeared at the door. "His Lordship is not at home, miss, but the staff was told to expect you. Please wait in the drawing room while I summon Miss Emily."

"Thank you, Grimm. Lizzie," she said to her abigail, "perhaps you might find refreshment for yourself down in the kitchen. I wish to speak to Emily alone."

"Very well, miss," Lizzie said with a curtsy. She followed a footman from the foyer, and Grimm showed Meg to the drawing room.

"I'll summon Miss Emily," he said, then left her to her own devices.

The drawing room was decorated in the Chinese style. Ocean-blue silk wallpaper covered the walls and gave a fine background for the jade statues and delicate vases that rested on every available flat surface. The sofa she sat on had carved wooden feet that resembled the paws of a tiger and was covered with red silk with a black dragon pattern swirling through it; the dark green pillows bore tassels at the corners. All in all, it was not the style she had expected from Lord Rathmore. It seemed a little too . . . in vogue. Rathmore was a man with his own likes and dislikes, society be hanged. And she couldn't see him honestly enjoying the Chinese style.

Though perhaps he had done it as one of his efforts to placate the fashionable world.

"Hideous, isn't it?" Emily said as she wandered into the room. "Grandfather had terrible taste. His last amour, Mrs. Pelton, convinced him that Chinese was 'all the rage.'" She rolled her eyes as she said the last three words, clearly conveying her opinion of *that*.

Meg, on the other hand, was rather astonished at the child's casual acceptance of her grandfather's "amour."

"Did it bother you that he let her decorate the house?" Meg asked.

Emily laughed and plopped down with an irreverent bounce in a nearby red silk-covered chair. "No. Grandfather was lonely, and Papa explained

to me that the ladies were good company for him.
He would never have married her."

"I see."

"Shall I have Grimm send for refreshments?"
Emily asked in a mature tone that belied the child-
like way she had jumped into her chair.

"No, thank you," Meg replied. "You don't seem
surprised to see me."

Emily shrugged. "Cousin Justin said you would
come to call today. No doubt he wants you to have
a talk with me. What have I done now?"

Meg stifled a smile at the impatience in Emily's
voice. "What makes you think you've done something wrong?"

"Because Cousin Justin told me you were coming to visit and then ran off to inspect the tenant
cottages at the far side of the estate. And he *hates*
inspections," she added with a smirk.

"I see. Well, your cousin did ask me to speak to
you," Meg said, deciding that honesty might work
best with the girl. "He would like you to go with
him to Lady Presting's house."

Emily curled her lip. "I *thought* that was what
this was about."

"Well, you were right, clever girl. And since you
are so smart, perhaps you'll listen to me when I explain why you should go."

Emily slouched back in the chair, her mouth
pursing in a petulant scowl. "Can I stop you?"

Meg frowned. "You know, Emily, I came here today to talk to you because I know that you're

grown up enough to understand the fine nuances of what is really going on around you. But with the way you're acting, I don't know if I can confide in you after all."

Emily sat up quickly, her sulky pout vanishing. "What nuances?"

"There are things going on around you that no one has told you about because they think you are a mere child," Meg explained. "I, however, know that you're smart enough to understand some of what's happening to your cousin, and I trust that you are mature enough to want to help instead of make things more difficult."

"What are you talking about?"

She clearly had the girl's attention now. "Emily, your cousin is not well liked by most of society at the moment."

"Who can blame them?" she muttered with a little snort.

Meg ignored the comment and continued. "This is a serious problem. There are people in society who would see your cousin barred from many of the events if not for his title and wealth. And this ostracism would extend to you if something is not done."

"*Me?* I didn't do anything!"

"You are related to the Earl of Rathmore," Meg said. "When you were a little girl, there was an accident here at Rathmore Hall, and a woman died."

The girl paled. "I remember that."

"Do you? I would have thought you too young."

Emily shook her head, and the yellow ribbon threaded through her curls drooped over one eye. With a growl of impatience, she ripped the ribbon out of her hair and crushed it between her fingers. "I had nightmares for years after that happened. When I was little, Cousin Justin always used to make the bad dreams go away, but he was gone by then."

"He was gone because some people thought he had something to do with the lady's death," Meg told her. "Your father and grandfather thought it best if he left the country until the scandal died down."

"So it wasn't me?" Emily asked with such vast relief that Meg could almost feel it. "I always thought I had done something to make him angry. The day before he left, someone had stolen his favorite cravat pin from his room." Her voice softened. "He thought I had taken it because I always loved it so. But I didn't take it!"

"Of course you didn't," Meg agreed.

"He was angry at me, and then the next day he was gone."

"But it had nothing to do with you." Meg leaned forward and touched the girl's hand. "Your cousin loves you very much. Some people are spreading those old rumors and making things very difficult for him right now."

"Cousin Justin didn't have anything to do with that lady falling down the stairs," Emily scoffed. "He's a tyrant, but he wouldn't hurt a fly. And if society doesn't understand that, then they're all stupid."

Meg had to chuckle at the child's candor. "I agree with you there, but the rumors are spreading nonetheless. That's why this invitation to Lady Presting's is so important."

Tears shimmered in the girl's eyes. "But why do I have to go? Why can't he just go and talk to this lady himself?"

"Because he's doing it for you."

"I don't understand."

"Emily, what affects him affects you. He's trying to fix things now so that when you come out in society, you won't have to deal with these ugly rumors. He wants the best for you."

"Sure he does." The bravado of the words faded as the girl's voice quavered.

"He really does, Emily." Meg gave her a reassuring smile. "I understand from what your cousin has told me that you had some difficulties with the other girls at the academy."

Emily nodded. "I came home when Papa and Grandfather died, and I told Cousin Justin that I didn't want to go back. He let me stay here."

"Why didn't you want to go back? Because of the other girls?"

Emily hesitated, then nodded again. "They think I'm strange," she whispered. "They say I act like a boy."

Meg laughed. "There's nothing strange about you," she said. "I was just like you when I was a girl. All I wanted to do was run races and climb trees. My mother despaired that she would ever make a lady of me."

"Really?" Emily looked her over, her disbelieving gaze moving over Meg's perfectly coifed hair and green-sprigged white muslin gown. "But you . . . you *look* like a lady."

"I can be both, can't I? And so can you."

"I can?" The girl wrinkled her nose doubtfully. "I don't know about that."

"Let me tell you a secret." Meg leaned forward and lowered her voice. "I still like to run races and climb trees. I still like to ride my horse faster than the wind. I just can't do it all the time anymore. Sometimes I have to play the lady for the sake of my grandfather, so I won't embarrass him. But that doesn't mean a lady is *all* I have to be."

"But what if this Anne girl cares only about fashion?" Emily asked. "What would we talk about?"

"You can simply tell her that due to your mourning over your father and grandfather, you haven't been keeping up with the latest fashion. Then ask her what's *à la mode* these days. People love to talk about their own interests. It will be boring, but your secret will be safe." Meg gave her a conspiratorial smile. "And if you absolutely cannot stand the girl, then simply plead a headache. It's the lady's way of getting out of a difficult situation."

"I can do that?"

"Of course you can. And your guardian will not

be vexed with you, as long as you are polite and *appear* to be a lady the whole time."

Clearly not believing her, Emily arched her brows in a way that reminded Meg strongly of Rathmore. "So all I have to do," Emily said, "is pretend to be a lady, and no one will bother me?"

Meg laughed. "My dear girl, moving about in society is all about appearances. People will believe you to be whatever you appear to be. Go visit Lady Presting's daughter. Spend at least a half hour, and if the girl completely bores you silly, simply claim a headache, and your cousin will bring you home." Meg lowered her voice to a mock whisper. "I guarantee you that your guardian will be all too happy to have an excuse to escape Lady Presting's drawing room." She winked.

Emily giggled. "All right," she said. "I'll go visit this Anne girl. And if she is completely horrible, I will plead the headache and ask Cousin Justin to take me home."

"And you must act the lady the whole time," Meg reminded her.

"I know," Emily sighed with a dramatic roll of her eyes. "Don't worry, I can pretend to be a lady for a half hour."

"That's all anyone is asking of you."

Activity outside the door drew Meg's attention, and her heart sped up as she recognized Rathmore's voice out in the hallway. Moments later the man himself opened the drawing room door.

He was dressed in riding clothes that accented

every inch of his lean, muscular frame. He paused
near the doorway, and the heat in his dark eyes as
he noticed Meg made her pulse skip wildly.

"Good afternoon, my lord," Meg said, wincing
at the breathless tone of her voice. Goodness, she
sounded like an infatuated schoolgirl!

Rathmore didn't seem to notice. "Good afternoon, ladies. Am I intruding?"

"No, we're done here," Emily said, in the dismissive tone one would use with a servant.

Meg sighed.

Rathmore narrowed his eyes. "What happened
to your hair, Emily?"

Emily parted her lips to utter some undoubtedly
scathing remark. Meg caught her eye and mouthed
the word "lady." Emily sighed, then slid out of the
chair, her hair ribbon dangling from her fingers.

"I seem to have lost my ribbon," she said to
Rathmore, her manner as regal as a queen's. "I
shall have someone fix it at once."

Meg pressed her lips together to keep from smiling as Emily sailed past the earl, then paused in the
doorway for maximum dramatic effect.

"By the way," Emily announced, "I have decided
to accompany you to visit Lady Presting's daughter
on Thursday."

With those words, she left the room altogether,
and Rathmore faced Meg, his expression completely dumbfounded. "How did you do that?"

Meg shrugged. "I simply explained the situation
to her."

His curious expression swiftly changed to one of fury. "You did *what*?" he roared.

"I told her the truth," Meg repeated, then glanced at the open door with a frown. "Really, my lord, do keep your voice down."

"This is *my* house." He slammed the door shut. Turning back to her, he pinned her in place with the sheer power of his furious gaze. "And if I want to shout, I will do so."

"Open that door," Meg demanded, rising.

"Not until I get an answer from you." He folded his arms across his chest. "What did you think you were doing, filling that child's ears with gossip?"

"I wasn't gossiping." Meg put her hands on her hips as her own temper surged to life. "Emily is twelve years old, Lord Rathmore, not a baby. She's old enough to understand some of what is going on."

"Understand what? That everyone in society thinks I killed a woman? I'm just now forging a relationship with the girl, and you tell her that people think I'm a murderer. I'm certain *that* will make her feel safe with me."

"For your information," Meg shot back, "Emily thinks that the rumors are ridiculous. She finds you overbearing but does not believe you had anything to do with Ophelia's accident."

"Accident? Is that what she thinks?"

"Yes." Meg glared at him. "I am not stupid, my lord. I let her think it was an accident and that you are merely the victim of thoughtless gossip. I also

explained that you were trying to repair your reputation and that her visit with Anne would help do
that."

He frowned. "And she agreed?"

"Yes, she agreed. And by the way, she has always
thought that your departure from her life had to do
with a cravat pin that went missing at the same
time. She said you thought she had taken it."

"How is it that she tells you all this?" he asked,
wonder overtaking anger. "I've been trying to get
through to her for the past year."

"Maybe because I'm a woman. Or maybe because I'm a stranger." She shrugged, her own fury
fading. "At any rate, she promised to go to Lady
Presting's with you *and* to act the lady, but if she
complains of the headache, my lord, you are to
bring her home straight away."

"Emily's never been sick a day in her life," he
scoffed.

"My lord, you don't understand. If Emily complains
of a headache, it's because she's bored with Anne. I
promised her that you would bring her home."

"She can't get out of doing something she doesn't
want to do just by saying she has a headache."

"Of course she can. It's the way ladies do
things."

He stared at her. "No, it's not."

"Ask Penelope if you don't believe me. The point
is, my lord, that you must promise to bring Emily
home if she claims a headache. Otherwise, I can't
predict what she might do."

"Fine, I'll do it."

"Thank you, my lord."

"Will you *stop* calling me that?" he snapped. "My name is Justin. Or Rathmore. You'd think with what we have between us, you can manage to call me something besides 'my lord.'"

She stiffened. "There's nothing between us, *my lord*, except one or two lapses in judgment."

"Is that what you think?" In two strides he reached her, and before she could move away he had cupped her face in his hands. "Do you really think that what's between us is a lapse in judgment? Or is the lapse in trying to ignore it? God knows, I've been trying to do just that."

Dear God, he was too close. And he smelled too good and looked too handsome. And the way he gazed at her made her feel as if she were the only woman in the world.

"Don't," she managed to say, though her mouth had suddenly gone dry. "Please don't make this any harder than it is."

"So you admit it's hard to resist me." He smiled, a wicked, sinful smile that made her think of every warning her mother had ever given her about the primitive nature of men.

Rathmore definitely looked primitive. And she had to admit, she was feeling a bit primitive herself.

"I admit that this is improper," she said.

He laughed. "Improper? Wasn't it you, dear Meg, who told me that I made you think thoughts no lady should think?"

She closed her eyes as heat swept into her cheeks. "I shouldn't have said that."

"Is it the truth?" His insistent tone made her open her eyes. He was so close now, his mouth a mere breath from hers. "Is it, Meg?"

"Yes," she whispered. "Please . . ."

"Please what?"

"Please kiss me." She looked straight into those dark eyes of his, eyes that seemed endlessly hungry. "Justin, kiss me before I change my mind."

"I never disappoint a lady." He kissed her, his mouth finding hers with unerring accuracy. At the first touch of his lips, her body seemed to explode with a myriad of emotions. Hot, uncompromising passion roared through her, smothering doubt and awakening desire. She arched toward him, sliding her arms around his neck and clinging as he took her to a place she had never been.

Everything. She wanted everything from him. He was so handsome, so sinfully sensuous. She wanted to gobble him up like dessert, tangle her fingers in his hair, press her passion-starved body against his. She wanted to feel his skin beneath her hands, to explore the strange and unfamiliar planes of his body, to learn what pleased him.

She wanted to know what it felt like to be physically taken by the man she loved.

Her thoughts scrambled and her breath hitched. Loved? Was she in love with Rathmore? Madness. Sheer madness.

But such delicious madness. Fear and panic

drowned beneath the onslaught of need that possessed her. Later. She would think about it later.

Right now she couldn't think, only feel.

"You make me insane," he murmured, leaving her mouth to trace teasing kisses down her throat, sucking lightly on her flesh.

"This *is* insane," she whispered, "and I don't care."

"Neither do I." He scooped her into his arms, and she let out a squeak of surprise.

He turned and sat down on the sofa with her cradled in his lap. She could feel the hard ridge of his . . . reaction . . . against her buttocks. Instead of shocking her, it thrilled her.

She had done that to him.

He buried his face in her neck, licking at the base of her throat with a gentleness that belied the insistence of his hands holding her in place. Her head fell back, eyes closing, and she moaned softly as pleasure swept over her.

He shifted, closing one hand over her breast.

Her eyes popped open. "What are you doing?" she gasped.

"This." He pinched the nipple lightly through her dress, watching her face as the nub hardened between his fingers.

"Sweet Lord," Meg whimpered. He caressed her breast through her dress, drawing lazy circles around the now stiff nipple with a touch so light she could barely feel it. But the longer he did it, the more aroused she became.

He bent his head over her other breast and breathed through the thin muslin, teasing the hard little peak with the heat of his breath. Then he flicked her nipple with his tongue, and she nearly shot out of his lap.

He chuckled, soothing her now writhing body with experienced hands.

"Justin." She reached for him, completely lost in the passion to which he had introduced her. Bringing her mouth to his, she kissed him hungrily, running her tongue lightly against his lower lip.

He gave a low growl of response, but let her continue to explore his mouth as she willed. His hand stroked over her body, her breasts, her belly, her thighs. She curled her nails into his shoulders and nipped his lip.

He pulled back, his face taut with male hunger, then tugged down the front of her dress, pulling away the gown and chemise in one experienced movement, exposing one breast to his gaze.

Shock held her immobile, and their gazes met. His expression dared her to object, but she remained mute. She wanted this, wanted to know what it felt like, wanted it with Rathmore and no one else.

He bent his head and took her naked nipple in his mouth, and her head fell back again on a long moan of abject surrender.

He lifted her up to his mouth with the arm beneath her back, alternately licking at her nipple and gently tugging it with his teeth. His other hand slipped beneath her dress, stroking up her bare legs, caressing her thighs.

Then he cupped her womanly mound and pressed his thumb against that one, secret spot. She arched her back, her legs parting to allow him more.

"Yes," he murmured against her breast. "Yes, let me show you."

He stroked between her thighs, stoking the fire that burned in her until she writhed in his arms, desperate for something that was just out of reach.

"Please," she whimpered. "Justin, please . . ."

She didn't even know what she was begging for. Just that she ached—oh, how deliciously she ached—and that she needed something, had to have something that only Justin could give her.

"I know, love." He kissed her deeply, tangling his tongue with hers as his fingers caressed her slick folds. She clung to him with her arms around his neck, tension building so fast and so hard that she thought she might snap in two.

And then she did snap. With a low moan of release, she stiffened in his arms, then shuddered as her body exploded. Hot pleasure flooded her veins, rippling across her skin, her entire body awash with new sensation.

"That's it," Rathmore whispered, kissing her cheek, her lips. "Yes, that's what I want."

She slumped against him, drained and dazed, burying her face in his chest. He stroked her body, petting her, soothing her, brushing his lips against her forehead.

Occasionally she shuddered, but for the most part she lay utterly content in his arms, waiting for strength to return, for the world to go back on its axis.

"God, you were beautiful," he groaned, burying his face in her hair and hugging her tightly. She shifted in his lap and noticed with amazement that his "reaction" had gotten bigger. Harder.

"Is it always like this?" she asked.

"No," he said. "This is rare."

"I thought so. Otherwise you'd be quite uncomfortable most of the time."

He lifted his head. "What?"

"This." She moved her bottom against his hardness. "It can't possibly be like that all the time."

He made a sound that was part laughter and part groan. "No, it only gets like that around you."

"That's what I thought."

"Much like this." He flicked her still exposed nipple with one finger and watched it harden immediately. "That's what you do to me."

"So if I did that to you . . . to your male part, I mean . . . then the same thing would happen?"

The stunned expression on his face gave way to intense arousal. "Love, if you touch me that way, I'll explode."

"Oh. I was just wondering."

"Wonder all you like. Tell me your thoughts, ask me your questions. No doubt I will find them all amazingly interesting."

His blatantly sexual tone made her flush, despite

what they had just done together. Suddenly shy, she tugged her dress back into place.

He watched her action with a hint of regret on his face. "It's a shame women have to hide their beauty under so many layers of clothing."

She laughed nervously and tried to slip out of his lap. The passion had ebbed, and she was a bit shocked at her own brazen behavior.

"Where are you going?" He caught her before she could rise and settled her in his lap again.

"Please, Justin. Someone could come in at any moment."

"You're right." His expression grew serious. "Meg, you know I didn't intend for this to happen."

"Neither did I." She untangled herself from his arms and got shakily to her feet.

"I had no intention of getting involved with you at all." He sighed. "You make me forget myself."

"You make me forget myself, too." She gave a nervous laugh. "Which is probably not the thing to say to a known rake." To buy herself time to calm herself, she walked over to the mirror hanging above the mantel and examined her appearance. By some miracle, her hair was more or less still in place, though she had to adjust the bodice of her dress.

She watched in the mirror as he rose from the sofa and approached her. "Meg, you know this was more than a moment's dalliance. You mean more to me than that."

His hair was mussed—from her own hands, she

realized with a start—and his eyes still simmered with male need. His trousers fit so tightly that she could see every detail of the hard bulge of his manhood. The sheer size of it made her heart flutter. Dear Lord, however did one accomplish the deed with something that big?

It was all she could do not to go back to him and ask him to show her.

But if she did that, if she gave in to these dangerous, unladylike impulses, they would both be trapped into marriage before she could blink. And that wasn't what she wanted.

Not that she wasn't tempted. But there had to be more.

"We should just forget this happened."

"I can't forget." He laid his hands on her shoulders and turned her to face him. "Meg, I meant what I said. You mean something to me. But until I clear my name, I can't think of taking a wife."

There it was again, talk of marriage.

"I don't expect you to marry me."

"You should." Guilt flickered in his eyes. "I took advantage of you."

"You did nothing I didn't want you to do." She met his gaze. "Justin, I'm not helpless. I knew what I was doing."

"I know you're not helpless. You're beautiful. Spirited. Smart." He cupped her cheek in his palm. "You're everything I want in a woman. And I have no right to even speak to you of this until I can offer you everything you deserve in a husband."

She shook her head. "Justin, you're very persuasive, but I would not marry you even if you felt free to offer."

"What?" He scowled, affronted male pride written all over his face. "Why not? I've a title and wealth. I'm pleasant enough to look at. I'm a considerate lover. Aside from my reputation, I'd be the prime catch of the Season. What more do you want?"

"If you don't know, then I can't tell you." Strangely disappointed, she turned back to the mirror and tucked a stray curl back into place. "Look at us, Justin."

He met her eyes in the mirror. "We look good together."

"Appearances." She gave a little smile. "The mirror shows only a reflection of the true person. Much as the face we show to the world only reflects one small part of a person."

"What are you trying to say?"

"I'm saying I don't know you, Justin, and you don't know me. Not the real me. And until you do, until you can know and *love* the real me, and I can know and love the real you, then I cannot even consider marrying you. I will not wed a stranger."

"Love can grow in a marriage," he said.

"Love should be the start of marriage."

His jaw tightened, and for a moment he looked every inch the Devil Earl. "Is it because of the rumors? Because you believe I really did kill Ophelia?"

She couldn't ignore the pain in his voice. "No, Justin. I don't think you killed her."

"That's something at least."

"I do believe you." She met his gaze in the mirror. "Really, I do. It has nothing to do with that."

"I can't formally offer until I prove my innocence," he said. "But once I do, you can be sure I will be paying my addresses to your grandfather."

"You're not listening. There's more we both need to learn about each other before we can ever consider marriage." She turned away from the mirror to face him again. "Justin, you taught me something today—a lesson of passion. Because of you, I know what it feels like."

"I haven't begun to show you everything." He stroked his fingers down her cheek. "Give me a chance, Meg. I want to show you everything."

She closed her eyes against temptation and took a deep breath. Then she stepped back from his touch. "You don't understand, Justin. It's not about you or what you can give me. It's about *me* figuring out where I belong. Until I discover that, I will not marry anyone."

"I don't understand."

"I would have gone from being somebody's sister to somebody's granddaughter to somebody's wife," she explained. "When do I get to just be Meg?"

"What do you want me to do?" he asked, frustration adding a bite to his words.

"There's nothing you can do. Only time can help."

"Time, is it? Time enough to clear my name, perhaps?"

"I told you—"

"—that it doesn't matter. Well, it does to me." He turned that fierce, unblinking stare on her, the one that made her think he would shed the constraints of a gentleman at any moment and lead her most willingly down the path to wickedness. Shivers of arousal rippled down her spine.

"I will give you time, Meg," he continued, "but only as long as it takes me to find Ophelia's murderer and regain my honor. After that, I intend to make you my wife."

The utter determination in his voice thrilled her even as it unsettled her.

"Of course I cannot stop you," she said. "But you cannot guarantee that I will consent. Good day, my lord."

With a polite smile, she exited the room, leaving him standing there, staring at his own dumbstruck expression in the mirror.

Chapter 11

Miss Anne Harcroft, daughter of Lord and Lady Presting, was a picture of a nobleman's fashionable daughter. She was blond and blue-eyed with beribboned curls and a frilly, pale blue dress. Her manners were impeccable, her demeanor demure, her posture painfully straight. She responded to each of her mother's dictatorial directives with a soft voice and downcast eyes.

A weak-minded ninny, Emily thought disdainfully. And her heart sank with despair. She had hoped that perhaps Anne might be the friend she had so longed for, but instead it looked as if her worst fears had been realized.

A headache would no doubt be swift in coming.

"Now you entertain your guest, Anne, while your father and I entertain Lord Rathmore," Lady Presting ordered.

"Yes, Mama," came Anne's dulcet reply.

Emily glanced at her guardian, who seemed just as dismayed as she was. He glanced from her to the fragile-looking Anne and then back to her, and his forehead creased with concern.

"Perhaps you girls would like to view the latest fashions?" Lady Presting asked. "I have recently received the latest issue of *La Belle Assemblée*."

Emily winced. It was bad enough she had to keep company with the insipid Anne. If she had to do so while pretending to be enraptured by fashion plates, she didn't know if she could possibly maintain the façade.

She spoke up on impulse. "Lady Presting, I've heard wonderful things about your gardens. Do you suppose we could take a turn through it so I might admire your lovely flowers?"

"I don't know," Lady Presting replied. "I do worry about Anne's skin in the sun. Freckles, you know."

"I would be delighted to show Miss St. James the gardens, Mama," the ever courteous Anne replied. "I promise we shan't be long, and I will stay out of the sunshine."

"Well . . ."

"My ward is very fond of gardens," Cousin Justin said. "I can't see the harm in it."

"Very well," Lady Presting relented. "But do bring your parasol, Anne."

"Yes, Mama," Anne said obediently.

Emily rolled her eyes, and Cousin Justin cleared his throat loudly. The stern look he sent her way spoke volumes.

"Would you care to borrow one of Anne's parasols?" Lady Presting asked Emily. "I'm certain she has one in willow green that will match your lovely dress."

Emily bit back the words she would have liked to say and instead replied politely, "No, thank you, my lady. I am not troubled by freckles."

"Lucky girl," Lady Presting said.

Emily caught her guardian's sigh of relief out of the corner of her eye. Once she might have delighted in speaking her mind about such nonsense, but not after what Meg had told her. She wished Cousin Justin would stop waiting for her to do something horrific. She wasn't a baby, after all.

Lady Presting sent a maid for Anne's parasol, a frilly thing that almost exactly matched her dress, and then they left the house for the gardens as Emily's guardian and Lady Presting retired to a sitting room.

The two girls walked in silence. Emily searched her mind frantically for something to say, but she could think of nothing. Anne clearly wasn't much of a conversationalist.

"Can you still see the house?" Anne whispered suddenly.

Startled, Emily glanced backward. "No, the hedges are in the way."

"Finally!" Anne closed the parasol with a snap and handed it to Emily. "Hold this, will you?"

Bemused, Emily took the ridiculously frilly thing and watched as Anne pulled a small jar from the pocket of her dress. "What's that?"

"A cream I had my maid acquire from the apothecary. It prevents freckles. Mother would turn puce if I got even one." She began to dab the white cream across her nose. "Want some?"

"No, thank you. My guardian doesn't care if I get freckles or not."

"You're very lucky," Anne said, now smearing the cream on her hands and rubbing until it disappeared into her skin. "Mother is obsessed with the fear that I will get a freckle and than no man will want to marry me. I think it's because she's a redhead and freckles easily." She dropped the jar into her pocket again. "I'm so glad you suggested we tour the gardens! If I had to look at *La Belle Assemblée* one more time, I might not be able to restrain myself from screaming."

"I know the feeling." As Anne briskly started down one of the garden paths, Emily trailed behind, still toting the parasol, fascinated by the vivacious girl who had taken the place of the vapid Miss Anne Harcroft. "At least Cousin Justin doesn't make me look at fashion plates."

Anne shuddered. "Heavens, I do hate the things. However, it does appease Mama, and that means I can do what I want when she's not around. I certainly don't want her watching me too closely."

Anne came to a gate that led to a huge field and opened it.

"Where are we going?" Emily asked.

"To the stables. I hope you like horses."

"I *adore* them."

"Me, too." With a mischievous grin, Anne snatched back the parasol and opened it. "I'll have to play the game to get us into the stables, but then we're safe. Ebbie, the head groom, has kept my secret for years."

Impressed, Emily could only shake her head in admiration.

"Oh," Anne added, "by the way, Miss Anne Harcroft is frightened of horses running loose in the paddock, so she always goes inside the stables where the beastly animals are kept in stalls." She flashed that engaging grin again. "Once we're inside, I'll introduce you to Pharaoh, my father's prize stallion."

"Sounds like fun," Emily said, and meant it.

"Let me tell you about my mare, Guinevere . . ."

Chatting amicably, the two girls made their way toward the stables.

Lady Presting's drawing room was done in the Greek style, rife with vases and screens portraying Greek heroes and goddesses. Feeling a bit as if he were being called to the carpet for some transgression, Rathmore perched on the edge of a rather delicate looking lyre-backed chair and tried not to think about what would happen if the legs of the thing were to snap off beneath him.

There was a robust-looking sofa in the room that would have managed his weight quite well, but Lord and Lady Presting had taken that for themselves, and between the tall, Junoesque Lady Presting and the shorter but more corpulent Lord Presting, there was not an inch to spare for a mouse, much less an earl with broad shoulders and unusually long legs.

"I called for refreshments some time ago," Lady Presting said, scowling at the clock on the mantel. "Peter, I swear the servants are getting slower and slower. It is not to be borne."

"Yes, dear," Lord Presting replied. He blinked rather owlishly and stared out the window.

"I do apologize for this, Lord Rathmore," Lady Presting said. "So hard to find good servants in the country."

"Not at all," Rathmore replied. He, too, glanced at the clock on the mantel. Emily and Anne had been gone for ten minutes. No screams had reached his ears, no crying, no crashes. And best of all, no Emily claiming a headache. The silence was either a good omen or a bad one. Either Emily was getting on with Miss Harcroft, or she had tied her up in a closet somewhere.

Which was not such a farfetched notion, as she had done just that to governess number two.

After another moment of strained silence, Lady Presting rose. "Please excuse me, Lord Rathmore. I shall see about the delay with the kitchen." She made her way to the door and opened it to speak to the footman standing just outside.

Lord Presting glanced at his distracted wife, then reached into his coat pocket and withdrew a small, silver flask. "Care for a nip?" he whispered to Rathmore.

"No, thank you."

Lord Presting shrugged. "You'll need it after an hour with Euphrenia." He uncapped the flask and took a quick drink.

"I hope to even last an hour," Rathmore muttered.

"What's that?" Lord Presting capped his flask and slipped it back into his pocket just as his wife returned.

"Nothing," Rathmore said.

Lady Presting smiled a bit tensely as she reseated herself on the sofa. "Refreshments will be along directly, my lord."

"You are too kind, Lady Presting." Rathmore glanced at the clock again. Twenty minutes.

"Do you have another appointment, Lord Rathmore?"

Rathmore jerked his gaze around to Lady Presting, who watched him with narrowed eyes. "Not at all, my lady. I was just wondering how my ward and your daughter were getting on."

"I'm certain they are getting on famously," Lady Presting assured him. "My Anne is an obedient, sweet child. I have no doubts that she and Miss St.

James will get on splendidly. After all, they are both gently bred young ladies from fine families."

"One of them is," Rathmore mumbled.

"I'm sorry, what did you say, my lord?"

Rathmore forced his lips into a polite smile. "I said of course, you're right. I'm afraid I haven't the benefit of your years of experience when it comes to Emily, my lady."

Lady Presting nodded regally. "Naturally you are concerned about your ward's social behavior, Lord Rathmore, especially as she is without any female relatives to advise her. However, I can assure you that I perceive her as all that is amiable, if a bit unpolished yet. Perhaps she will learn a thing or two from Anne to smooth out her rough edges."

"That, my lady, would be most welcome."

"Catch it!" Anne squealed, jumping up and down.

"I've almost—drat, it's headed for your side!" Emily darted around the pile of hay after the pale gray kitten. "Quick, come around this side!"

Anne raced around the hay after the little creature. The kitten, realizing it was trapped, turned abruptly and disappeared into the haystack. Anne squealed and leaped into the hay after it.

"You dig on that side, and I'll dig on this side," Anne gasped, pawing at the hay. Straw clung to her curls and the lace of her dress. "If we go at it from both sides, we are bound to find him."

"I've always wanted a pet," Emily said, getting

down on her hands and knees in the straw. She dug as feverishly as Anne, straw pricking her fingers like tiny gnat bites. "How fortunate your barn cat had kittens."

"And how *un*fortunate that we opened that stall door," Anne said. "Who knew the little thing could run so fast?"

"I just wanted to pet him." Emily spread her hands through the straw, scattering it everywhere. "At least he ran into *this* stall. And thank goodness it was empty."

"With the door closed, he shan't be able to get away," Anne said. "We'll find him soon enough."

"I hope Cousin Justin lets me keep him," Emily said, "even if I have to keep him in the barn." She scowled at the strewn hay. "Where did the little fellow go?"

"Perhaps if we stay very still, he will think we have gone away," Anne said. She swiped at a piece of straw hanging from her sleeve. "He's bound to come out as soon as he thinks we're gone. I think we frightened him."

"I think you're right."

Both girls stayed very still and quiet, and moments later they were rewarded when a section of the straw moved, followed by a tiny mew from the distressed kitten. A moment later, the animal's little head popped out of the straw.

Anne scooped the cat up in her arms, then settled back on the straw, shushing kitten as it mewed piteously. "There, there, now. We won't hurt you."

Emily scrambled over the hay to where Anne sat and reached out to scratch the tiny cat behind its ears. It immediately stopped mewing and arched its head toward her. Moments later, the cat's little body began to vibrate as it started to purr.

Anne giggled. "His whole body is shaking from his purring. Keep scratching."

"I will." Emily stroked her hand down the animal's back, pausing to scratch its haunches. The kitten raised its tail in the air, making both girls giggle. "I think I shall call him Lancelot."

"To go with your Guinevere." Anne sighed. "I wish Mama would let me have a more spirited horse to ride, but the only one she allows me to mount is old Dulcinea, who I have ridden since I was a baby. I don't think Dulcinea even knows how to gallop."

"Aren't ladies supposed to know how to ride?" Emily asked.

"Of course, but only sidesaddle and at a sedate pace." Anne made a face. "I often think that Mama wouldn't even let me do that much if it weren't a socially acceptable pastime."

"I shall have you come visit at Rathmore Hall," Emily said. "You can go riding there."

Anne shook her head. "Even there, Mama would insist I be mounted on the oldest, gentlest nag available."

"That's all right," Emily said. "We'll ride out and when we're away from the house, we'll switch horses, and I'll let you ride Guinevere. Cousin

Justin doesn't insist on coming with me if I bring a footman along."

"You'd do that for me? You are indeed the best of friends!" Anne reached out to give Emily a one-armed hug, and the poor kitten let out a squeal of complaint as it was squished between their bodies. Giggling, the two girls parted, and Anne handed the cat to Emily. "Here you go. He's yours now."

"Mine," Emily said with wonder. She scratched the kitten behind the ears again, sending the little feline into rapturous purring. "I don't know how I shall get him home, though."

"Don't worry about that," Anne said. "I shall have one of the footmen deliver him to your guardian's estate. Is there someone in the stables who you can trust to watch out for him?"

"Peeves, our head groom. He's known me since I was born."

"Then tomorrow I shall send Lancelot to Rathmore Hall, care of Peeves the head groom." Anne brushed at her hair. "Do I have straw everywhere?"

"I'm afraid so. Do I?"

Anne nodded. "We shall have to tidy up before we return to the house. Mama would send me to Scotland to live with my maiden aunts if she knew I was romping about in the hay."

"I'll straighten your hair, if you straighten mine," Emily offered. "That way one of us can hold Lancelot."

"Done. I'll do yours first."

Emily wiggled around until she sat with her back

to Anne. The other girl slipped the willow-green ribbon from Emily's hair and began to finger-comb the straw out of her curls.

With Anne straightening her appearance and her new pet cuddled in her arms, Emily was overtaken by a feeling of contentment such as she had never known. Never before had she had a friend, a girl her own age with whom she could giggle and exchange secrets. Someone who understood her and liked her anyway.

And to think she had resisted this visit! If Meg hadn't persuaded her to come, she would never have met Anne, never known what it felt like to be accepted for who she was.

Moved almost to tears, she glanced back over her shoulder. "Anne, I never—"

"Shhh," Anne hissed, pausing in her ministrations. "Someone's coming."

Emily held very still. For her own sake, she didn't care if she got caught rolling around in the hay and chasing kittens around the stables. But she knew that Anne would get in trouble, and she wanted to keep her new friend. She stayed quiet.

"You're back early, my lord," a gruff male voice said.

"That's Ebbie," Anne whispered. "He's our head groom. He won't say anything if he sees us."

Emily nodded.

"The horse threw a shoe," came a drawling, cultured voice, ripe with annoyance. "And I had to walk all the way back here down that muddy lane with the creature. And look! My boots are ruined!"

"My apologies, my lord," Ebbie said calmly. "Would you care for another mount?"

"Not until I've changed my boots. Just look at them. My valet will be in hysterics."

"I can have Solomon ready for you in a thrice, Lord Fenton."

Anne scrunched up her nose in distaste. "It's that nasty Lord Fenton," she whispered. "He's always shouting at the servants."

Emily nodded and swallowed hard as the nobleman's voice rose.

"Is that all you have to say?" Lord Fenton snarled, sending a shiver of alarm rippled through Emily. "My boots have suffered because of your shoddy work, and I will be late for my appointment."

"Horses throw shoes all the time," Ebbie replied. "All I can do is apologize to Your Lordship and fetch another mount for you."

"Impertinent oaf!" Lord Fenton roared. "You will do as you are told!"

"He can't talk to Ebbie that way!" Anne gasped as the groom once more apologized to Lord Fenton.

Emily squeezed the kitten tighter and began to tremble. "Stay quiet, Anne," she begged.

Anne cast her an annoyed glance. Then the irritation faded from her face to be replaced by concern. "What's the matter with you? You're shaking."

"Lord Presting will hear of this!" Lord Fenton roared.

Emily winced and shut her eyes. "I can't stand the yelling," she whispered. "I wish he would stop yelling."

"He won't harm you." Anne sat beside Emily and slipped her arm around her shoulders. "It's all right. He won't harm you."

"I know. But I'm scared anyway." A tear slipped down her cheek. "Ever since I was a little girl, I have become terrified whenever men yell. And I don't know why."

"Did you hear me, man?" Lord Fenton shouted. "Your master will hear of this outrage! You will be seeking a new position before the sun goes down."

"I heard you, Your Lordship," Ebbie replied evenly. "And Solomon will be ready when you come for him."

"Don't you dare walk away from me!" A crash sounded.

Emily cringed.

"Ebbie!" Anne whispered with alarm. She touched Emily's shoulder. "I'll be right here. I just want to look and make sure Ebbie is all right."

Emily nodded, still clinging to the kitten, and opened her eyes to watch Anne peer out the stable door.

Muttering could be heard, and pacing. Then footsteps storming off. Anne gave a sigh and sat back down beside Emily. "Well, Lord Fenton is gone. It looks like he simply kicked a bucket of feed

across the stable. He probably got angry when
Ebbie walked away from him. Lord Fenton is very
high in the instep."

"I'm glad he's gone." Embarrassed, Emily said,
"You must think me a wet goose."

"Not at all. Everyone is afraid of something,
and Lord Fenton in a temper is *very* frightening."
Anne smiled. "You should see how I react to the
sight of a spider. A veritable bedlamite, that's what
I become."

Emily managed to laugh, but her entire body felt
as if it were made of pudding. "I think perhaps we
should go back to the house, Anne. I suddenly
don't feel very well."

"Of course. Stand up now." She helped Emily to
rise, then took the cat from her arms. "I'll give
Lancelot to Ebbie with instructions to send him on
to Rathmore Hall. Then we shall take turns brushing the straw off each other."

Emily nodded and leaned against the wall of the
stall. Her legs didn't seem to want to support her.

Anne paused before leaving the stall. "I'll be
right back," she assured Emily. "And I'm holding
you to that promise about Guinevere."

"Done." The weak smile Emily managed to
form faded from her lips as Anne left to see to the
cat. Drained, she closed her eyes and willed her
limbs to stop trembling.

She hadn't been exactly honest with Anne. Yes,
she was terrified of men who shouted when they
were angry. Men who grew violent in temper,

throwing things or kicking them or striking out at the people around them.

Cousin Justin sometimes shouted when he got vexed with her, but she always managed to maintain her calm until she left the room. *Then* she would give in to her weakness.

But this time, it had been so much worse than before. Something about this incident had sapped the strength from her body and left her a trembling mass of terror. Something about Lord Fenton's tone or his manner had struck a chord in her. She had heard something like that before.

In her nightmares.

The door to the drawing room burst open.

"Presting, I demand—" Lord Fenton stumbled to a halt mid-tirade. "Rathmore. Sorry, didn't see you there."

"Lord Fenton, what a surprise." Lady Presting rose to her feet and glanced nervously from Rathmore to Fenton. "I thought you were on your way to the village."

"I was, but the horse threw a shoe." Fenton slapped his riding crop impatiently against his thigh and looked at Lord Presting, who was surreptitiously slipping the flask back into his pocket. "Presting, I have come to complain about your head groom. He was most impertinent with me."

"Impertinent? Ebbie?" Lord Presting's brow furrowed. "I'm certain you are mistaken, Fenton."

"He accepted no responsibility for my horse

throwing a shoe, just stood there and boldly asked if I wanted another mount. Didn't even care that the mud has ruined my favorite pair of boots."

"Shocking," Rathmore drawled.

"Seems to me he did as he ought," Lord Presting said, pursing his lips in thought. "Offered another mount, did he? Well, then. There you go."

Fenton let out an exasperated breath and looked expectantly at Lady Presting.

She smiled weakly. "Good help is so difficult to find in the country, my lord."

"Obviously." Fenton glared at Lord Presting. "I expect you to do something about this, Presting."

Not liking the demanding tone of Fenton's voice, Rathmore suggested smoothly, "Perhaps you should have a talk with your man, Presting. Straighten out the matter."

"Indeed. Quite so. Thank you, Rathmore," Lord Presting said. He looked at Fenton. "I shall have a talk with Ebbie, Fenton. Sorry about your boots."

Lord Fenton shook his head and with a snort of disgust, whirled on his heel and stormed out of the room.

A moment of uncomfortable silence descended.

"I apologize for that, Lord Rathmore," Lady Presting said, sitting down slowly. "I expected Lord Fenton to be in the village all day."

"It's quite all right, my lady." Rathmore managed to utter the words calmly enough, though inside he was reeling with shock. Had Lady Presting just *apologized* to him for Fenton's presence?

"Not quite." She folded her hands. "I understand that you and Lord Fenton have come to some sort of . . . understanding. But I had still hoped to arrange things so that the two of you would not have to meet."

"As I said, it's of no consequence."

"Hear that, Euphrenia? No consequence at all." Chuckling, Lord Presting slapped his hand on the arm of the sofa. "Grown men, the both of them. Let it be."

Lady Presting flushed and glanced at her clearly intoxicated husband. "As you wish, Peter."

Anne entered the room at that moment, her arm hooked through that of a pale, somewhat shaky Emily.

"Mama," Anne said, "Miss St. James does not feel quite the thing."

"Oh, dear!" Lady Presting rose and helped Emily get seated.

Rathmore glanced at the clock. Wonder of wonders, the girl had lasted nearly an hour.

"Have the two of you been out in the gardens all this time?" Lady Presting asked. "Too much air is not good for a young lady's constitution."

"We were not outside very long," Anne replied demurely.

"Be that as it may . . ." Lady Presting shook her head. "Never mind. How may I assist, Miss St. James? Do you feel faint? I can have my maid fetch some hartshorn."

Rathmore rose, deciding the charade had gone

on long enough. "What's the matter, Emily?" he asked. "Have you the headache?"

Instead of the affirmative answer he expected, Emily weakly shook her head and instead laid her hand across her stomach. "I feel ill, Cousin Justin."

Rathmore frowned at the frail sound of her voice. Coming to stand beside her, he noted that his ward looked unusually wan. The sparkle was gone from her eyes, and she had the uncertain expression of someone who might cast up her accounts at any moment. He took her hand in his and was alarmed to find it clammy and trembling.

Good God, she really was ill!

Shaken, he dropped her hand and took a step back. Think. He had to think. What was he to do?

"Cousin Justin," Emily whispered plaintively. She reached for him.

"I'm here," he said, once more taking her cold hand in his.

"Shall I summon the physician?" Lady Presting asked.

"No," Emily whimpered. She clung to Rathmore's hand with surprising strength. "Take me home, Cousin Justin. I just want to go home."

"Then you shall." Scooping his ward into his arms, he paused to give a nod to Lord Presting and then faced his lady. "Please forgive the abrupt departure, my lady."

"Of course, of course." Lady Presting waved her hands dismissively. "Do let us know how she fares, my lord."

"Anne," Emily whispered.

"Yes, Miss St. James?" Anne stepped toward Emily, but her mother's hand stayed her.

"Not so close, Anne," Lady Presting murmured.

"Don't forget, Anne," Emily said.

Anne smiled. "I shan't." She glanced up at Rathmore, and he was startled to see a lively spark in the girl's blue eyes. "Do take good care of her, my lord. We have become bosom bows."

Rathmore inclined his head. "I shall do that, Miss Harcroft."

With a nod to the assembled company, he left the drawing room, his ward cradled protectively in his arms.

Chapter 12

Meg sat in the music room at Knightsbridge Chase and frowned once more at the clock. Her music instructor was almost a half hour late. Most unusual.

Though she had taken only two lessons with Signora Vitessa, Meg was becoming more and more confident that music might be her calling. Already the signora had described Meg's voice to be "as nothing she had ever heard before." The former opera singer had recommended many lessons to help Meg develop her ear for music.

Meg was flattered that the signora considered her so talented. Music was certainly turning out better than botany or dog breeding.

She frowned at the clock again. Signora was now forty minutes late. She had gotten the date right, hadn't she? Thursday at three o'clock.

Thursday, the same day Emily was to go visit Lady Presting's daughter.

Meg scowled. Drat it all, she hadn't wanted to think of Rathmore today. His talk of marriage on Sunday had taken her by surprise, as had the passion he'd shown her. Why was the man suddenly so determined to wed her? It couldn't be that he had fallen in love with her.

Of course not.

Meg sighed and ran her fingers over the keyboard of the pianoforte. The notes hung in the air like unspoken words between lovers, then dissolved into silence.

If he loved her, it would be worse, she assured herself. After all, since he *didn't* love her, then it was easier to resist him.

Wasn't it?

Dear Lord. Meg sat down heavily on the bench of the pianoforte and poked aimlessly at the keys. *Plink, plink.* She could barely resist him as it was. If he figured out how vulnerable she was to him . . .

Plink, plunk. Maybe he already had. Maybe that . . . incident in his drawing room had given her away. Did he suspect? Did he know that it had taken everything she had to walk away from him?

Plunk, plunk, plunk. She had to refuse him. She had meant what she said. All her life, she had lived in the shadow of being Garrett Lynch's sister, and her brother had overseen her every movement as if she were a babe. Then she had escaped to England to meet the grandfather she had never known, onl to discover that she was now known as the Duke of Raynewood's granddaughter, and that English society was just as restrictive as her old life had been.

As much as she longed to make her own way in the world, as much as she had bragged of it to Rathmore, she was enough of a realist to understand that she probably would have to wed at some point. It was either that or live under her brother's thumb. But before she did marry, she needed something to cling to, something of her own that lived in her heart, some *place* where she was only Meg.

And until she found that place, she dared accept no one's offer of marriage. Especially Rathmore's.

How *had* Emily gotten on with Lady Presting's daughter? She was mad to know.

She ran her fingers down the keyboard, then pounded hard. A deep *thrum* sounded through the room. She lost herself in the note, eyes closed, just the music and her heartbeat.

Someone cleared his throat.

Meg's eyes popped open. Algie stood in the doorway of the music room.

"My apologies, cousin," he said. "The servants heard the pianoforte and panicked . . . I mean, came to fetch me so that I might bring you some bad news. I'm afraid Signora Vitessa will not be coming today. Or any other day for that matter."

"Why not?" Meg rose from the bench. "Is she ill? Has something happened?"

"Not at all." Algie cleared his throat, looked at

the wall, the ceiling, the floor. "The truth is, I paid her to never give you voice lessons again."

"*What*? Whatever possessed you to do such a thing?"

Knightsbridge winced as her tone grew louder. "Now, cousin, let me explain."

"Please do." Meg folded her arms across her chest and tapped her foot.

"I am lord here," he said, "and it's my duty to protect those on my lands and in my house."

"Algie, please get to the point."

"Very well. The point is . . ." He took a deep breath. "Your singing voice is awful, cousin."

"Hence the reason I hired a voice teacher."

"Yes, well." Algie cleared his throat again. "The thing is, the housekeeper threatened to quit if one more crystal goblet shattered."

She narrowed her eyes. "Are you saying that my voice shattered your crystal?"

"It could be a coincidence, I suppose, though it did happen every time you sang. And then there were the dogs."

"The dogs?"

"The howling was disturbing to the servants."

"The howling."

"Yes." Finally, he looked at her. "Cousin, I do not believe music is your forte. Perhaps you should consider something else."

"I am running out of things to try!" Frustrated, she plopped down on the bench of the pianoforte. "I thought at least I would be able to learn to sing

even if I wasn't born with the gift for it. Those who
embrace music seem to take such joy in it. I had
hoped to find some of that for myself."

Algie scratched his ear. "Meg, I'm trying to understand what you want to do, but I admit, I'm baffled. Most ladies of my acquaintance aspire to
marriage and motherhood. You puzzle me."

"Algie, isn't there some hobby that you're passionate about? Something that you simply love to
do? Something that you're good at?"

"I am rather good at cards," he said. "And fencing. I do love the intricate dance of fencing, the
swish of the rapier, the skill of a good opponent."

"That's what I want," Meg said, leaning forward
earnestly. "I want to know that there is something
in the world that I do well, something that gives me
joy just from doing it."

"Hmm." Algie shrugged. "I wish you luck in
finding it then. As long as it doesn't involve singing."

Meg sighed. "I fear I shall have to give up on
singing. What else do gently born English ladies do
to pass the time?"

"Gardening—"

Meg shook her head.

"Yes, well, we know what happened there. Music, needlepoint—"

Meg made a face. "Needlepoint would bore me
to tears."

"Watercolors—"

"Watercolors," she repeated. "Painting. That
might be a possibility."

"Indeed," Algie agreed. "Many ladies engage in watercolors. And I understand that painting can be quite the consuming passion."

"That might be the thing," Meg said. "Painting. But not your insipid watercolors." She gave him a huge smile. "*Oils*."

"Oils? But they make a terrible mess and smell awful."

Meg gave him a look. "I can always call Signora Vitessa."

"However," Algie continued without skipping a beat, "painting is *quiet*, isn't it? And I imagine we can put you in a room away from the rest of the house where the smell will remain contained."

Meg leaped from the bench and clapped her hands. "Algie, you are the best of cousins!"

He flushed a bit. "Yes, well, at least painting is a lady's pursuit, quite unobjectionable."

"I believe I shall go to the village immediately and see about obtaining the necessary materials." Meg came forward and impulsively kissed his cheek. "Thank you, Algie."

Knightsbridge blushed even redder, and Meg hurried out of the music room. "Bold American baggage," he called fondly after her retreating form.

Her laughter echoed back to him from the hallway.

Rathmore cradled the slim body of his ward close beside him in the carriage. Her thin fingers clung to his arm, a testament to the extent of her illness. Normally she avoided touching him if at all possible.

She seemed so small, all the defiance gone from her. Now she looked like what she was: just a child who'd been orphaned and depended on him to make her world right.

He leaned his head back against the carriage seat, the sheer weight of responsibility robbing the breath from his lungs. His heart pounded in his chest. His fingers trembled as he stroked her hair.

He was terrified.

What did he know about children, much less sick ones? All he could think to do was to get Emily home as quickly as possible and then summon the physician. Certainly that was the right thing to do? The physician would know how to help her.

"Please don't worry, Cousin Justin," Emily said softly. "I'm certain I will feel better soon."

"I'm calling the physician as soon as we get home," he said. "Don't worry, Emily. I'll take care of you."

She said nothing more, but snuggled closer to him. He laid his head on top of hers.

"I'll take care of you," he whispered again.

"I can't believe there are no oil paints to be found in any of the local shops," Meg said. Her determined stride down the village's main thoroughfare echoed her impatience with the situation. "We shall have to send to London for them, I expect."

"Not much call for that sort of thing in the country," her maid Lizzie remarked, hurrying after her. "Most ladies use watercolors."

"I'm not most ladies." Meg halted. "Lizzie, isn't that Lord Rathmore's livery?"

Stopping just short of crashing into Meg, Lizzie caught her balance and squinted. "Do you mean the coach outside the physician's cottage? It certainly looks like Lord Rathmore's crest, miss."

"Someone must be ill." Meg started forward at an even quicker pace, Lizzie scurrying after her, and reached the coach just as the doctor rushed out of his cottage, his black bag in his hand.

A footman jumped down from the coach and opened the door so the doctor could climb in. Meg recognized the servant from her previous visits to Rathmore Hall.

"What's happened, Matthew?" Meg demanded of the footman. "Is someone hurt?"

"It's Miss Emily," Matthew replied. "She took sick at Lady Presting's house this afternoon." He slammed the door of the coach.

Meg moved to block him as he went to climb back on top of the coach. "Was it a headache?"

The footman shook his head. "No, miss, she's all shaky and such. His Lordship sent the coach for Dr. Peters."

The doctor stuck his head out the window. "And I can't help the girl until you get me there, so stop chattering!"

Matthew bobbed his head in acknowledgment and climbed to his perch.

Meg yanked open the coach door. "Wait! I'm coming, too!"

"Miss Stanton-Lynch!" Lizzie protested.

Meg scrambled into coach and into the opposite seat from the doctor. Then she closed the door with a final-sounding snap and peered out the window. "Lizzie, take our carriage back to Knightsbridge Chase and let my cousin know where I am."

"But, miss—" the maid began.

"Miss Stanton-Lynch," the physician interrupted from the other side of the coach, "you do know this is not exactly proper."

"Propriety has no place in the face of a young girl's illness, Dr. Peters." Meg folded her arms across her chest and glared at him. "I know Miss St. James quite well, and I might be able to help. I'm going." She lifted her chin and narrowed her eyes, silently daring him to argue further.

He studied her for a moment, then sighed. "You're American, correct?"

"I am."

"That explains it." He stuck his head out the window. "On, driver!" he called.

"That explains it?" Meg repeated as the coach lurched into motion. Somewhat insulted, she gave the doctor her haughtiest look.

He merely shrugged and made himself comfortable in the luxurious seat. "I've known a few Americans. Stubborn as mules, the lot of them."

"Oh." Mollified, Meg watched the countryside race by. "That's all right then."

* * *

Rathmore paced the foyer. Where was the
bloody doctor? He had sent his own coach with his
fastest horses to fetch the physician more than a
quarter of an hour ago. What was taking so long?

Perhaps he should have sent for Meg after all.

No. He couldn't keep running to Meg every time
some difficulty arose with Emily, especially not
since she had so roundly rejected him. He didn't
want her to think him useless. Lost without her. Incapable of raising his ward.

Though he felt all of those.

No, if he was ever going to be a successful
guardian to Emily, he needed to learn how to handle such emergencies himself.

If only he knew for certain that he was doing the
right thing.

The rattle of coach wheels in the drive drew his
attention. He yanked open the door even before
Grimm could reach for the knob and bounded outside as the coach pulled to a stop.

"What took you so long?" he demanded as
Matthew the footman hopped down to open the
coach door.

"There was a bit of a complication, my lord,"
Matthew replied respectfully.

"What kind of complication?" Rathmore demanded. "Was the physician away?"

"No, my lord."

"Then what?"

"I'm afraid I am the complication," Meg said, appearing in the doorway of the coach.

Rathmore could only stare at her, dumbfounded. How could she be here? It was as if he had summoned her by mere force of will, and he was so pitifully grateful for the miracle of her presence that he could do nothing more than silently offer his hand and help her descend from the coach.

Once her feet were on the ground, she faced him squarely. "I was in the village and inflicted myself on your footman. I'm afraid he couldn't stop me from coming." Unable to believe she stood before him, he said nothing. Silence stretched between them, and uncertainty clouded her blue eyes. She dropped her gaze. "I'm sorry if I have trespassed where I should not have, my lord," she whispered.

He found his voice at last. "Not at all." Emotion nearly choked him. She looked so beautiful in her pale green walking dress, and at this moment he would have found her exquisite even if she were the homeliest woman in England. Somehow her mere presence calmed him. "You are most welcome, Meg."

"Thank you, *my lord*."

Her emphasis on his title reminded him that they weren't alone, and he turned his attention to the short, thin man who clambered down after Meg. "You are the doctor? I am Lord Rathmore."

"I am Dr. Peters, my lord. Where is Miss St. James?"

"My housekeeper will show you the way." He indicated Mrs. Milton, who hovered nearby.

The physician gave a brisk nod and followed the plump housekeeper into the house.

Rathmore turned back to Meg. She watched him calmly, and already he found some of his anxiety easing. Holding her gaze, he lifted her hand to his lips. "Thank you for coming."

Her smile chased the shadows from his soul. "I couldn't stay away."

He offered his arm and escorted her inside.

Meg allowed Rathmore to lead her into the house. She handed her bonnet and gloves to the butler by rote, aware that Rathmore watched her every movement with those enigmatic dark eyes. He could stand amazingly still when he wanted to, and his gaze tended to pierce one with its intensity. Butterflies fluttered in her stomach as she turned to face him.

"Would someone please show me the way to Emily's chamber?" she asked.

"I will escort you myself."

The words, though said casually enough, flustered her. Just the thought of ascending the stairs to the sleeping quarters with him filled her mind with all sorts of improper ideas.

Emily. She must think of Emily.

"Thank you, my lord," she said with a polite smile. But as they made their way up the long staircase toward Emily's bedchamber, she was very much aware of Rathmore's presence at her heels.

Upon reaching the girl's room, Meg knocked softly, and a maid cracked open the door.

"I've come to see Miss Emily," Meg whispered.

"Yes, miss. She'll be glad to see you." The maid opened the door wide enough for Meg to enter, but when Rathmore made to follow, the woman gasped with alarm.

Meg glanced behind her and understood the situation immediately. She turned back and blocked Rathmore when he would have entered the room.

"What are you doing?" he demanded. "I want to hear what the doctor has to say."

"My lord, wait." Meg lowered her voice and held fast to the door as the maid retreated into the sickroom. "Emily is in a state of undress. It's not proper for you to see her like this."

"To the devil with her state of undress," he growled. "The girl is ill. I am her guardian, blast it!"

"I know that, and you have every right to know what is happening." When he would have barged through the door, Meg laid a hand on his chest. He froze. Taking a sharp breath at the wild look in his eyes, she dropped her hand. "My lord, has it occurred to you that Emily might be embarrassed if you were to see her in her current indisposed state? That it might make her illness worse if she were distressed?"

The fury faded from his features. "I don't want to distress her."

"Then allow her some privacy. The doctor will report to you the instant he has finished examining her. You will be informed of everything, I promise you."

He sighed and rubbed a hand wearily over his face. "Very well. Send the doctor down to my study when he has finished his examination."

"I shall do that," she promised.

He glanced past her into the room. "She looked so pale coming home in the carriage. So small."

"All children get ill," Meg reassured him. "By tomorrow, she will probably be arguing with you again."

"I never thought to say this, but I sincerely hope so." He reached out and touched her cheek, then dropped his hand to his side. "I'm trusting you with her, Meg. Take care of her for me."

She swallowed hard, her pulse galloping from that brief, tender touch. "I shall, my lord. You have my word on it."

Firmly, she closed the door.

She leaned back against the portal, closed her eyes, and took one deep breath. Then another. Still her heart raced, and her body sang. Even during this serious time, the attraction between them burned hot enough to rob her of her senses.

She had to do something about Rathmore. She just didn't know what.

Emily saw her then and called her name. Pushing the too attractive earl from her mind, Meg turned her attention to the child who needed her.

Chapter 13

Rathmore sat behind his desk and stared at the ledgers and papers strewn across the surface. What had ever made him believe he would be able to work while waiting for the doctor's verdict?

It had seemed like a good idea at the time, but now that he tried to execute his plan, he found he couldn't concentrate long enough to add a column of numbers or read a letter. His mind would always drift to the drama being enacted upstairs.

He reminded himself that children got sick all the time. He had learned from his housekeeper that children not only got sick, but often they were very dramatic about it, casting up their accounts and growing feverish from the slightest ailment. But this wasn't just any child. This was Emily.

What would he do if the news was bad? What if

Emily had contracted some deadly disease? How would he handle such dreadful tidings?

Until now, he had not realized how completely he loved that child. She was the one member of his family who had never criticized him, never looked down on him. On the contrary, she had always looked *up* to him, often calling him her "white knight" when she was a little girl. Even at the age of six, Emily had been fascinated by stories of knights and their ladies and monsters slain.

How could he bear it if anything happened to her?

His hands shook at the thought, and he carefully put down the pen he held. Emily would be all right. She had to be. He refused to think anything else.

But what if she wasn't?

He shoved away from the desk and rose to stalk the room. She *would* be all right. If it was at all in his power, she would recover completely and be plaguing him again by tomorrow.

A soft knock drew his attention. "Enter!" he called.

Grimm pushed open the door. "Dr. Peters to see you, Your Lordship."

"Thank you, Grimm." The butler stepped aside to let the physician enter the room, then quietly retreated. Rathmore faced the doctor, gripping the back of his desk chair with both hands. "Well, Doctor?"

"Your ward will be fine, my lord."

Relief sapped the strength from his body, but rather than allowing his knees to buckle, his breeding and pride kept his spine straight and his expression impassive. "She's all right then? What was the problem?"

"The nearest I can tell, Lord Rathmore, is that something seems to have frightened the girl out of her wits, which brought on a severe attack of the vapors."

"The vapors!" Rathmore didn't realize he had shouted until he saw the physician flinch. "Dr. Peters, my ward didn't swoon, as is usual with an attack of the vapors, and she gave no indication that she was fighting the urge. Are you certain of your diagnosis? Her skin was pale and clammy, and she felt nauseous."

"Which are all signs of the vapors as well."

Rathmore scowled at the quietly confident physician. "And you say something frightened her? Did she say who? Or what?"

The doctor shook his head. "That is my own conclusion, my lord. Is Miss St. James afraid of anything? Insects? Horses? She did say she was near the stables when the illness struck."

Rathmore gave a bark of laughter. "Emily's not afraid of a blasted thing. And as for horses, the girl is a veritable Diana in the saddle."

"Then I have no other explanation, my lord. She suffered some sort of fright or shock. Only she can tell you why."

Rathmore frowned and tapped his fingers against the back of the chair. "What must be done to speed my ward's recovery, Dr. Peters?"

"Since I don't know what caused the ailment, I can only treat the symptoms," the physician replied. "I recommend she stay in bed for the remainder of the day. Draw the curtains, keep her quiet, and keep her meals light for now. Broth and some bread should do nicely. I've left some laudanum to help her sleep."

"Very well."

The doctor hesitated, then said, "It really would be best if you could convince her to sleep, my lord. It's the best thing for her right now."

"I thought you just said you had given her laudanum."

"No, I said I *left* the laudanum." The physician gave a little chuckle. "Your ward is a very stubborn young lady, Lord Rathmore. She refused to take the laudanum until she was permitted to speak privately with Miss Stanton-Lynch. She dismissed the rest of us from the room."

"Indeed." Rathmore cast a curious glance at the ceiling, as if he could see right through it to the bedroom above. What did the little hoyden have to tell Meg that was so important she needed total privacy? Was she even now confiding who or what had frightened her?

Whatever had happened, he needed to know. How else could he protect her?

"By your leave, Lord Rathmore, I should like to return to the village now," the physician said, drawing the earl's attention back to him. "I shall stop by tomorrow to see how Miss St. James is faring."

"Of course. Thank you, Doctor."

Dr. Peters bowed. "My pleasure, my lord. Please do send for me if you have a need."

Once the physician had left the room, Rathmore gave in and sank into his chair. The utter relief at hearing that Emily would swiftly recover had left him feeling as weak as a newborn foal.

And just as shaky.

What would he have done if he had lost her?

The mere thought sent him out of the chair and across the room to the brandy decanter he kept in the study. His nerves were raw, and his hands shook. "Like a damned woman," he muttered.

Taking the decanter and a glass with him, Rathmore sat down behind his desk and poured the first glass.

What could have frightened Emily so much that she succumbed to so feminine an ailment as the vapors? Had young Anne been unkind to her? Perhaps pulled some sort of prank to frighten Emily? The two girls had seemed amiable enough, but if Anne had injured Emily's feelings in any way . . .

Well, someone would pay.

He only wished he knew what had transpired. While it stung that Emily would not confide in him, he took comfort in the fact that Meg would get to the bottom of things—and then she would, of course, tell him what happened.

Funny, but once upon a time the idea of depending on someone else to help solve a problem of his would have galled him. But because it was Meg . . . well, it didn't really bother him at all.

Pouring his second glass of brandy, he stared out the window and attempted to calm his nerves while waiting for Meg's arrival.

The vapors.

Meg had heard the doctor's pronouncement, but she would never have thought that a young lady as active and fearless as Emily would ever succumb to such a female ailment. Still, the girl *was* beginning her journey into womanhood. Maybe that had something to do with it.

She sat down in the chair beside Emily's bed and smothered a smile as the girl imperiously dismissed both the servants and the physician. Despite her fragile appearance, Emily's spirit remained undaunted.

Once the door closed behind the banished, Emily turned to Meg and scoffed, "What a quack!"

"I don't think so," Meg replied blandly. "Dr. Peters seems most competent."

"Miss Stanton-Lynch, really." Emily's exasperation was echoed by the rolling of her eyes. "He said I had *the vapors*. He will have Cousin Justin thinking me a complete widgeon!"

"I don't believe your guardian will think any such thing," Meg replied. "He was very worried and will no doubt be relieved that your illness is something so commonplace."

Emily snorted. "Something so missish, you mean."

"Well, at least you didn't swoon."

"Thank *God*." Emily's eyes widened in horror, emphasizing her pallor. "I would have been mortified!"

"Well, you didn't, so don't even think about it." Meg leaned forward to tuck the bedding in around the girl's slender frame. "What did you want to talk to me about? You sounded so fierce as you dismissed everyone from the room."

Emily giggled. "I was trying to sound like Cousin Justin."

"Well, it worked. You were most imperious."

"But I didn't yell." The smile faded from her face. "Miss Stanton-Lynch, there is something I want to talk to you about. Something peculiar happened today."

"Was it Lady Presting's daughter?"

"Oh, no." Emily beamed. "Anne is wonderful! I do believe we shall become the best of friends."

"I'm glad to hear it."

"I need friends, Miss Stanton-Lynch." Emily sat back against the pillows, her expression subdued. "I am so very much alone."

"My dear girl." Impulsively, Meg rose and gave the child a fierce hug. "You are not alone. You have me, and you have your Cousin Justin."

"I like to think that we are friends," Emily said,

"or even sisters, as I daresay you are not old enough to be my mother."

"You are correct," Meg said with a laugh. "And since we are friends—or nearly sisters, as you put it—you must call me Meg."

"Meg." Emily tried out the name with the air of someone who was tasting a new food for the first time. "I'm so glad I met you in the woods that day. Sometimes I need someone to talk to."

"You can talk to me."

Emily nodded. "Which is why I dismissed the servants. I do need to talk to you."

"You could also talk to your guardian," Meg reminded her. "He loves you very much."

"If you say so." Emily's disbelieving expression said it all. "He's always dictating to me and shouting. He used to be so much fun."

Her voice dropped to a tone so rife with longing that Meg reached out and squeezed her hand. "You missed him while he was gone, didn't you?"

Emily nodded. "One minute he was there, walking his horse around the stables with me in the saddle. Then he was gone without a word. Without a note. And Papa wouldn't tell me where he had gone."

Meg sighed. "Men tend to want to protect the people they love, Emily. I can only guess that your papa was trying to protect you from being hurt by the rumors about your cousin. You do realize that you were practically a baby and certainly incapable of understanding the whole mess."

"They could have told me *something*." Emily

clenched her small hands into fists. "I waited and I waited that day for Cousin Justin to come play Arthur and Guinevere with me. I waited all day, and he didn't come." Her voice broke.

"Oh, Emily." Meg shifted to sit on the edge of the bed and pulled the child into her arms. Emily didn't protest. She buried her face in Meg's shoulder, fists still clenched even as her slender arms held tight. Meg stroked her back soothingly. "Emily, please understand that your cousin loves you. He wasn't allowed to contact you. Your father and grandfather forbade it."

"But why?" Emily wailed. "I needed to know what had happened to him. Why did Papa do that to me?"

Meg sighed again. "As I said, men tend to be protective, sometimes overly so. Perhaps your father thought that you were so young you would forget about Justin in time."

"I never forgot! Never!"

"I know you didn't." She stroked a hand over the child's hair. "Everyone makes mistakes, Emily. Even parents."

"I always thought it was my fault." Emily sniffed and sat back against the pillows again.

"And now you know it wasn't." Meg went back to the chair beside the bed. "What happened today, Emily? What frightened you so?"

Emily hesitated. "I'm not exactly sure. Anne and I were in the stables, and a man came in. He started yelling at the groom, and suddenly I couldn't breathe right. Suddenly I felt like—" She stopped, took a deep breath.

Meg placed her hand over the girl's. "It's all right, Emily. You're safe here."

Emily swallowed hard, as if the terror still held her. "Suddenly I felt as if I were in the middle of one of my nightmares," she whispered.

Though gravely concerned, Meg kept her expression mild. "You have nightmares?"

"I used to. Not so much anymore."

"I'm glad to hear it. What was it about the man that scared you? Do you remember?"

The child frowned. "Something about his voice seemed familiar somehow. It was the yelling that made me afraid."

Noting Emily's distress at even talking about it, Meg let the incident drop. She smiled reassuringly. "Well, you're safe now. No doubt your guardian will be up to see you soon."

Emily gave her a shy smile. "He hugged me in the carriage, Meg. And he carried me out of Lady Presting's house, just as Lancelot would have done."

Meg blinked at the blatant worship in the girl's voice. Apparently she didn't hold Rathmore in complete dislike. In fact, she had cast Rathmore in the role of knight in shining armor. This boded well for the future.

"See?" Meg said. "I told you he still cares."

"So you did." Emily beamed at her. "I should change into something more appropriate to receive Cousin Justin, don't you think?"

"Excellent idea." Meg rose. "I shall send for your maid before I go downstairs and speak to your guardian."

"Thank you." Emily stretched. "I'm feeling much better already."

"I'm glad to hear it." Meg went to the door. Emily stopped her when her hand was on the knob.

"Meg, will you stay with us awhile? At least for dinner?"

Even though she knew that she shouldn't stay, that Rathmore was a dangerous temptation, she couldn't resist the plea in Emily's eyes.

"I shall send word to my cousin," Meg said, "provided your guardian agrees."

Emily folded her arms, a determined gleam in her eyes. "I shall see to it."

Meg laughed. "You're incorrigible, Miss St. James." The girl's giggle warmed her heart as she left the room in search of Rathmore.

Rathmore had just finished his second brandy when Grimm announced that Miss Stanton-Lynch wished to speak with him.

It was about time. At least he wouldn't have to chase her through the house to get his answers.

"Send her in, Grimm," he said, then rose as Meg entered. "And, Grimm, see that we're not disturbed."

Grimm nodded, then retreated, leaving the door ajar.

Meg put her hands on her hips and eyed him supiciously. "I have come to discuss Emily."

And nothing else. She might as well have shouted the words, so clear was the implication.

"I have every intention of discussing Emily," Rathmore replied. He raised one black brow. "Unless, of course, you would rather discuss matters of a more personal nature."

"I should say not. I have said all I intend to say on that subject."

Rathmore swept a hand at an empty chair. "Then do sit down, Miss Stanton-Lynch, and we will discuss my ward."

Meg took the chair he indicated, and he settled back into his own seat. "I'm sure Dr. Peters spoke with you," she said.

"He did." He leaned back in his chair, rather liking the way she looked in his study. Now that he was in control again, he could dismiss his earlier moments of weakness when he had feared for Emily's life. His ever-present attraction to Meg felt familiar and right. It reinforced that he was a man, not some softhearted weakling. "The doctor also tells me that Emily asked to speak privately to you."

"Yes, she had some things she wanted to talk about."

"Would you care to share any of them?"

"No, my lord, I would not."

Rathmore blinked. "Did I hear correctly? You're *not* going to tell me what she said to you?"

"You heard correctly. Emily has had a traumatic experience, and she trusts me. I will not violate that trust."

He frowned. "Meg, I am the girl's guardian. It's the doctor's opinion that something scared her. Don't you think I have the right to know what that was?"

Meg nibbled her lower lip. Rathmore watched the motion like a cat eyeing a mouse and enjoyed the arousal that simmered within him.

"Actually, my lord—"

"Justin," he corrected.

She gave him a look that should have sliced him in two. "There are one or two points I feel I can share with you, as it would be better for Emily's well-being."

The truth at last. "And those would be?"

"For one thing, she dislikes it when you yell. It frightens her."

"What!" he shouted. "Me? She dislikes it when *I* yell?"

Meg winced. "Quite so."

Rathmore scowled. "Are you implying that I am somehow responsible for Emily's illness?"

"Not at all," she replied. "But nevertheless, your tendency to bellow like a mad bull does make her nervous. I thought you would want to know."

"A mad bull?" He drummed his fingers on the arm of his chair, debating how to respond to such an insult. "Have a care, sweet Meg. I have no liking for being compared in such a way."

She got that stubborn glint in her eye and tilted her chin. "Then perhaps you will think before raising your voice in the girl's presence in the future."

Rathmore leaned forward in his chair, hunger for her rising in him. She was magnificent. How in blazes did she expect him to live without her by his side? "Do you dare to dictate to me, my dear?"

"I am just giving you some advice to help your relationship with your ward." She gave him a sweetly sarcastic smile. "Of course, you have been doing *so* well on your own."

"You grow bold, Meg. Don't think that just because you refused my suit that I have given up the cause." He grinned like a pirate as her eyes widened. She swallowed hard.

"I have given you my answer, my lord."

"My name is *Justin*. You certainly didn't have any trouble using it the last time you were in my home."

Color flooded her cheeks. "Much has happened since then."

"Indeed." He sat back in his chair again, master of his house. "And who knows what might happen after this moment."

She gripped the arms of her chair, and he smirked. The lovely American was not as immune to him as she tried to appear.

She cleared her throat. "Emily is waiting for you to come see her, my lord. I'm certain you won't want to disappoint her."

"Of course not." He rose, and she quickly leaped to her feet. "Is there something else, Meg?"

"Yes."

She had to tilt her head to look up at him, and he relished the smooth curve of her neck, the swanlike grace of her throat. Remembered the taste of her there.

"Lord Rathmore, Emily has asked that I stay for dinner. Under the circumstances, I believe it would be better if you were to refuse the request."

"Refuse my ward's request when she's so ill?" Rathmore shook his head and nearly chuckled at the dismay that flashed across her face. "I would never dream of doing such a thing. You must stay for dinner, Meg. After what happened today, I'm certain it's the best thing for Emily."

"Perhaps a tray in Emily's room would be agreeable," Meg said.

"The doctor said she should sleep." He gave her his most charming smile. "Surely you're not afraid to dine with me?"

She narrowed her eyes at him. "I'm not afraid of you, my lord, but I am here for Emily. Please try and remember that."

"I am well aware of that fact." Satisfied with the way events had come to pass, he swept an arm gallantly toward the door. "Would you care to refresh yourself? One of the maids can show you upstairs."

"That would be most welcome, my lord."

"Justin," he corrected again. And this time he did chuckle at the annoyance that glittered in her eyes.

"*Lord Rathmore*," she said, her voice tight with impatience, "I would appreciate it if you would send word to Knightsbridge Chase as to the circumstances. And please do let them know that the only reason I am staying for dinner is your ward's request."

"Of course, my dear. I never thought otherwise." He took her arm to escort her from the room, chuckling when she stiffened. "Calm yourself, Meg. While you are tending to your needs, I will go look in on Emily."

"I am calm," she hissed.

"Indeed." Amused and encouraged by her skittishness, he escorted her to the foyer and summoned a maid to attend her. "I shall see you at dinner, Miss Stanton-Lynch."

"Perhaps, my lord." Her frosty tone and the way she stiffened her spine as she followed the maid conveyed her feelings most clearly.

He wanted to laugh out loud. Meg was far from indifferent to him. He watched the sway of her skirts as she ascended the stairs ahead of him, more determined than ever to make her his bride. This last emergency had decided him. Meg would be his wife.

He needed her, reputation be damned.

And all he had to do to win her was prove his innocence—and make her fall in love with him.

Chapter 14

She should leave.

Meg glanced at the clock on the mantel. It was nearly half past seven. Dinner was over, Rathmore was enjoying his port, and she had withdrawn as a lady should to the drawing room.

Why was she waiting? She should go now, before he joined her.

Yet she stayed. She could lie to herself, say it was for Emily. But Emily, poor child, had followed the doctor's advice and taken the laudanum, falling into a deep and restful sleep long before dinner began.

Leaving Meg to dine with Rathmore alone.

She should have left before dinner. As soon as she had seen Emily slumbering in her bed, she should have hied herself with all haste back to the safety of Knightsbridge Chase. But she had been worried that the girl might awaken and discover that Meg had broken her promise to stay to dinner. So she had eaten with Rathmore, alone in the huge formal dining room that seemed oh so much smaller with the big, handsome earl in it.

Rathmore himself was another problem altogether. He had barely eaten his meal and had instead watched her every movement with those dark, dark eyes. His peculiar talent for remaining so still for so long put her in mind of a panther, and she had felt much like a tasty young gazelle while sitting across the dinner table from him. Her polite small talk had fallen on deaf ears, and it was with great relief that she had escaped to the drawing room.

She should leave—now. Despite his silence at dinner, despite his hungry stare, she still wanted him. And that was very dangerous indeed.

Her resolve to be her own woman weakened in the face of his obvious desire, but she dared not give in. The alternative—accepting a proposal of marriage—would lead exactly where she didn't want to go, to a life where all her time and energy would go to her husband and her husband's pursuits, leaving nothing for herself. Meg Lynch would cease to exist, and everything that made her a unique person would fade away.

If ever she did marry, she would do so only if the man she chose understood her need to remain an equal partner in the marriage. She could accept nothing less.

But marriage had nothing to do with pure animal attraction, and she was tempted to give in to passion and forget everything else. All she wanted to do was fall into Rathmore's arms and surrender to his sweet persuasion.

The surge of heat that shot through her at her wanton thoughts brought home the point as nothing else could. If she stayed, she would end up in his bed.

Unsettled by the strength of her response, she headed toward the door at a speedy clip. Good manners or not, she was leaving—before she did something foolish.

She flung open the door to the drawing room and nearly walked right into Rathmore.

"Surely you're not leaving, Meg?" His seductive purr wrapped around her senses like warm silk as he took her arms to steady her.

He was much too near, his touch much too distracting. "I'm certain Algie must be wondering where I am." Since he was blocking the doorway, she stepped away from his hold and walked back into the drawing room.

"You'll need my carriage," he reminded her, following her into the room.

"Of course." She clenched her fingers together to still their trembling and tried for a polite smile. "If you'd be good enough to summon one . . ."

"In due time."

The gleam in his eyes put her on guard. "Lord Rathmore, I do feel that I should return to my cousin's house. Emily is asleep and will no doubt remain that way through the night."

"We're alone now, Meg." He reached out and caught her chin in his hand. "Call me Justin."

She moved away from him. "It's not proper."

"Proper be damned." He pulled her into his arms and held her close. The boldness of the action sent her senses spinning. "There's more between us than social convention."

"That's exactly the problem, my lord." She squirmed in his embrace. "I came here for Emily, not to dally with you."

"You're not the type of woman a man dallies with, Meg."

"Then let me go."

He held her tighter. "I'm glad you were here today."

The break in his voice made her realize that something more than his lust drove him. She stopped trying to free herself and looked deeply into his eyes, noting the almost wild gleam that had nothing to do with desire.

"Good heavens." She cupped his face with one hand, making him hold her gaze when he would have looked away. "You were frightened today."

"The earls of Rathmore do not get frightened."

"Nonsense. You were afraid for Emily." She smiled softly. "It's all right to admit it, you know. It's quite natural."

"I was somewhat concerned." At her knowing look, he sighed. "All right, I admit that I was worried that something was terribly wrong with the girl."

"I was worried, too. But she's fine now."

"Yes, she's fine, but I'm not." Rathmore shrugged away her touch and strode across the room. "How can I run these estates and battle society's opinion if I cannot maintain my equilibrium when it comes to one small girl? I detest weakness, most especially in myself."

"It's not weak to admit that you care."

He spun to face her. "I do more than care for Emily, Meg. I *adore* her. I would be completely lost if anything happened to her." He let out a harsh laugh. "The child has me in the palm of her hand, if she but knew it."

"Justin—"

"Do you know how glad I was to see you today?" he interrupted. "I was so happy when you stepped down from that coach that I almost dropped down on my knees and kissed your feet. And not because I thought you could help with Emily but because I didn't want to go through this alone. Pathetic, wouldn't you say?"

She shook her head. "I was glad to help."

"At least I had the sense to call the bloody doctor."

"You did very well. No one else could have done any better."

"She seemed so small in the coach," he murmured, clearly lost in memory, "so helpless. *I* felt helpless."

"Stop it," she ordered. "Considering you're a man who is not used to children, I think you did fine. And the depth of your love for Emily is nothing to be ashamed of."

"I know, I know." He slashed an impatient hand through the air. "I just . . . it felt . . . uncomfortable."

She gave a snort of laughter. "Justin, this myth that men do not feel the softer emotions is ridiculous. We are all human. We all love, we all feel fear, and sometimes we feel helpless. There is no shame in any of that."

He gave her a sheepish grin that made her heart do a long, slow tumble in her chest. "I'm still learning how to be a parent."

Meg only smiled as she searched desperately for words to dissolve the intimacy that had fallen over them. Rathmore was devastating when he was being wicked, but Lord above, she found the man even more attractive now that he had revealed his vulnerability. And she suspected he knew it, if the look of awareness that crept across his face was any indication.

The clock chimed eight.

"I should go," she said, absurdly grateful for the reminder of the hour. She bustled toward the door. "Algie will be wondering what's become of me."

"Stay."

His soft entreaty made her pause. She looked over at him and almost melted at the utter longing on his face. "I should go," she whispered.

"Why? Knightsbridge knows where you are." He came to her and took her hand. "Please, Meg.

This has been a hellish day, and I would enjoy your company for a while more."

His warm hand holding hers distracted her. Such a tiny thing, the touch of flesh on flesh. Yet it was enough to alert her every sense, to speed her pulse and pinken her cheeks.

"I shouldn't." Was that her voice, so husky and inviting?

"I shall behave the perfect gentleman." A wicked grin spread across his face. "If you want me to."

"Of course I want you," she said. Then her eyes widened in horror. "I mean, of course that's what I want."

"Is it?" He moved a step closer. "Perhaps you were right the first time."

She closed her eyes against the lure of that too-handsome face. But she could still feel the heat of his body, could still smell the sweet tang of his cologne. "Perhaps I was, but we've already talked about this, Justin."

"We've talked about marriage," he corrected. "Not about this." He took her chin in his hand and coaxed, "Look at me."

Slowly she opened her eyes. He was too close, that beautifully shaped mouth only inches from hers. This near to him, she could see that his infamous black eyes were actually a warm shade of dark brown with little flecks of green in them.

Silly to be thinking of his eyes when he was clearly an inch away from kissing her.

But with his slow, knowing smile, the world

tilted on its axis. The room fell away, as did her urgency to go home. There was only Rathmore and the soft, intoxicating emotions in his eyes.

"I need you," he said. "I need you in ways that have nothing to do with the physical. Today would have been unbearable if not for you."

"I'm glad I could help." His simple honesty utterly seduced her, more than pretty words ever could.

"You're the only woman who looks at me as if I'm a man." He lifted her hand to his lips, his eyes never leaving her face. "The only woman who doesn't expect ravishment or worse from me."

"You would never hurt anyone," she breathed. And suddenly she believed it. She knew utterly and completely that Rathmore had not had anything to do with Ophelia's death. He was a good man, yet he had been banished from his home, his relationship with Emily ripped asunder, his good name destroyed.

"How can you stand it?" she asked, her heart softening as he continued to hold her hand.

"I hate it." The words singed the air, and his fingers tightened around hers. "I hate every moment of it."

"Oh, Justin." Feeling for him, she wrapped her arms around his neck and hugged him. He jolted with surprise, then returned the embrace, pulling her tightly against his body and burying his face in her hair.

Improper though it was to be in his arms, she

couldn't ignore the quiet desperation of his embrace. Here was a man unjustly judged by his peers, a man who felt emotions so deeply that they unnerved him. A man who adored his young cousin with all the zeal of a true parent.

How could she not love such a man?

The realization shook her. Good Lord, it was true. She was in love with Rathmore.

She didn't want to be in love with him. He was dangerous to her plans. But she couldn't ignore the truth in her heart. She loved him.

And he must never know.

Yet when he raised his head to look at her, her resolve to resist him faded. And when he bent to kiss her, she couldn't push him away.

She wouldn't let her feelings for him override her need to find her own path; to do so would be to destroy her soul. Even for Rathmore, she could not surrender who she was. So she would never marry him.

But perhaps she could have this one thing from him, this moment, these feelings. They were completely alone, and he wanted her. And she wanted him right back. She wanted to know what it felt like to be in the arms of the man she loved.

So she melted into his arms, responded to his kiss, and gave herself up to passion.

She felt his surprise, then his eagerness as she opened her mouth to him, wrapped her arms around him, pressed her body against his.

Sinful.

Hungry now, and insatiably curious, she tangled her fingers in his hair. Soft. Who knew a man's hair could be so soft, so silky?

His hands moved over her back in a slow but restless pattern, smoothing over her shoulders, stroking down her spine, cupping her buttocks. His bold caresses first made her stiffen with surprise, then sigh with pleasure.

"Meg," he murmured, nibbling along the curve of her throat. She moved her head to give him better access, and he nuzzled his face into her bosom.

"Justin." She tugged at his hair.

"It's all right," he soothed. His breath drifted across the bared portion of her breasts that were exposed by the fashionable neckline of her gown. Her nipples hardened as he pressed gentle kisses across the exposed skin.

Heat shot through her from breast to groin. And when he hooked a finger in the neckline of her dress and bared one breast completely, she grew dizzy from sensation.

"So lovely." He stroked her pale pink nipple with his thumb. She arched her back with a low cry of discovery, then moaned outright as he dipped his head and took her nipple in his mouth.

She uttered his name again and tightened her fingers in his hair.

He chuckled at her reaction, and the sound vibrated against her aroused skin, bringing new sensation. He pulled back, tugging her nipple playfully between his teeth before releasing it. Then he soothed the pebble-hard flesh with a slow, sensual lap of his tongue before carefully replacing her dress.

"That," he whispered, "was a truly delicious dessert."

As if in a dream, she untangled one hand from his hair and stroked his cheek. "Why did you stop?"

Surprise lit his eyes, followed by the swift rekindling of desire. "My dear girl, you should be glad I did."

"Kiss me again."

He shut his eyes and shook his head. "You don't know what you're asking."

"I do." She let her fingers drift over his jaw to his mouth. "You've shown me enough that I do know what I'm asking. I'm not one of your sheltered English misses."

"Indeed." He swallowed hard as she stroked her fingers over his ear and down his neck to trail along the edge of his neck cloth.

"I want you, Justin," she said, meeting his eyes with bold intent. "I want to you to teach me all you know. And then I want to discover if what you've taught me has the same effect on you as it does me."

Trailing a finger down his chest, she held his gaze for a long moment, then went over and deliberately shut the door.

"Bloody hell, Meg," he muttered, his voice rough with arousal. "Think of your reputation."

"There's no one here but you and me." Stepping

closer, she pressed her mouth to the smooth flesh beneath his ear. His pulse thundered beneath her lips.

"Meg." He gripped her shoulders with the clear purpose of moving her away. But then she touched her tongue to his throat and he groaned, pulling her closer instead. "Meg, you must stop. A man can only take so much before . . ."

"Before what?" She licked experimentally at his ear.

He shuddered, and his arms tightened around her. "Before his baser instincts take over. Meg, please stop. I don't want to hurt you."

"My dear Lord Rathmore," she said with a flirtatious little laugh. "I have no intention of stopping."

"Meg—"

She pulled back so she could see his face. "Don't you understand, Justin? I want you. The only way you can hurt me is by pushing me away."

He let out a long, shaky breath. "Then heaven help both of us, Meg, for I'm only human."

He reached for her.

He would make it right later.

The thought drifted through his mind as he swept Meg into his arms, nearly groaning with pleasure at the feel of her lush young body against his. She wanted him. She wanted *him*, the Devil Earl or not. And she didn't give a fig for his reputation.

Her mouth was eager beneath his, her hands curious as she smoothed them over his shoulders. He shrugged out of his coat, mad to feel those dainty female hands on his flesh, and she helped him remove his cravat, the precise folds crumpling beneath enthusiastic fingers. With a soft cry of discovery, she pressed her mouth to his exposed throat.

He swore softly as her innocent kisses aroused his flesh to nearly painful hardness. He must be mad to take her here, in the drawing room. He wanted to wait. But as she withdrew the pins from her hair, the inky dark curls tumbling like black satin over her shoulders, he knew he couldn't resist her.

It would be here, and it would be now, and nothing short of a pistol to his head could stop him.

Perhaps not even then.

He took hold of one of her curls, gently tugging her closer, then bent and sampled the creamy skin of her shoulder with his lips. He trailed a string of kisses along the milky flesh, down to the edge of her gown, then moved aside the material that was in his way.

She helped him undress her. Everywhere he unfastened a button or tugged on a ribbon, she eagerly assisted. Soon her lovely dress lay discarded on the floor, and Meg stood before him in only her thin white chemise.

The nearly transparent garment hid nothing from him.

"You are so beautiful." Trailing a finger over her skin, he playfully slipped a strap off her shoulder.

"I want to be beautiful for you." Ignoring the dangling strap, she smiled at him, then nuzzled her nose into his chest.

"You are, dear girl. You are." He slipped the

other strap off her shoulder so that the only thing holding the chemise in place was her erect nipples. With a mischievous grin, she gave a sinuous swivel of her hips, and the garment slithered to her feet.

Meg was standing naked in his drawing room.

For one wild moment he nearly called a halt. But then she smiled at him the same way Eve must have smiled at Adam just as she held out that apple, and he was lost.

Meg would be his tonight.

He gave a thought to locking the door, but then Meg reached for his shirt. "You are overdressed, my lord."

He raised a brow. "Am I?" With a grin, he removed his shirt and tossed it on the floor with her garments. "How about now?"

"Much better." Licking her lips, she came forward and smoothed her hands across his hairy chest. "You are truly a magnificent specimen, Justin. I thought so when I first saw you."

"I thought *you* were mad." He hissed in a sharp breath as she licked his nipple. "I see I was right. This *is* madness." He gripped her head, tangling his hands in that silky mass of dark hair, and held her face to his chest as her tongue played with his sensitive nipple.

"This is marvelous," she corrected. Her hands drifted to his waist, toyed with the waistband of his trousers.

With a hoarse laugh, he removed her wandering

hands. "Not so fast, my girl. I don't think you're quite ready for that yet."

"Perhaps I am." She leaned against him, her breasts silky soft as she rubbed against his chest.

"Let's see." He slipped a hand between her legs. The slick heat of her nearly made him lose control. "Perhaps you are at that."

"Don't stop touching me," she whispered, closing her eyes and moving against his hand. "Sweet heaven, if you stop I shall die, I just know it."

"I have no intention of stopping." He rested his forehead against hers and struggled for control. The scent of her arousal filled his senses. "The sofa," he said. "Let's get to the sofa."

Somehow they made it. They tumbled onto the sofa in a tangle of limbs, male atop female in the age old position of mating. He pressed himself against her, savoring the heat of her even through his trousers.

"Justin . . . my goodness." She shifted. "I don't believe you've ever had a . . . reaction . . . that severe before."

"I've never had you naked beneath me before." His instincts screamed at him to bury himself deeply inside the hot female folds only inches away, but he knew it was her first time and was trying for some semblance of control.

Deliberately ignoring the distinctive scent that called to him, he dipped his head and suckled her breasts. She gave a soft cry and arched her back, instinctively pressing her feminine mound against the hardness straining the buttons of his trousers.

God, she was so damp. So ready for him.

He had to make it good for her. Sucking strongly at her breast, he slipped a hand between her legs and stroked her gently, seeking the tiny bud that would ignite her ecstasy. She mewed in the back of her throat, hands gripping his shoulders to find purchase, back arching off the sofa.

"Justin, Justin, Justin," she chanted.

Still he stroked gently at her feminine flesh, finding and caressing the center of her pleasure. She panted, she clung, she whimpered his name. With every noise, with every movement, his own need clawed at him, demanding release. His forehead beaded with sweat as he fought back the urge to thrust hard and deep.

Suddenly she cried out, hips lifting off the sofa as a great tremor wracked her body. Her nails dug into his shoulders as the evidence of her pleasure drenched his caressing fingers.

"Yes," he murmured as she slowly slumped back against the sofa again. "Yes, that's how it should be. That's what I wanted."

A delicate flush spread across her face and breasts, and she opened heavy-lidded blue eyes to look at him in wonder. He smiled at the look of utter satisfaction in her eyes, then nearly exploded as she brushed her fingers across the front of his trousers. "More."

That one word shattered the last of his control.

He managed somehow to release himself from the confines of his trousers, though removing the skin-tight garment entirely was impossible. Her eyes widened at the sight of him—no doubt her first glimpse of a fully aroused, naked man—but there was no missish blushing or stammering, no maidenly lowering of eyes. In fact, she reached out to touch him, caressing the engorged tip of his erection with honest curiosity.

He muttered a harsh curse, then took her tormenting hand in his, twining their fingers together as he positioned himself against the hot, damp entrance of her body. She reached up her other hand, and he held that one, too, as he slowly entered her.

A soft, shaky moan slipped from between her lips as he pressed home with slow, shallow strokes that tormented even as they tantalized. Then he came up against her maidenhead. With a barely coherent apology, he took her mouth in a fierce kiss as he thrust through the thin barrier.

She made a sound of distress and stiffened, but he couldn't stop. Not now, not so close. She felt so right, so warm, it was like coming home. He gentled his strokes as much as he could, murmuring endearments against her lips. One lone tear slid down her cheek, but gradually her body stopped trembling with pain. She shifted on the sofa, bringing her legs up around his hips, driving him deeper still. With a groan of surrender, he slipped over the edge, shuddering as he emptied himself inside her.

His climax triggered something inside her. She

stiffened suddenly and pulsed around him, her cry of release muffled beneath his mouth. She tightened her legs around his waist, pulling him closer, her fingers clenching in his.

Then it was over. She slumped bonelessly beneath him, and he buried his face in her neck, utterly spent.

She was his now, and he wasn't about to let her go.

Chapter 15

Long moments slid by, the silence broken only by the ticking of the mantel clock and the sound of their heartbeats. Replete with satisfaction, Rathmore gradually became aware of the air cooling his bare skin and the soft limbs of the woman beneath him. His conscience pricked him. He knew what they had done was wrong, but he couldn't bring himself to regret it completely. Meg was his now, and she would remain his. This act had made it inevitable.

The only obstacle now was his reputation. Would the duke allow them to marry?

He lifted his head, then leaned up on his forearms to look at her. "I'm too heavy for you."

She gave him a smile and lazily stroked her hand through his hair. "Not at all."

"I am." He moved off her, gently disengaging

their bodies and getting to his feet. He stood there for a moment, looking down at her, all soft and warm from their lovemaking. "Well, we've certainly done it this time."

"We certainly have." She stretched sensuously, grinning like a cat who had just gorged on a barrel of cream. "And it felt wonderful."

He loved knowing that he had put that look on her face. But honor weighed on him. He tugged up his trousers—good Lord, he hadn't even undressed completely!—and buttoned them. "Since your grandfather is away, I shall pay my addresses to Knightsbridge tomorrow."

Surprise flickered across her face. "There's no reason for that."

"No reason?" He stared at her, aghast. What lady of breeding would dare refuse an offer under these circumstances? "My dear girl, has it escaped your notice that I've just taken your innocence?"

"And without even taking your trousers off completely," she teased, but her eyes glimmered with panic. "Perhaps next time we should have your valet assist."

"You think this is funny?" He picked up her chemise and tossed it to her. "Do you realize, you misguided little baggage, that the door was unlocked the whole time? That someone could still walk in at any moment?"

"Oh, dear." Biting her lip, she took the chemise and quickly pulled it over her head. "I wouldn't want that."

"No, because then everyone would know what had happened here." He picked up his shirt and donned it. "I have every intention of asking for your hand, so you had best get used to the idea. It's the right thing to do."

She got up off the sofa and tugged her chemise into place over her hips, a mutinous light coming into her eyes. "No, my dear Lord Rathmore, *you* had best get used to the fact that I will not marry you. We've already discussed this."

"Damn it, Meg!" Anger bubbled up to overtake guilt, and he swiped his wrinkled cravat off the floor and hung it around his neck, ends dangling. "I know you have this notion about discovering your true self or some such nonsense before you wed, but you must face reality. Things have changed now. We must marry. It's a matter of honor, both yours and mine."

"Nonsense?" she cried, putting her hands on her hips. "What do you mean, nonsense? My personal quest is just as important to me as proving your innocence is to you!"

"Meg, you must see reason. Things are different now."

"Not as far as I'm concerned." She poked a finger in his chest. "Do you think just because I shared my body with you that you have some sort of claim on me now?"

"Well . . . yes. That's usually how these things work."

She shook her head and stood on tiptoe to bring

her face close to his. "You won't win me that easily, my lord. Only a man who truly understands and respects who I am will win my heart. And my hand." Scowling, she backed off and glanced around the room. "Where, by all that's holy, is my dress?"

Clenching his jaw, Rathmore glanced around, then discovered her garment tossed haphazardly over a footstool. "I apologize for my remark," he said as he handed it to her. "But you must realize what's happened here, Meg. I've compromised you. Honor demands that we wed. You cannot in good conscience go on as you were before."

"You didn't compromise me," she snapped, searching through the folds of her dress for the proper way to put it on. "If you recall, Lord Rathmore, *I* lured *you* to the sofa. I quite deliberately trod your scruples into the dust and had my way with you. So if anyone should propose marriage, it should be me."

"That's ridiculous."

"So's the reason for your proposal." She found the bottom of the dress and pulled it over her head.

"A proposal of marriage is never ridiculous. I took your innocence, damn it!"

"Wrong." Her head popped through the neck of the dress, and she shoved her arms into the sleeves. "I *gave* you my innocence, Justin. There's no reason for you to sacrifice yourself on the altar of marriage."

"It would be no sacrifice." He came to her, touched her cheek. "I would be honored to have you as my wife, Meg. I do believe we could be happy together. Marry me."

She closed her eyes against the anticipation on his face. She had to admit, she had secretly fantasized about a man asking her to marry him, and more recently her imaginary suitor had taken on Rathmore's features. But where were the words of love? What was he feeling?

Would she lose all chance with him if she didn't say yes? Dreading the answer, she asked the question uppermost in her mind. "Do you love me, Justin?"

He hesitated. "Love comes, Meg. In time, I could love you most easily."

She kept her face expressionless lest he see how his words had crushed her budding hopes. "If you don't love me, why are you so insistent I be your wife? Physical desire is not usually enough to compel a man of your position to wed."

"I do desire you," he said. "And now that we have acted on that desire, we must marry. Honor is at stake." When she didn't reply, he went on. "Don't you see, Meg? My reputation has been destroyed these past few years for something I never did. But *this* sin I did commit, and I must rectify it. Surely you understand."

"I do understand." And her heart broke because of it. "Justin, I will not marry out of obligation."

He gaped at her. "I've offered you everything I value," he whispered in disbelief. "My name. My honor. And you have thrown both back in my face. Again."

"I know." Tears threatened, but she refused to let them come. She realized what he must think of her. Of course he would blame her refusal on his blackened name, but she couldn't tell him the real reason—that she wanted him to love her.

She had tried to tell him. If he still didn't understand, she wasn't about to spell out the words to him.

"What more do you want?" he demanded, clenching his fists at his sides. "I've compromised you, and I've come up to scratch. Any other woman would be in raptures."

"I'm not 'any other woman,'" she reminded him. "I'm an American, and I do things differently."

"I'm tempted to put you over my knee," he growled. "You're acting more like a child than the independent woman you claim to be."

"I know what I'm doing." She hoped.

"I don't think you've thought this through. You could even now be carrying my child."

"Oh, my." Eyes wide, she laid a hand over her belly. "I hadn't thought of that."

"You haven't thought at all from what I can see. Meg, you *must* marry me. For the sake of the child."

Her conviction wavered for a moment, then she firmly shook her head. "Justin, there may not be a child."

"But what if there is? This is not a simple matter. I am an earl, and you're the granddaughter of a duke. Our child would be my heir."

"Justin, I am *not* going to marry you for the sake of a child who may not even exist!"

"What if he does exist?" he demanded. "What then? I will not have my heir be born a bastard!"

"*If* I am with child," she said tightly, "only then will we discuss what should be done."

He hesitated, the muscles of his jaw working. "I don't like this. Honor demands that I go to Knightsbridge in your grandfather's absence and offer for you immediately."

"No, I won't have it!" She adjusted the neckline of her gown, tugged her sleeves into place. "I will not have you going to the one man in England who does not think you a dishonorable beast and confessing your sins to him! What would that do to your friendship with Algie? *If* I am with child, *then* we will go to him together and decide what to do."

"What of Emily?"

She paused in adjusting her dress. "What about Emily?"

"If you married me, Emily would have the mother she so desperately needs."

She sent him a look of disbelief. "Really, Justin. No woman wants to be proposed to because she would make a good mother! And you hardly need my help with Emily."

"But I do." He took her hand. "Meg, I do need your help. I have no idea how to raise a child, much less a young girl as active as Emily. Every day I'm terrified I will do something wrong."

Her heart melted. "You're doing fine, Justin."

"I'm not," he insisted. "Look at what happened today. I thought I had lost her, and the enormity of it nearly struck me down. If you hadn't arrived when you did, I'd be raving in Bedlam by now."

She gave him a tender smile and gently removed her hand from his. "Justin, I know you're uncomfortable with these softer emotions, but please believe me when I tell you that they aren't weak or unmanly. Knowing how much you care for Emily only makes me more certain that you will be able to give her the sort of love she needs in order to grow into a woman."

"But she needs a woman's influence."

"Perhaps. But I needn't marry you for that. We can continue as we have been, and I will be certain to spend as much time as I can with Emily."

He gave a growl of frustration. "I've compromised you beyond repair and still you won't wed me. You won't marry me for honor or because of a child we may have made together. Now you won't even be my wife for the sake of my ward. *What do you want from me?*"

Meg winced as his roar echoed through the room. "If you can't figure it out, Justin, then I'm doing the right thing by refusing you."

"Between you and Emily, I shall be dead of apoplexy in a week's time."

"Hardly." Turning her back to him, she glanced at him over her shoulder with a sweet smile and said, "Now be a dear and do up my dress for me?"

Rathmore scowled at the rows of hooks and ties

presented to him. Her creamy flesh peeked from between the edges of the dress, and even now, even when he was so furious with her, he was still tempted to kiss his way down her spine and make her sigh with pleasure.

But he'd be damned if she was going to toss his honor in his face and then expect him to wait on her like some lovesick pup!

Turning away from the enticement, he began to do up his dangling cravat. "It seems to me, my dear girl, that if you want so much to be an independent woman, you had best learn to do such things for yourself."

Her outraged gasp brought a cynical smile to his lips. With effort, he resisted the temptation to look back at her.

"Justin, you cannot leave me like this!" Meg exclaimed. "Even the most independent woman doesn't have eyes in the back of her head."

"A pity." Twisting his cravat into a simple knot, he turned to face her, clucking his tongue in sympathy.

"Justin!" Her expression of pique changed to a coaxing smile. "Please help me do up my dress. Someone could walk in at any moment."

He cocked his head, amused at her wiles. "Have I heard aright? Did the words 'please help' pass through your lips?" He raised his brows, making no effort to hide his mockery. "Can it be that the independent woman needs the help of a mere man?"

"Don't be difficult, Justin."

"*I* am difficult?" His veneer of indifference dropped away. "*You*, my dear, are the one who doesn't care a whit for your reputation—or mine, for that matter. *You* are the one who has refused a perfectly respectable offer even under these extreme circumstances, an offer any lady of breeding would rush to accept. Yet *I* am difficult?"

She sighed, something that looked to be regret in her eyes. Whatever her reasons, refusing him was not an easy task for her. "Justin, all I ask is your assistance in fastening my dress, not your immortal soul."

"And there's the rub." Anger ebbed, dissipated by her genuine distress over the matter. He came to her, stroked his hands over her shoulders before gently turning her around so that her back was to him. Bending to his task, he whispered near her ear, "For I wanted to give you my soul, dearest Meg, and you have rejected it."

He waited for a sharp reply, but instead she only hung her head forward, her long hair shielding her face, as her shoulders slumped in silent surrender.

Guilt tugged at him. Emotions were high, and she was really quite young, for all her American bravado. Had he been too hard on her?

Perhaps.

But her refusal still stung, and anger still simmered, and so he elected to keep quiet as he slowly began to do up the back of her dress.

Yet what began as a tedious task gradually turned into a feast of sensuality. His fingers brushed her silken skin with each hook he fastened, each ribbon he tied. Despite his will, his caresses became more deliberate. Her breath caught with each touch, urging him to continue. And when he bent forward and pressed a soft kiss to the nape of her neck, she let out a tiny moan.

And that was how Knightsbridge found them.

Chapter 16

As the door to the drawing room opened, Rathmore raised his head to growl a warning at the intruding servant. But the words froze in his throat as he met Knightsbridge's shocked gaze.

"What the devil—!" Knightsbridge slammed the door before the inquisitive servants could peer inside. "Unhand my cousin at once, Rathmore!"

"Algie!" Meg jerked her head up. "What are you doing here?"

"Looking for you." Algie stalked over and yanked her away from Rathmore. "It's after nine o'clock, and Penelope was concerned for your reputation. I told her not to worry, that you were with Rathmore, but she insisted it wasn't proper." He turned a sneer on Rathmore. "And apparently she was right."

"Stop it." Meg pulled her arm from her cousin's grasp, the stricken look on both his face and Rathmore's making her heart sink. "You're in a taking over nothing."

"Nothing!" Knightsbridge indicated the disarray of her hair and her half-fastened clothing. "You call this nothing?"

A blush heated her cheeks, but she met her cousin's gaze squarely. "I'm not a child, Algie."

Knightsbridge dismissed her with a look and rounded on Rathmore. "And you! What have you to say about all this? You're supposed to be my friend, devil take you! I stood by you always, and *this* is how you repay my loyalty?"

The sharp words made Meg wince. Rathmore looked at her over Algie's shoulder, the growing pain in his eyes bringing home to her the enormity of the situation.

When only she and Rathmore had known about their assignation, it was easier to ignore the consequences. But now that Algie knew . . . it would be much more difficult for her to continue to refuse Rathmore.

It was obvious from the stone-chiseled expression on Rathmore's face that he wanted nothing more than to roar at Algie, but he clenched his jaw and controlled his temper with visible effort.

"I have no excuse," Rathmore said in a rather calm tone. "I will, of course, do the honorable thing and wed your cousin."

"By the devil, you will at that!" Algie vowed, shaking a fist.

"Let's not be hasty." Meg moved between the

two men. Algie looked so hurt, and Rathmore's shattered dignity tore at her heart. She hadn't realized how much it meant to him that they follow tradition. She didn't dare accept his offer, not without knowing that he loved and understood her as she was. But by refusing to go along with accepted social standards, would she end up losing him?

It was a chance she had to take. Her soul was at stake.

She looked at her cousin. "Justin has already offered, and I have refused. It's over."

Algie slowly lowered his fist. "You've already offered, Rathmore?"

"I have." Rathmore scowled. "Several times, in fact. But the stubborn chit won't have me."

"What!" Algie glared at her. "Are you daft? You must accept the man."

"I won't." Meg tilted her chin, determined to hold her position despite her heart's urgings to give in. "I didn't accept him before, and I certainly am *not* going to marry him just because you walked in on a private moment."

"A private moment?" Knightsbridge threw up his hands. "Meg, you're the granddaughter of a duke. 'Private moments' with a man are simply not permitted."

"This is none of your affair, Algie."

"I'm responsible for you, so it bloody well is my affair." Face red with emotion, Algie took her arm again and pulled her aside. "Put yourself to rights,

Meg, while Rathmore and I discuss this rationally."

"I will *not* be dismissed like a foolish child." Again Meg shook off his hold. "The man has proposed marriage already. I have refused."

"I don't understand this." Algie turned to Rathmore. "Why didn't you come to me? We could have contacted the duke and had the two of you betrothed before she ever knew about it."

"You wouldn't dare!" Meg searched her cousin's face and then Rathmore's. Surely these two men who both claimed to care for her wouldn't betray her in such a way?

"Indeed I would," Algie replied with a nod.

Rathmore shrugged. "Such things are done all the time."

A chill came over her as she looked from one man to the other. "So you would go behind my back and arrange a marriage without my consent? Even though I have expressly refused Lord Rathmore's offer?"

"Females rarely know what's best for them," Algie said. "Don't get yourself in a taking, Meg."

"Don't get myself in a taking?" Her tone rose on the last words. Algie seemed oblivious of her rising temper, but Rathmore grew very still, his eyes narrowing as he focused on her.

"It hardly matters now," Algie said. "Under the circumstances, there's no other choice."

"There bloody well *is* a choice! And my choice is no."

"Meg, your language!" Algie stared at her, shocked.

"You'll have to worry about more than my language if you don't start listening, Algie."

Algie took a step back. "Now, Meg, you know I have your best interests at heart."

Meg gave a snort of disbelief and received a quelling look from Rathmore, who stepped forward before Meg could fire off a blistering reply. "You have my deepest apologies for this incident, Knightsbridge. But it's all water under the bridge now, and I am more than willing to come up to scratch and wed your cousin."

Knightsbridge rubbed his temple wearily. "I just wish you had followed tradition, Rathmore."

"I wanted to." Rathmore assumed a look of humble regret.

"We will need the duke's permission," Knightsbridge said. "With her brother absent, he is her guardian."

"Excuse me," Meg interrupted, ignoring Rathmore's signal to be quiet. "Did neither of you hear the part where I said I *will not* marry Lord Rathmore?"

"What you want has no bearing here," Algie said with a dismissive wave of his hand. "You must do what's right."

Meg propped her hands on her hips. "There's one little detail you're forgetting, Algie. You need me to agree when I am standing at the altar, and I can assure you, I will *not*."

Clearly startled, her cousin opened and closed

his mouth several times. "But you must," he finally spluttered.

Meg folded her arms. "I'm nearly twenty-three years old, Algie, and you can't force me to do anything."

"But . . . but . . . I shall inform the duke," he said. "Yes, I shall summon him from Bath, and he will make you see reason."

Guilt made her hesitate. Did she really want to upset her grandfather?

No. And neither did Algie.

Slowly, she shook her head. "My grandfather is extremely ill, Algie, and it would be very bad of you to distress him over what is really a trifling incident. If he had another attack, it would be all your fault for distressing him."

"*My* fault?" Algie echoed.

"Trifling?" Rathmore said with arched eyebrows, his voice heavy with innuendo. "Really, Meg."

She flushed. "Do behave, Justin."

"But we can't just pretend this never happened," her cousin exclaimed. "You have been ruined, Meg. Don't you understand that?"

"I will only be ruined if news of the incident reaches London," Meg said. "And since just the three of us know about it, there's no reason to believe that will happen."

Rathmore laid a hand on Algie's shoulder when her cousin would have protested again. "Let me talk to her," he murmured. "Perhaps I can make her see reason."

"As you will, but I'm not leaving the room." Clearly dismayed at the way events had come to pass, Knightsbridge turned to sit on the sofa.

Rathmore grabbed his arm before he sat. "Not there," he said. "May I suggest the chair by the hearth?"

A knowing look passed between the two men, and Algie followed Rathmore's suggestion, coloring in embarrassment as he took the seat by the hearth.

"I hope you don't expect me to swoon in your arms and say yes," Meg warned as Rathmore approached her. "I already told you I won't marry you."

"Meg." His voice was soft, his touch tender as he reached out to tilt her face to his. "You're making your cousin uncomfortable."

Dear Lord, did he have to be so attractive? Already she felt herself melting beneath his touch, and she struggled to concentrate on standing her ground. "No one asked him to come barging in here," she muttered, matching his low tone.

"Meg." Rathmore took her hand. "He cares for you. He wants you to do what's right."

"I am doing what's right. What's right for *me*."

"Are you?"

"Yes." Fighting sudden tears, she pulled away from him and began to coil her hair into a knot at the nape of her neck. "And if I was at all unsure, then the way you and my dear cousin have just treated me has removed all doubt. Both of you insist on dismissing my opinion as if I were a brain-less ninny."

"I don't think you're brainless." He sighed. "This is a complex situation, Meg. It goes against every grain of breeding in my body to know that I dishonored you and you won't let me make it right."

"And it goes against *my* grain to marry a man simply because of obligation." One by one, she stuck the hairpins into her hair. "Justin, marriage is forever. And I can't spend forever with a man who sees me as a convenience."

"You're more than that."

"Am I?" Hair in place, she met his gaze, her own determined. "Justin, you're not offering for me because you've spent time getting to know me and letting me get to know you. You're proposing because there's a social rule that says you should. And because you need a mother for Emily." She smiled sadly. "And because I'm one of the few women of good family who will even talk to you. None of these are the right reasons to marry. I need more."

"There is more. There's passion." He took a step toward her. "I can give you passion, Meg. And chil-dren. And wealth and a secure social position."

"It's not about what you can give me, Justin." She shook her head. "We're getting nowhere with this."

"Tell me what you want."

"I have told you. You just don't seem to under-stand it. And until you do, until you can meet me as an equal and convince me that you love me, I won't wed you."

"This isn't a fairy tale, Meg. Many couples marry for reasons other than love, though the love eventually comes."

"That's not enough."

"All right." He fixed those dark eyes on her. "But I intend to win you, Meg," he warned in a voice that sent a shiver of desire through her. "Whatever it takes."

"I hope you do, Justin. I truly do."

He changed the subject. "Turn around. Your fastenings are all askew."

"You try doing this without a lady's maid," she grumbled, but obeyed him.

"I say, Rathmore—" Knightsbridge protested.

Rathmore silenced him with a look. "Do you want your cousin to leave the room *en dishabille*, Knightsbridge? I'm only setting her appearance to rights."

"It isn't proper," Knightsbridge muttered.

"I think we can all agree my relationship with Meg passed proper some time ago."

Algie subsided into brooding silence, and Rathmore efficiently refastened her dress. "There you are. Quite the proper lady once again."

Meg glanced back over her shoulder. "Not quite the same," she murmured for his ears alone, "but no one will be the wiser."

He squeezed her shoulder, then stepped away from her. "I will be attending the Friday night assembly tomorrow, Meg. I hope to see you there."

"You might, my lord." She sent a meaningful look at Algie. "If my cousin doesn't imprison me at Knightsbridge Chase."

Knightsbridge rose. "Neither of you seems to be taking your situation seriously."

"And you're taking it *too* seriously," Meg replied tartly.

"Meg, why don't you look in on Emily before you leave," Rathmore suggested. "One of the maids can escort you."

"I believe I shall." With a last, resentful look at Algie, she sailed from the room.

"Demme, but I forgot about your ward with everything at sixes and sevens," Knightsbridge said. "How is the child?"

"It was nothing serious. She'll be fine." Rathmore sat down in a nearby armchair and met his friend's gaze squarely. "I hope you understand that I hate this situation as much as you do, Knightsbridge. You know I would never do anything to damage our friendship."

"I know that." Knightsbridge sat down again in the chair by the hearth. "But Rathmore, the girl is ruined. You know it, and I know it."

"Yes." Rathmore drummed his fingers on the arm of the chair. "But your cousin is no milk-and-water miss, Knightsbridge. She means what she says. Unless I can convince her otherwise, she will refuse to wed, right at the altar if it comes to it."

"If the duke finds out . . ."

"I know. Meg's good name is not the only one at

stake." He clenched his hands. "The duke would ruin me utterly. There would be no way I could ever recover my reputation. And Emily would suffer for it."

"You must convince Meg to do what's right," Knightsbridge said. "I know you. You've always been able to coax women to do your bidding. Surely my cousin isn't all that different." He gave a bitter laugh. "In fact, you've already proven that she isn't."

"I do care for her, you know," Rathmore said quietly. "I would never have been so careless otherwise. She *will* be my wife. I just need some time to convince her."

"Well, you had better do so," Knightsbridge said, rising from his chair. "For if you don't, I fear things may never be the same between us."

The words hung in the air between them.

"I understand," Rathmore said finally. He rose as well. "I value your friendship, Knightsbridge. I should hate to lose it."

"And I should hate to withdraw it." Knightsbridge's expression wavered between fury and hurt. "Damn it, man! It's bad enough that my boyhood friend has compromised my cousin, but with *your* reputation . . ."

Guilt pinched once more. "I can't undo what's already been done," Rathmore said quietly. "All I can do is to make it right."

"See that you do." Knightsbridge sighed and

gave a helpless shake of his head. "What am I going to tell Penelope?"

"Tell her nothing. The fewer people who know what happened, the better."

"You're right, of course, but I'm not in the habit of keeping things from my wife. And the duke returns from Bath in a month."

"Give me that month." Rathmore clasped Knightsbridge on the shoulder. "If I have not convinced Meg to marry me, by then you are free to follow your conscience and do whatever you feel you need to, even if it means telling the duke. But I swear to you, Knightsbridge, Meg *will* be my bride."

"She had better be." Knightsbridge stepped away, leaving Rathmore's hand to drop away to his side. "I had best take my cousin home now."

Rathmore watched him leave the room, his heart heavy. Knightsbridge had been a true friend to him through the long years of his exile. Algie had always believed him innocent and had even gone out of his way to invite him to his wedding. Knowing that he had disappointed his closest friend pierced his heart.

How was he going to convince Meg to marry him? How could he make things right?

He had made a complete botch of his whole courtship by taking her innocence. Tempting her with passion had been his best chance of wooing her to the altar, and now he had lost that precious advantage. Not that he had intended to compromise her. His honor would never allow him to deliberately ruin a lady.

Still, when Knightsbridge had walked in on them, he had wondered if Fate had smiled on him. Through no machination of his, they had been discovered alone together. Compromised. Undone. By the rules of society, they *had* to wed. Meg would be his, reputation or not.

Unless the duke had him transported first.

He heard voices outside in the hallway, then the sound of the front door closing. He fancied he could even hear the hiss of the carriage wheels as Knightsbridge took Meg back to Knightsbridge Chase.

The house fell silent, except for the soft footfalls of the servants going about their duties. With Meg's departure, it seemed as if she had taken all the joy and warmth of his home with her. Loneliness crept over him like a shadow.

Were tonight's events a blessing in disguise or the death knell to his chances of sharing his life with her?

The true severity of his situation crashed over him. Giving in to passion had been a monumental mistake. Now, not only did he still have the burden of restoring his good name in society, but he had taken the chance of damaging it further just as doors were starting to open for him. If Meg's grandfather discovered their circumstances, the duke could ruin him forever, and Emily's future with him. And with that would also go Knightsbridge's valuable friendship.

And Meg would never be his.

That possibility was unacceptable. It would take all his considerable charm to woo her in the mere month he had allowed himself in his agreement with Knightsbridge, but in the end, he was determined to win her. She would make an excellent countess and a good mother for Emily.

And he needed her.

It was a hard thing for a man of his stamp to admit, but it was the truth, and he believed in never hiding the truth from himself. He hadn't lied to Knightsbridge; he did care for Meg. And he needed her in ways he had never needed a woman before, ways that had nothing to do with satisfying his physical desires.

He wanted her to be there at his side through good times and bad. He wanted to laugh with her and hold her when she cried. He wanted her to be the mother of his children.

And the only thing standing in the way was Meg herself. Meg and her determination to find . . . whatever it was she was looking for.

What was it that she searched for, that elusive, insubstantial discovery that she sought to make? It could take her years to find it, and he had only a month to win her.

Perhaps he should make it his business to find out what she was trying to do. If it was that important to her, he really couldn't dismiss her needs lightly. Meg was not a typical woman, and it was time he stopped using typical methods to try and win her. She was unique.

Tomorrow when they met at the Friday night assembly, he would not so much as kiss her hand. Meg's mind was the key to winning her; their courtship had become a battle of wits. And he was up to the challenge.

Chapter 17

Meg entered the assembly room right behind Algie and Penelope. A quick glance around revealed that Rathmore was not present.

She wasn't certain if she was relieved or disappointed. The events of yesterday seemed almost like a dream, except for the very real twinges of soreness in her muscles this morning—twinges that sent a glow of warmth through her as she remembered their cause. She didn't regret giving herself to Rathmore, but she did regret the consequences. Not only had their discovery hurt Algie and left things tense between her and her cousin, but Rathmore's longtime friendship with him had been damaged as well.

And the only thing that would fix everything in everyone's eyes was if she were to marry Rathmore.

Oh, how tempting the idea was. She was drawn

to Rathmore as she had never been drawn to any other man. Everything about him fascinated her—his vulnerability, his wicked sense of humor, his bone-deep sense of honor. And now that she had lain with him, she wanted nothing more than to spend her life in his arms.

Yet that path was dangerous. It was so easy to fall prey to a handsome face and hot passion, and even more so to a man unafraid to voice the depths of his feelings. Indeed, she was tempted to just accept Rathmore's offer and lose herself to the blissful warmth of his embrace forever.

But losing herself was just what she was trying to avoid.

Knightsbridge and Penelope paused to greet acquaintances, and Meg smiled and murmured the appropriate social pleasantries even as her mind continued to work on the dilemma at hand. Rathmore was a strong-willed man, and since he had taken her innocence—however freely given—his honor demanded that they wed. Being a man of strong convictions, he would not be satisfied until she was his bride.

And yet *she* would not be satisfied being merely a wife. She needed more, and she would not give up—or give in—until she found it.

The way Algie and Rathmore had started to plan her wedding, completely ignoring her own thoughts on the matter, had only served to make her more determined than ever to wed only when *she* was ready. Not a moment before.

The woman who was Meg Lynch would not be sacrificed on the altar of matrimony just to satisfy society's whim.

She was brought back to the present as a whisper rippled through the crowd, and she heard Rathmore's name. Glancing at the doorway, she saw him standing there, resplendent in formal black.

Her insides melted. Lord, he was irresistible.

He spotted her then and made his way through the suspicious throng to her side. Knightsbridge stiffened as Rathmore joined them, but Penelope smiled and held out her hand with a warm greeting.

"Lord Rathmore, how lovely to see you this evening."

"Lady Penelope." Rathmore bowed over Penelope's hand, then straightened and gave a short nod to Algie. "Knightsbridge."

Algie responded in kind. "Rathmore."

Penelope frowned at the formality between them as Rathmore turned to Meg.

"Good evening, Miss Stanton-Lynch," he said. "Might I interest you in a glass of punch?"

She couldn't refuse. His dark eyes warmed as he took in her appearance, and as much as she wanted to resist him, she couldn't do it. Just his smile was enough to lure her.

"Why thank you, Lord Rathmore," she said, laying her hand on his extended arm.

"Meg—" Algie began.

Meg sent him a sharp look. "I shall be back directly, Algie."

"See that you are." His frown at Rathmore said clearly that he would come looking for her if she wasn't.

Rathmore gave Algie one of his cool, unmoving stares.

Tension rose. Just as Meg began to worry that they might come to blows in the middle of the assembly room, Penelope broke the silent communication between the two men.

"Algernon, you're certainly out of sorts tonight," she said with a frown. "Come dance with me."

"Perhaps when Meg returns," Knightsbridge replied stubbornly.

Penelope raised one delicate blond brow. "Oh, stop fussing, Algernon. Meg will be fine with Lord Rathmore, and they'll be right here in the assembly room the entire time."

"Quite so, my lady," Rathmore agreed.

"Very well," Knightsbridge said grudgingly. "But I'll be watching the both of you."

"Understood." Rathmore gave Algie a brief nod before escorting Meg away.

"I've never seen Algie act this way," Meg said as they made their way to the refreshment table.

"Can you blame him?" Rathmore's lips curled in a self-mocking smile. "After all, I've already proven that I cannot be trusted alone with you."

"Really?" Meg sent him a sidelong look. "I thought *I* was not to be trusted alone with *you*, my lord."

He laughed. "Impudent chit. How you can poke fun at our situation amazes me."

"There is no situation, Lord Rathmore." They stopped at the refreshment table, where Rathmore gallantly procured her a glass of the insipid punch. "Only you, I, and Algie know what happened, and he will not tell tales."

"You're a fool if you think it's that simple." He steered her away from the punch bowl and the curious, eavesdropping bystanders. "There is the little matter of whether or not you carry my heir."

She flushed and glanced around. "Justin, this is not the place to discuss the matter."

"So concerned with the proprieties all of a sudden?"

She stopped and gave him a look. "You know that's not what I mean."

He shrugged. "It hardly matters." He began to steer her through the crowd again. "The truth will come out, my dear. It always does."

"Speaking of which," she said, quickly changing the subject, "how goes your quest to prove your innocence? Have you discovered anything of note?"

"Perhaps tonight."

"What do you mean?"

He smiled mysteriously. "It's nothing for you to be concerned about." They stopped in a quiet alcove in full view of Knightsbridge and Penelope on the dance floor, but far enough away that no one could overhear their conversation. Rathmore glanced down at her, his dark gaze softening. "I meant to ask you, are you all right today? No discomfort?"

"No." Her face heated, and she looked away.

"I would hate to cause you any distress," he murmured. "I tried to be as gentle as I could, but it's quite normal for a woman to be sore after her first time."

"My lord, this is hardly the time to discuss such things." Placing her untouched punch on the tray of a passing servant, she snapped open her fan and rapidly waved it in front of her burning face.

"My apologies, my dear. Given your actions yesterday, I had thought that you didn't care what the gossips said."

"I see you're still angry." She slanted him a look brimming with challenge. "I'm sorry if your pride has been hurt, but this wasn't easy for me, either."

"So you're saying you do want to marry me?"

She opened her mouth, then shut it again. "I can't marry you, Justin. I told you why."

"So you did." The set ended, and Rathmore swept a hand toward the dance floor. "Would you care to dance?"

She started to accept, then thought better of it. How could she possibly continue to resist him if she didn't stay out of his arms? So she shook her head. "No, thank you."

A bleak light flickered in his eyes for a moment, but then his familiar impassive expression came back. "As you wish. Allow me to return you to your cousin."

Without another word, he escorted her back to Algie and Penelope, then walked away. Meg stared after him with a heavy heart. She wanted nothing more than to call him back, to apologize for refusing him. To accept his offer.

And that was exactly why she remained silent, watching him until he had disappeared into the crowd.

"Odd behavior for Lord Rathmore," Penelope mused.

Meg met Algie's glance in a moment of shared understanding, then turned to Penelope and said, "I believe he's still shaken over Emily's illness yesterday."

"Ah, yes, of course." Penelope smiled. "He's so fond of that girl."

"Yes, he is." Another reason that she loved him, Meg thought with a bittersweet pang.

Already she missed his presence.

Rathmore made his way through the crowd, the taste of rejection still bitter in his mouth. Meg seemed alarmingly adamant about keeping distance between them—so much so that now she even refused to do something as innocent as dance with him.

He could have forced the issue. He knew she wanted him physically, and he could have charmed or seduced her onto the dance floor with him. But he wanted her willing, not coerced. Better to have walked away than let his black temper worsen the situation.

With effort, he pushed Meg to the back of his mind. He had other business to conduct tonight, business that he had neglected in pursuit of that stubborn American female.

A sultry laugh reached his ears, a familiar sound that drew his attention as a hare drew a hound's. Following the distinctive laughter, he made his way to a secluded alcove where a group of eager men gathered around a short, buxom blond. Though he knew her to be well past her thirties, the years had made no negative impact on her impressive figure, and she entranced the crowd of men as easily as Eve had beguiled Adam.

Mrs. Imogene Warington.

She spotted him as soon as he stopped at the edge of her coterie of admirers. Her hazel eyes widened, and her lush lips parted in a seductive smile. "Well, well," she purred in her unusually deep voice. "Good evening, Lord Rathmore."

At the sound of his name, a startled murmur went through the suitors, and the group parted to let him through.

Rathmore gave a brief bow. "Mrs. Warington. I understand that congratulations—and condolences—are in order."

"You wicked man," the lady replied, tapping his arm playfully with her fan. "Have you no manners to recommend you?"

"I think not. However, I see that you still dazzle Devon with your smile."

Pleasure flickered across her face, nearly masking the calculation in her eyes. "And you, Lord Rathmore, are as charming as ever."

He offered his arm. "May I have this dance?"

She hesitated barely a moment, then nodded. "A pleasure, my lord." With a wave of her hand, she dismissed her swains, then rested her fingers lightly on her arm. "I had thought you never wished to see me again."

"People change," he replied. "Six years have gone by."

"Indeed they have." They neared the dance floor. "And you have grown into quite a man, Lord Rathmore."

He didn't miss either her flirtatious tone or her greedy glance at his groin.

He swallowed his distaste and said, "You've always been an attractive woman, Mrs. Warington. Perhaps I was hasty in refusing your offer all those years ago."

"You were a mere boy," she said with a forgiving smile and a toss of her blond curls. "And your uncle would have disapproved."

"I'm not a boy anymore." Gaze fixed on hers, Rathmore took his position for the dance.

"No, not anymore." Desire crept into her voice. "The offer is still open, my lord."

So she was between lovers. That made his job all the easier.

He gave her his wickedest smile. "Let's talk a bit about old times, my dear Mrs. Warington, and then we can decide what the future might bring."

"I'm at your disposal, my lord." The eager hunger in her eyes belied her submissive tone.

He leaned an inch closer, all the while wishing she were dark-haired and American. "Let's talk in private after the dance," he murmured, then fell into line as the music began.

Her inviting smile was all the answer he needed.

"Good evening, Knightsbridge." The man who stopped beside Algie was short with a round, baby-like face and curling blond hair. "May I congratulate you on your marriage?"

"Good evening, Fenton." Uncertainty flickered across his features, but Algie nonetheless turned to Penelope. "My dear Penelope, may I present Lord Fenton to you?"

"Lord Fenton." Penelope extended her hand as was polite, but her smile discouraged further pleasantries.

"A sincere pleasure, my lady." Fenton bowed over Penelope's hand, then turned his dark blue eyes on Meg. "Might I beg an introduction in this quarter, Knightsbridge?"

"This is my cousin, Miss Stanton-Lynch," Algie said. "Meg, this is Lord Fenton."

"Good evening, Lord Fenton." Meg extended her hand, unsure how to react to being introduced to Ophelia's brother.

"Enchanted." He bowed over her hand, then said, "May I have the honor of this dance, Miss Stanton-Lynch?"

Since she hadn't been at the assembly long enough to get her dance card filled, she had no excuse to refuse. Nodding, she gingerly put her hand on Lord Fenton's extended arm and allowed him to lead her to the floor. They took their places in the set with the other couples.

"Was that Lord Rathmore I saw you with earlier?" Fenton asked.

"It was." Meg sent him a warning look. "He's a friend of the family."

"Yes, I do recall that he and Knightsbridge were close as brothers at Eton." The music began, and Fenton stepped into the dance. "I once counted Rathmore among my friends, Miss Stanton-Lynch."

"Indeed?" She turned, stepped, moved to the next position.

"Quite so. Until the tragedy." His blue eyes suddenly filled with sadness. "I'm certain you know the tale."

"Some of it." She would have pressed for details, but then she caught sight of Rathmore dancing with a lushly curved blond beauty. Meg nearly threw her dance partner out of step as she stretched to look at them.

Rathmore acted as if he hadn't seen *her* at all.

"Miss Stanton-Lynch?"

She whipped her gaze back to Lord Fenton and

gave him a sympathetic smile. "My condolences on the death of your sister, my lord."

"Thank you." He sighed. "So tragic for a beautiful girl to die so young."

She glanced at him sharply, but met only bland innocence in his eyes. Had she imagined a warning in his words? "Indeed, my lord. Quite tragic."

"I should hate to see such a thing happen again." They came around again, right past Rathmore and the blond woman, whose décolletage was so low, she might as well not have worn anything at all. Rathmore never took his eyes from his companion.

Who was she, and why was Rathmore dancing with her?

Because you wouldn't.

"It can do you no good to keep company with Rathmore, Miss Stanton-Lynch," Fenton said, and Meg jerked her attention back to him.

She gave him her most quelling look. "You overstep yourself, Lord Fenton."

"I know I do," he said apologetically. "But I do so out of concern for your welfare."

"I told you Lord Rathmore is a family friend. He would never harm me."

He smiled sadly. "No one ever thought he'd harm Ophelia, either."

She nearly stopped in the middle of the dance floor. "Sir, I find your conversation offensive."

"My apologies, Miss Stanton-Lynch. Shall we change the subject?" He glanced over at Rathmore and his partner, and Meg realized she had not been as discreet in her interest as she had hoped. "That's Mrs. Warington," he said. "She just buried her sixth husband. She and Rathmore are . . . old friends."

Old friends? Meg narrowed her eyes as the blond woman moved a little too close to Rathmore as they danced. Had they been lovers?

Had she lost him after all?

Lord Fenton seemed to realize that he had said enough, and he confined the rest of his conversation to a monologue about the weather.

Rattled by the encounter, Meg was glad when the dance ended and Lord Fenton escorted her back to Algie and Penelope. He didn't linger, merely made his bow and left directly.

"I don't like that man," Penelope murmured to her husband.

"Neither do I." Knightsbridge frowned at Lord Fenton, where he stood talking to someone across the room. "Though I suppose one can't fault him, given what happened six years ago."

Meg wasn't looking at Lord Fenton; she was watching Rathmore escort Mrs. Warington from the assembly hall, her laughter trilling behind them.

She didn't want to contemplate where they might be going. And she didn't like the mournful wail that her heart gave as she considered that she might have finally succeeded in pushing Rathmore away.

Algie frowned. "Meg, are you all right?"

"Quite certain." She rubbed her temple, though t was her heart that ached. "I believe I'm developing a headache. Perhaps I will find a quiet corner to sit in for a while."

"Did Lord Fenton upset you?" Penelope asked, laying a hand on her arm. "We can take our leave if you like."

"No, don't do that. We only just got here."

"Did Fenton say something inappropriate?" Knightsbridge demanded.

"It was just the usual gossip," Meg replied with a sigh. "He thinks Lord Rathmore killed his sister."

"I wouldn't take what he said to heart," Penelope advised. "He has a unique perspective on the situation."

"No one seems to believe that Lord Rathmore is innocent."

"I'm sorry to say that I didn't, either," Penelope said. "It was Algie who convinced me."

"Yes, I believe him innocent." Algie's mouth firmed. "At least of murder."

Penelope frowned. "Algernon, what's bothering you this evening? Have you and Lord Rathmore had a falling out of some kind?"

Meg held her breath. Algie looked at her, conflict clear on his face. Then he shrugged and said to Penelope, "A minor quarrel is all. Less than nothing."

"Then pray don't let it affect the evening," Penelope replied. The orchestra struck up a waltz and she looked eagerly at her husband. "Do dance with me, Algernon. You know how I adore the waltz."

A small smile curved Algie's lips as he gazed at his wife. "But dearest, if we dance twice in one night, the gossips will talk. And if we dance three times, your father will expect me to offer for you."

"Such a scandal," Penelope laughed. "Come, Algernon. Dancing the waltz with you is one the benefits of being an old married lady."

"Only *one* of the benefits?" Algie murmured with a playful leer.

Meg had to smile at their antics. What would it be like to be loved as Algie clearly loved Penelope? They were so perfect for each other.

She sighed, drawing the attention of the couple.

Penelope's smile dimmed. "Oh, dear, I had forgotten about your headache, Meg." She cast a longing glance at the dance floor, then turned back to Meg, clearly determined to take her responsibility as chaperone seriously. "Come. Let's find someplace quiet to sit for a while."

"But what about the waltz?" Meg asked.

"It will wait for another time."

"Absolutely," Algie agreed. "Your well-being comes first."

"I won't have it." Meg looked at Algie as she spoke, her tone carrying meaning only he would understand. "Please don't let my problems ruin your evening. I'll find a quiet chair near the dowagers, and I'll sit there until you have finished your waltz."

"Are you certain?" Penelope asked, but Algie was already shaking his head.

"No, I don't think that will do," he said. "There

are too many lowborn fellows at these assemblies, and it's our duty to protect you from them."

"I'll be sitting with the pillars of society," Meg reminded him. "Look, I see Lady Hemmingford right over there. She's a friend of your grand-mother's. Surely I will be safe enough with her." She gave him a pleading look. "Please, Algie. I don't want to ruin the evening for you and Penel-ope, not when you've been so kind to me."

Algie hesitated, and Penelope laid a hand on his arm, her own expression hopeful. "Very well," he said at last.

Penelope gave an undignified squeal of delight, bringing a smile to Algie's face.

"Let's get you settled with Lady Hemmingford," he said to Meg.

Moments later Meg sat beside the nearly deaf dowager and watched Algie and Penelope join the whirling dancers on the floor.

She hadn't lied; she did have a headache, stem-ming no doubt from the unpleasant scene with Rathmore and the shock of seeing him with Mrs Warington.

Didn't he care for her at *all*?

She just wanted to go home, but Algie and Penel-ope had been so kind to her, she hated to ruin their evening. And it was good to see a smile on Algie's face again. He had become so stern and protective of her that she wondered if she would ever hear him laugh again.

And it had broken her heart to see the rift in his

friendship with Rathmore and to know that she caused it.

Lady Hemmingford was chatting with an acquaintance on her other side, leaving Meg to close her eyes and rest her weary head against the wall behind her. The music was soothing, and as long as she didn't watch the swirling dancers, it actually seemed to help her headache. Sitting with the formidable Lady Hemmingford on her right and a large potted palm on her left shielded her from ardent suitors pursuing a place on her dance card.

There was only one man she wanted on her dance card, and he had already left for the evening . . . with another woman.

"Did you see them together?" a female voice said, coming from the other side of the palm. "Do you suppose it's true that he's going to offer?"

"That's what's been buzzing all over Devon," another woman answered. "He only attends events where she is likely to be."

Meg smiled a bit as she listened to the typical gossip heard at every social event. There was always talk and speculation regarding who pursued whom, who possessed the greatest fortune, and who needed to marry one. It was comforting in the fact that it was so normal. So harmless.

"I'm surprised he's even invited to anything," the first woman said. "I had thought he wouldn't be received after what happened."

"No, no, no," said the second woman. "It's because of what happened that he *is* invited everywhere. Really, would you want the Devil Earl's wrath turned on you? Look what happened to poor Ophelia Haversham."

Meg sat straight up in her chair. They were talking about Rathmore!

"I suppose you're right. But what is his relationship with Miss Stanton-Lynch? Do you really think he plans to wed her?"

"Of a certainty." The woman lowered her voice, and Meg leaned closer into the palm leaves to hear her. "Haven't you noticed how people have changed toward him since he began keeping company with her? She's the granddaughter of the Duke of Raynewood, and her brother will inherit when the old duke dies. Allying himself with that family will open doors that have long been closed to Lord Rathmore."

"But what if she refuses him?"

"I doubt she will. The two of them have been smelling of April and May since she came to Devon."

"Well, he is rich, not to mention handsome. His mother was French, you know."

"Really!"

"Indeed." Clearly delighted to share this scandalous tidbit, the second woman urged, "Tell me more."

"I can't right now, as my husband is signaling me from across the room. Do come to call this week, and I will tell you all I know about the Earl of Rathmore and Miss Stanton-Lynch."

Their voices began to fade as they walked away

from their corner. "Everyone knows he's pursuing her," the first woman was saying. "And if she refuses him, it's bound to ruin him for good."

"No one wants to cross the Duke of Raynewood," the other agreed, her voice growing fainter. "And if the duke refuses the match, then everyone will know the rumors are true . . ."

The two gossips had moved out of hearing distance, and two debutantes took over the corner behind the palm tree, whispering in excitement and measuring their various suitors as if they were comparing one bonnet to another.

Meg sat stunned, not even wincing at the high-pitched giggling of the young girls.

Everyone knew Rathmore was pursuing her? Everyone expected him to offer? And if he did offer and was refused . . .

Good Lord, she'd had no idea it was so complicated.

She sat back in her chair, staring blindly at the dancers. It made perfect sense that an alliance between her family and Rathmore's would go a long way toward repairing his reputation and securing Emily's future. But was that the only reason he wanted her?

Had their lovemaking been a calculated move to get her to the altar so that her reputation could repair his?

Betrayal rose like a lump in her throat as she struggled to hold back tears. Rathmore and his blasted honor would break her heart.

His honor.

She sat up straight, swiping at the tears before anyone saw them. Rathmore was a man of honor. While he may indeed have been pursuing her for her social standing as the granddaughter of the Duke of Raynewood, she didn't think he would have deliberately compromised her to win her hand. He was too dratted honorable.

If only he loved her . . .

She shook off her maudlin thoughts and turned her attention to another new discovery. If it became common knowledge that she had refused Rathmore's proposal, then nothing he did would ever restore his good name. And Emily would suffer for it as well.

By marrying Rathmore, she risked losing a piece of herself that might never be recovered. But by not marrying him, she condemned both him and Emily to lifelong ostracism. Emily would be forced to accept some less-than-desirable offer in order to survive.

She had seen how grim a woman's situation could be when she was raised to be a lady of breeding and was forced by circumstance to wed the first man who asked her. Her sister-in-law, Lucinda, had been in such a situation when Meg had first met her. Buried beneath her late husband's debts and pursued with illicit intent by her lecherous brother-in-law, Lucinda, the well-bred daughter of a famous general, had essentially been hired by the duke to teach Meg to get on in English society.

Though employment was the worst sin a woman of good family could commit, it had nonetheless been the only way Lucinda could continue to go out in society where she could find another husband and therefore survive. She managed to keep her true position in the duke's household a secret until Meg's brother, Garrett, married her and took her away to America.

While Lucinda's story had had a happy ending, the thought of Emily being forced into such a situation appalled her.

And Rathmore . . . He was an earl. He needed an heir. If she continued to refuse him, soon he would give up and look elsewhere for a wife. Yet with his reputation in shreds, neither his title nor his wealth would be enough to lure a woman of acceptable birth to marry him.

If she didn't marry Rathmore, she condemned both him and Emily to a life of banishment and misery. If she did marry him, Rathmore's reputation would be safe, as would Emily's future, but Meg herself might lose something of great value—her soul.

There had to be another way.

Knightsbridge and Penelope approached from the dance floor, and it was then that the idea came to her. It was really so very simple, she was amazed that she hadn't thought of it immediately.

All she had to do was prove Rathmore's innocence.

Then they would both be free.

Chapter 18

He certainly had botched things, hadn't he?
Rathmore sat at his breakfast table and wondered if there was any way he could possibly have made the situation with Meg worse.

He had intended to go to the assembly and bewitch her with his wit. Dazzle her with his charm. Tease her with memories of their lovemaking and leave her hungry without ever touching her.

Instead he had gone there and let his temper get the better of him.

He couldn't forget her face when she had refused to dance with him, that expression of gentle regret. That was when he knew that the best plan was strategic retreat.

What was it she had she accused him of . . . seeing her as a convenience?

He had practical reasons for wanting to wed

her; it was true. Her affinity with Emily. Her social connections. The fact that honor remained yet unsatisfied.

The fact that even now she might be carrying his heir.

But scandal aside, it was Meg he wanted beside him as his countess. Meg with her American bravado and her clever wit. Meg, whose mere presence helped him focus in a crisis.

It was Meg he wanted in his bed at night.

The evening had not been a total loss, however. He had managed to get close to Mrs. Warington. Though *she* had obviously wanted to get even closer.

He grimaced and took a swallow of coffee as if to wash away the distasteful memory. Imogene had not changed a bit from when she had been his uncle's mistress years before. She still went after any man she wanted like a cat in heat. While he had deliberately used her own licentiousness against her so he could get her alone, he was lucky to have escaped ravishment.

He had lured her out into the assembly hall's tiny rose garden, hoping that the romance of the moonlit night would loosen her tongue. He had asked his questions, but she had playfully avoided each one, choosing instead to caress his arm, his face, his shoulder and even his thigh. And when the hand on his thigh had crept northward, he knew he wasn't going to get what he wanted.

But then again, neither was Imogene.

He chuckled aloud as he recalled the thwarted look on her face when he had removed her hand from his upper thigh and claimed it was time for him to retire. Her touch had made his skin crawl, and he realized that Meg had ruined him for any other woman. It was only his promise to see Imogene again that had kept her from throwing a tantrum on the spot.

And he did intend to see her again. In fact, he had come up with a plan where he would see *all* the house party guests again—and finally prove his innocence.

But he would need the help of his friends to do it. He hoped Knightsbridge still *was* his friend, and with luck Meg was still speaking to him. He'd caught a glimpse of her face when she'd seen him with Imogene. He hadn't dared look at her while he was trying to seduce the truth out of the lusty widow; Imogene would have immediately sensed his distraction and become piqued. And he had needed her at her most amenable so he could question her.

Now he just needed to explain all that to Meg.

"Good morning, Cousin Justin."

He shook off the memories of last night and looked over to see Emily standing hesitantly in the doorway, watching him warily.

"Good morning, Emily. Have you come to breakfast with me?" He indicated the empty chair at his right.

She cleared her throat. "I believe I shall, Cousin Justin."

"Delightful." He gave her his most charming smile. "Cook has made the eggs exactly as you like them. Shall I have one of the servants fix you a plate?"

"I can do it." Emily took up her plate, then selected eggs and sausage before sitting down at the table.

Rathmore regarded her critically. This was the first day she had been up and about since her mysterious attack of the vapors on Thursday. While her skin seemed pale, he noted no other indications that her illness still lingered.

But the way she kept watching him out of the corner of her eye bothered him. He thought they had come to some sort of truce. She had even cuddled up to him in the carriage on the way home from Lady Presting's house. Why did she look so cautiously at him now?

"I'm told you're fully recovered from your illness," he said, trying to make his voice as gentle as possible. "You had all of us quite frightened, you know."

Emily cast him a sidelong look while slicing her sausage. "Even you, cousin?"

"Even I." He gave a mock shudder. "I hope you never do that to me again."

His tone must have been gruffer than he intended, for rather than reply, she recoiled and returned her attention to her plate.

Blast it, now what?

He watched her slice her sausage into smaller

pieces and searched for a way to comfort her again.

"Emily," he said finally in the kindest tone he could manage, "you need never be afraid of me."

She gave him a wary look, then nodded and continued to eat her breakfast in silence. Not the response he was hoping for.

"Emily," he continued, "I know that sometimes I shout. But that doesn't mean you need to fear me. We used to be friends, you and I. Don't you remember?"

She put down her fork and looked at him. "That was a long time ago."

"I know Miss Stanton-Lynch explained to you that I had to go away for a while, that I couldn't contact you. And I'm sorry. But I'm back now, and I still want to be your friend."

She said nothing.

"We were friends on Thursday when you got sick," he reminded her.

"I know," she said finally. "I just feel so . . . stupid."

"Stupid?" He sat back in his chair, dumbfounded by the unexpected answer.

"Yes, stupid." She blushed. "I had *the vapors*," she whispered in a mortified tone. "Like some weak little girl."

He smothered a chuckle. "Everyone gets sick sometimes," he said. "I'm just glad it wasn't anything serious."

"I wish it *had* been serious."

"I'm glad it wasn't." He smiled at her. "I don't want anything to happen to you, Emily."

She blushed again, but this time it was with pleasure at his remark.

Rathmore smiled. At least he was making headway with one of the females in his life.

"What's the surprise?" Meg asked Algie the following morning. "Come, now, Algie. I'm beside myself with curiosity."

"Just follow me," Algie said, leading her through a little-used wing of the house.

"As if I can do anything else." Intrigued, Meg trailed along behind her cousin. He had appeared as she had breakfasted alone that morning and claimed to have a surprise for her. No cajoling would get him to tell her what it was; she was simply to trail along behind him so he could show her.

After last night, she needed some cheering up.

Algie stopped before a small, rarely used bedroom at the end of the third floor hall. He unlocked the door, threw it open and gestured for her to enter. "This is it."

Curious, she stepped into the room.

The lovely plush rug that had graced the floor had been rolled up and set along one wall. All the furniture was pushed aside and draped in Holland covers, forming a large empty area in the center of the room.

Not quite empty. An easel, several canvases,

and Meg's precious new oil paints stood waiting to be used.

Meg clasped her hands together in delight. "My studio," she whispered.

"No one comes down this hall much," Algie said, "so the smell of the oils shouldn't bother anyone. And Penelope has an old gown or two that you can borrow when you paint."

"It's wonderful!" With a squeal of delight, she hugged him and kissed his cheek. "You're the best of cousins."

Knightsbridge reddened. "Yes, well, it seemed to mean so much to you."

"Thank you, Algie." She went over to touch the easel, run a tentative finger along a canvas. "I'm surprised that you've done this for me, though, given what's transpired the past couple of days."

A pained expression crossed his face. "Let's not get into all that, Meg."

"How can we not? It stands between us, Algie."

He shook his head. "I don't know why you persist in your refusal of Rathmore. Don't you realize that your grandfather returns from Bath in a month? Sometime between now and then, I must find a resolution to this. I cannot let you go on as you are."

"There's nothing you can do about my situation with Rathmore," she said gently. "I will make that decision myself. But I hate what it's done to us."

"In the duke's absence, *I* am responsible for keeping you safe, and I have failed at that." He regarded her with a troubled expression. "Meg, don't you realize that Rathmore has taken something of great value from you? How are you to make an advantageous marriage when you are no longer . . . er . . ."

"Innocent?" she supplied.

His cheeks reddened. "Meg, you know that when a man marries, he needs his wife to be . . . ah . . . pure, so that he can know that his heirs are indeed his." He shifted, clearly uncomfortable. "I can't believe I'm forced to broach such an indelicate topic with you."

"I'm sorry you ended up in the middle of this. It should have remained between Justin and me."

"Meg, I'm sorry, but it could never remain that way." He came toward her, his hands spread in earnest. "You're the granddaughter of a duke. Rathmore is an earl."

"But we're people first."

He shook his head. "No. Meg, you must do what's right. You must marry Rathmore."

"Or what? You'll arrange the betrothal behind my back with Grandfather like you told Justin you would?" Struggling to keep the betrayal out of her voice, she stared blindly down at the colorful paints.

"Even that would have been difficult, but I would have tried for Rathmore's sake, because he's . . . he *was* my friend."

"He still is your friend." She looked up again. "Nothing has changed."

"*Everything* has changed." Algie rubbed the back of his neck wearily. "I trusted my friend with your care, and he's betrayed that trust."

"I encouraged him, Algie."

He held up a hand. "I don't want to hear the details."

"I'm surprised at you, Algie. You seem determined to condemn Justin without knowing the facts. You, the one man in England who believed in him when the rest deemed him a murderer."

"Now I wonder at the wisdom of that," he muttered.

"Oh, no, you don't! You're *not* going to rescind your support of him when it comes to Ophelia's murder." She came over and touched his arm, looked into his eyes. "Algie, Justin still is your friend. He's more than willing to do his part. *I'm* the one who won't cooperate. If you need to blame anyone, blame me."

He shook his head. "Rathmore knew better. He betrayed my trust."

"So did I, Algie." She stepped away from him. "Justin didn't overpower me and take advantage of me. Believe me, if anything, it was the other way around."

He flushed. "Meg, please."

"Can't you make some sort of concession? This man is your *friend*."

"I know he's my friend!" Algie burst out. "I've given him a month, haven't I? I've not called him out on a dawn appointment, though God knows, I should."

"What do you mean, you've given him a month?"

He winced. "Did I say that?"

"You did." She folded her arms across her chest and eyed him expectantly. "Now what exactly does that mean?"

"The duke returns in a month's time." He shrugged beneath her narrowed stare. "Rathmore knows I must tell the duke what happened. I *should* send a letter to Bath, but, well, the duke is ill."

"And Justin's your friend."

"Exactly. I told him I would wait to tell the duke what happened until he returns from Bath."

"And in that time, you hope that Justin somehow convinces me to marry him."

He gave a short nod. "Yes. I hope to God he does."

"Oh, Algie." She sighed.

"It's the best solution," Algie said firmly. "Except for his reputation, Rathmore would have been an advantageous match for you under normal circumstances."

"I don't think we should talk about this anymore," Meg said. "We clearly cannot come to an agreement on the matter, and I don't want to fight with you, Algie."

Though he looked as if he wanted to protest, her cousin finally nodded. "But we're not finished with this," he warned. "This isn't like the rose garden or the singing lessons, Meg. This is one scrape you've gotten into that I cannot ignore."

"Understood."

He turned as if to leave the room, then hesitated. "Also, I make no promises about the duke. If I feel he needs to know what happened, I will tell him. Make no mistake."

She wanted to protest, but the seriousness of his expression decided her against it. "I understand, Algie. And I'm sorry to put you in this position."

He gave her a strained smile. "Enjoy your new studio." Then he left, leaving Meg alone with her paints and her churning emotions.

At precisely three o'clock, Rathmore presented himself at Knightsbridge Chase. He considered it a good sign when the butler admitted him rather than tossing him out on his ear.

Knightsbridge and Penelope received him in the drawing room, tea and biscuits at the ready. "Lord Rathmore," Penelope said warmly. "How lovely to see you. Would you care for tea?"

"Yes, thank you."

Knightsbridge gave a brief nod. "Rathmore."

"Knightsbridge," he said, returning the nod, hating the stiff formality between them. He looked around curiously. "Where's Meg? There's something I'd like to discuss with the three of you."

At the mention of Meg's name, Knightsbridge gave Rathmore a disgruntled look, then settled onto the sofa and reached over to snag a biscuit from the towering stack on the tea tray.

"Don't eat all the biscuits, Algernon," Penelope scolded. Looking at Rathmore, she said, "I shall send someone to fetch Meg, my lord."

Before she could take two steps to do so, the partially open door flew open, and Meg burst into the room, hauling a canvas with her. "Algie! Penelope!" she cried. "Look what I've done!" She came to a sudden halt as she noticed Rathmore's presence.

Rathmore blinked at the sight of her. She wore an old blue dress that looked as if it were better suited for the rag bin. Her hair was pulled back from her face with a simple ribbon and tumbled down her back in unruly curls. And she was covered in paint.

A daub of red smeared her cheek. Splatters of green and blue and yellow covered the dress. White dotted her nose and decorated her hair in splatters that looked like snowflakes in her dark tresses. Her fingers were smudged with every color of the rainbow.

"Oh, Meg," Penelope moaned, clapping a hand to her cheek.

A flush crept across Meg's paint-smeared face. "Lord Rathmore. What are you doing here?"

"Meg," Penelope murmured, embarrassment flickering across her face. "Lord Rathmore has obviously come to call."

Meg's blush darkened. "My apologies, my lord. Do allow me a moment to change my dress, and I'll be with you directly."

"A moment please," Rathmore said. He stepped forward and gently pried the canvas from her fingers. "Let's see what you have here."

"It's still wet," Meg warned. "Do have a care for your fine coat."

"Don't worry about my coat." Carefully he held the canvas up so everyone could see it.

Silence fell over the room.

"Well," Knightsbridge said. "Isn't that . . . ah . . . interesting?"

"Very colorful," Penelope choked.

"Meg," Rathmore said, staring in awe at her work, "it's *wonderful*."

A riot of color swirled across the canvas in a dance of hues that sang of passion and laughter. Strokes of cerulean blue echoed vivid green with splashes of yellow and streaks of crimson that whirled in blissful abandon across the canvas.

Rathmore couldn't pull his eyes from it. The tumult of color reminded him of Meg, of her passion and her beauty. Of her impetuous nature. Of her love of life. He was riveted.

"What is it?" Algie asked, squinting.

"It looks like . . . um . . . a flower garden," Penelope said with a weak smile.

Rathmore and Meg stared at both of them.

"That's not a flower garden," Knightsbridge scoffed. "Anyone can see it's a rainbow."

"Are you both mad?" Rathmore asked. "It's neither. It's just . . . Meg."

Meg turned luminous eyes to him, a look of

amazement on her face. "Exactly, my lord. It's just me. What I feel."

"Marvelous," Rathmore said, regarding the painting with a half smile. "I don't suppose you'd consider selling this to me, would you?"

Knightsbridge's eyes bulged. "You want to *buy* this?"

"Why not? Don't you think it's about time I started redecorating Rathmore Hall in my own taste?"

"Certainly," Penelope agreed with a polite smile pasted on her lips. "And how lovely that you would consider our Meg's work for your own home."

"I do consider it. Meg is very talented."

"Thank you, my lord," Meg said with a dazzling smile. "Now if you will excuse me, this needs to dry before it's safe for you to take it home."

"So you'll sell it to me?"

"No. It's yours, my lord, as a gift." Taking the painting from him, she sent a brief smile to the very baffled Knightsbridges, then left the room.

"A gift." Rathmore grinned, foolishly touched by the gesture.

"Wonderful," Knightsbridge muttered, then helped himself to another biscuit.

Meg changed as quickly as possible and hurried back downstairs. She was strangely eager to see Rathmore again, considering how badly they had left off at the Friday night assembly. Still, his admiration of her painting had left her lighthearted. He genuinely seemed to think that she had talent.

She did, too. Never before had she felt so free as when she had been painting. She had been so caught up in her art that she hadn't even noticed the time going by. How embarrassing to find Rathmore in the drawing room when she was covered head to toe in paint! She must have looked a fright.

If he had noticed her appearance, his breeding had not allowed him to show it. But he *had* noticed her painting. Even upbringing as meticulous as his had not prevented him from showing his genuine appreciation. And his offer to buy the painting was outside of enough. There was nothing to be done but make a gift of it to him.

Especially since she had been refusing his marriage proposals for the past week.

Meg came back down to the drawing room, properly attired now in a dress of delicate pink with tiny flowers scattered over it. She met Rathmore's eyes as she entered the room, and she grew lightheaded at the genuine appreciation in his gaze.

If only he was in love with her . . .

Good heavens, what was she thinking? Having Rathmore in love with her would be the worst possible thing that could happen! Look how he pursued her when honor alone forced him to wed. How persistent would he be if his heart was engaged?

It was bad enough that she held him in too much

esteem. If he returned her affections, she would end up married to him before she could say Countess of Rathmore!

"I'm sorry to have kept you waiting," she said, seating herself in an armchair.

"It was worth the wait," Rathmore said gallantly.

She blushed even though she knew his words were nothing more than empty social pleasantries.

"We're all here now, my lord," Penelope said. "What was it you wished to discuss?"

He looked at Knightsbridge as he said, "I believe I've found a way to prove my innocence, but I need your help to do it."

"Really?" Algie sounded as if the only help he was willing to give involved the choosing of dueling pistols. "Do enlighten us, Rathmore."

"Someone must know what really happened to Ophelia," Rathmore said. "I suggest we recreate the house party where she died and question all who were involved. That's the only way to find the truth."

"That's a wonderful idea!" Truly thrilled with the idea of restoring Rathmore's reputation, Meg nonetheless felt a pang of regret. Once his innocence was restored, she would be able to publicly refuse his addresses without worrying about the social consequences for both him and Emily.

That was what she wanted, wasn't it? Then why this twinge of regret?

Rathmore gave a grim smile and continued.

"The problem is, none of those people is going to come anywhere near Rathmore Hall. If you remember, the Aggerlys attempted to cut me at Lady Denniston's ball."

"Oh, dear, that's true," Penelope said.

"So I would like to suggest," Rathmore continued in a strained voice, "that Lord and Lady Knightsbridge give the house party."

"What!" Algie exclaimed.

"That's brilliant," Meg said. "I remember that the Aggerlys were eager to curry favor with Algie. They won't be able to resist the invitation."

Penelope pursed her lips. "Meg is right. I have no objections, Lord Rathmore. I would be happy to help." She sent her husband a meaningful look. "And so would Algernon."

Algie looked pained. "I will agree to it, Rathmore, because it can't hurt to clear your name . . . for *any* situation you currently find yourself in."

Rathmore gave a nod of acceptance. "My thanks."

"They will come to a house party hosted by the Earl and Countess of Knightsbridge," Meg mused. "And we should keep Lord Rathmore's presence a secret until the last moment."

"Agreed," Penelope said.

Rathmore looked from one determined face to the other. "I thank you all for your assistance."

"Let's just hope it works," Algie muttered.

Chapter 19

As predicted, no one refused an invitation from the Earl and Countess of Knightsbridge.

Within a day of sending out the invitations, the acceptances began to pour in. Seated in the morning room, Penelope planned the menus for the event while Meg sorted through the acceptance notes.

"Everyone's accepting," Meg said. "And the invitations went out only two days ago."

Penelope looked up and gave Meg a confident smile. "And why shouldn't they accept? The Polite World is fascinated with my marriage to Algernon."

"Because it's a love match," Meg said. "That breaks all the rules."

Penelope laughed. "And I spent so much time following all the rules of society before Algernon offered for me! Perhaps if I'd been brave enough to bend a rule or two, he might have gotten his courage up and offered for me sooner."

"I can't even imagine you breaking any of the rules of society," Meg said. "You always know what to do in any situation."

Penelope nodded. "Which is why I was known as Perfect Penelope. Lud, how I hated that dreadful nickname! Do you know that was what kept Algernon from paying his addresses?"

"Your nickname?"

Penelope nodded. "Silly, isn't it?"

"Perhaps he simply wasn't ready for marriage."

"Nonsense," Penelope said with a laugh. "He knew his duty, just as I knew mine. Luckily for the both of us, our duty included a love match."

"So your duty was to get married."

"Of course. As is yours."

"But what if I don't want to marry?" Meg asked. "What if I'd like to do something else?"

"You're a duke's granddaughter. There's nothing else you can do."

"I was afraid you were going to say that," Meg replied glumly.

Penelope's face softened into a smile. "Meg, marriage is not a death sentence. There are many advantages to being a married woman, not the least of which is the freedom you have within society. There are many things a married woman can do that an unmarried girl simply can't."

"I suppose."

"There's the companionship of having someone to grow old with," Penelope continued. "The joy of bearing children. The satisfaction of being the mistress of your own home. Don't dismiss marriage as a prison, Meg. It's really the key to living a full and satisfying life."

Before Meg could reply, a frantic knock came at the door. Without even waiting for an answer, the housekeeper burst into the room.

"Mrs. Belton, what on earth—"

"Begging your pardon, my lady, but you must come immediately. It's Monsieur Corveau. He's threatening to give notice again!"

"Oh, dear." Penelope stood. "What is it this time?"

"The little dog, my lady. He got into the kitchen again, and that stubborn Frenchman has gone into a fearsome temper! Threatened to stuff poor little Pudding and serve him roasted, he did."

"He *what*!" Penelope's mouth thinned, and her eyes glittered. "We shall see who ends up stuffed, shall we? Come along, Mrs. Belton!"

Penelope swept from the room, the housekeeper wringing her hands and following behind. Noting the angry set to Penelope's chin, Meg had no doubt that Monsieur Corveau would soon find himself on the swiftest boat back to France.

She was still giggling about it when the butler announced Lord Rathmore.

Meg leaped to her feet as Rathmore entered the

room. Her pulse quickened at the very sight of him, which irritated her to no end. "What are you doing here?" she demanded.

"A fine greeting," he replied, raising his brows. "I've come to discuss the house party."

"Of course." She made herself recall her manners. "Please sit down. Would you care for some refreshments?"

"No, thank you." He gave her a wicked grin as he seated himself in an armchair. "Unless you count yourself among the refreshments."

"Justin!" Heat flooded her face—and a few other places. Curse the man! How was it one smile from him could make every sane thought flee her mind? Just this morning she had reaffirmed her vow to resist his charms. She couldn't succumb. She couldn't marry him. She had to stick to her principles.

But for some reason when he smiled at her like that, she had difficulty remembering why it was so important that she continue to refuse him.

"Haven't you thought about it?" he murmured.

"Thought about what?"

"About what it felt like to be in each other's arms."

"Of course I've thought about it," she snapped. "It's caused me no end of trouble, hasn't it?"

"Our being together hasn't caused you the trouble," he corrected. "Your own stubbornness has done that."

"How can you say that and still call yourself a gentleman?"

He grinned. "Sorry, my dear, but in your presence, my gentlemanly instincts seem to simply fade away."

"So I've noticed." Suddenly tired of the emotional twists and turns of the situation, she asked impatiently, "What brings you here this afternoon, Justin?"

The amusement faded from his expression. "I came to tell you that I'll be bringing Emily with me to the house party."

"Why? Seeking a murderer is certainly no task for a child."

"I know, and I had intended to leave her home, but her nightmares have returned." His expression grew troubled. "I dislike the idea of her calling for me at night when I'm not there. I'll provide someone to see to her safety, but she *will* be coming."

Meg's heart softened at his concern for the girl. "Then of course you must bring her."

"My thanks," he said with a curt nod. "Hopefully everything will turn out well and my innocence proven."

"I hope so, too." She stacked up a pile of letters, unable to look at him. "Clearing your name is the only way we can both get out of the situation we find ourselves in."

"Wrong, my dear. *Marriage* is the only way out, a path you choose not to take."

"I have my reasons."

"So you have stated. Very well, Meg, do tell me how restoring my reputation is going to undo the scandal of our lovemaking."

She flushed at his bold words. "Are you aware that there is gossip being circulated about us?"

"Of course," he said. "I'd be surprised if there *weren't* any rumors circulating."

"Our . . . friendship . . . has been noted, my lord, and the *ton* is waiting with great anticipation for you to offer for me."

"I've already offered. Several times."

She ignored the pique in his voice. "But you haven't officially spoken to my grandfather. Society is waiting to see if you are rejected as a suitor. If it becomes common knowledge that I've refused you, it will be believed that the rumors surrounding Ophelia's death are true, and both you and Emily will be ruined."

"I'm aware of that." He got to his feet. "That's why I proposed this whole thing."

Of course he would have considered the circumstances, she thought with a flush of embarrassment. He knew the rules of society far better than she did.

She cleared her throat. "We both know I have no intention of wedding you, Justin, but at the same time, I don't want my choice to be the deciding factor in your social fate."

"Awfully generous of you," he drawled with unveiled sarcasm.

"Therefore," she continued, casting him a look

of admonishment, "our only recourse is to try and prove your innocence. Then if I refuse you, there will be *some* gossip but it will be a tempest in a teacup and fade away quickly."

"I see you've thought of everything," he said. "But have you considered this?"

He leaned down and placed his hands on either arm of her chair, trapping her. Then he kissed her.

Her hands fisted on the arms of the chair. Despite her will, her body responded. Despite her many reasons for refusing him, her arms crept up around his neck. And despite their already precarious situation, she couldn't resist kissing him back.

He made a growling sound and swept an arm around her waist, lifting her to her feet and holding her tightly against him. He cupped the back of her head, held her in place, and kissed her as if there were no tomorrow.

Hunger vibrated through her. She wanted nothing more than to lose herself in his arms forever. But there was more to a marriage than passion. More to a partnership than desire.

She couldn't forget that, no matter how much she wanted to.

"Stop," she managed to whisper against his mouth. "Justin, we can't."

He pulled back, but only enough to break the kiss. Leaning his forehead against hers, he looked deeply into her eyes. "Not that easy to forget, is it?"

She closed her eyes. "I don't want to hurt you."

"Then marry me," he urged. "Make me the happiest of men."

"I wish I could." Opening her eyes, she looked at him for a long moment, then gently pressed a tender kiss to his lips. "But I can't, Justin. I can't take the chance that I'll lose everything I have."

"What about the things you don't have?" He pulled back from her. "A partner in life. Your own home. Children."

"Those things will come. Someday."

"Someday may be too late."

Voices sounded in the hall, and Rathmore quickly returned to his own seat. They were the picture of propriety when Algie entered the room.

"Pen—good Lord, Rathmore, what are you doing here?" Algie glanced at Meg, and his gaze dipped to her kiss-swollen lips. His eyes narrowed. "Never mind, I can see what you've been about. Name your seconds, sir!"

"Algie, no!" Meg cried, leaping to her feet.

"I did nothing the first time," Algie snarled, "but this time he has dishonored you in *my* home. And I demand satisfaction!"

Penelope entered at the end of this tirade. "Algernon, what, by all that's holy, are you doing? Have you just *challenged* Lord Rathmore?"

"I have," Algie said. "Now if he would but answer it—"

"Have you lost your mind?" Penelope exclaimed.

"They were in here alone," Algie said. "Where were *you* anyway?"

"A problem with the chef. Algernon, I do believe the excitement of the social whirl has affected your senses. As if Lord Rathmore would take advantage of Meg."

"Already has," Algie growled. "But this time I'm going to do something about it."

Penelope paled. "What?"

"Algie, stop it!" Meg cried. "You know Lord Rathmore has done nothing wrong."

"I know nothing of the kind. Rathmore, I await your response."

"Algernon, I demand to know what's going on!" Penelope took Algie by the arm. "Are you saying that Lord Rathmore has dishonored Meg? Here, in our drawing room?"

"No," Meg said defiantly. "He can't say that because it isn't true."

Algie's face reddened. "Not here. I mean, he has dishonored her, but it happened somewhere else, some days ago."

"*What!*"

"Knightsbridge, nothing happened here," Rathmore interjected smoothly. "Surely nothing to warrant a duel. Still, the rules say that an apology will dismiss the challenge, so please accept my humblest apologies for anything you think may have gone on here today."

"Don't patronize me, Rathmore," Algie warned. "Don't try to tell me that you were alone with Meg and nothing happened. Not after Thursday evening."

"It was on Thursday?" Penelope turned to Meg. "Lord Rathmore took advantage of you last Thursday, and this is the first I'm hearing of it?"

"He didn't take advantage of me," Meg protested. "It was entirely mutual."

"Good heavens!" Penelope swayed, and Rathmore moved to catch her.

"Unhand my wife, Rathmore!"

"Shall I allow her to drop on the floor?" Rathmore gave him a disgusted look. "Really, Knightsbridge, you're taking this whole matter way too far."

"Please release me, Lord Rathmore," Penelope whispered. "And then you will leave my house."

Stunned silence fell at her pronouncement. Rathmore first looked shock, then resigned. He inclined his head. "As you wish, my lady."

Algie looked uncomfortable. "Now, Pen, that's not necessary. Rathmore has offered to do the right thing, you know."

"He has?" Penelope shook off Rathmore's helpful hands and regained her balance. "Then why hasn't anyone told me? When's the wedding?"

"There's not going to be a wedding," Algie said. "Meg refused him."

For a moment, it looked as if Penelope would faint again. "She did what?" she whispered. Then, without waiting for an answer, she turned to Meg. "You *refused* him?"

Meg tilted her chin. "Yes, I refused him."

Penelope whirled on Algie. "And you're just telling me this *now*?"

"Uh . . . well . . ."

Penelope's lovely face settled into lines of icy formality. She pointed to Rathmore. "Let me see if I have this aright. You, Lord Rathmore, dishonored Meg last Thursday. Is that correct?"

Regret touched his features. "I'm afraid so."

"Are you willing to make amends by making Meg your wife?"

"I am."

"And you, Meg." Penelope's disapproval washed over her like melted snow. "After Lord Rathmore attempted to do the right thing, you had the audacity to refuse him?"

Meg swallowed hard. "I did."

"Then you're a fool. But I shall deal with you in a moment. Algernon?"

Algie stepped forward. "Yes, my sweet?"

"Don't try and charm me, husband. How is it that you kept such momentous events a secret all this time? Did you ever intend to tell me?"

"I *intended* to . . ."

Penelope waited, but although Algie's mouth moved, no other words were forthcoming. "Humph," she said. "It's obvious to me that you had no intention of saying anything about this."

"Now, Pen—"

Penelope held up a hand, and Algie fell silent. "We shall discuss this later in private, Algernon. Lord Rathmore, though I am very disappointed in what I have heard here today, I commend you on being willing to make things right. I will ask you to take your leave now. We will summon you if we need you."

Even a man as bold as Lord Rathmore didn't argue with Penelope when she was in her high ropes.

"As you wish, my lady." Rathmore bowed, then looked at Algie. "I trust the challenge is rescinded, Knightsbridge?"

Algie nodded stiffly.

"Good day, my lord," Penelope said pointedly.

Rathmore bowed again, then quit the room.

"Algernon," Penelope said, "please excuse us. I would like to talk to Meg alone."

"Of course, my dear." Looking somewhat like a man who had narrowly escaped execution, he quickly fled the room.

Meg found herself facing a fiercely angry and disappointed Penelope.

"Well, Meg, you've certainly made a muddle of things, haven't you?"

Meg gathered her dignity around her. "I never intended to cause so much trouble. All I want is to choose when I shall wed and whom."

"I'm afraid you no longer have that luxury." Penelope shook her head. "Dear heavens, girl, you have been *compromised*. And the man who dishonored you is more than willing to come up to scratch, and you *refuse* him?"

"I'm not ready for marriage."

Penelope's blue eyes grew huge, and her perfect nostrils flared. "*You're not ready for marriage? That's* your reason for disgracing yourself?"

"Well . . . yes."

Penelope pointed to the sofa. "Sit."

Meg sat.

Penelope sat down across from her and folded her hands in her lap. "Since your mother has passed on to her reward and neither Lady Agatha nor your new sister-in-law is here, it falls to me as your nearest female relative to advise you." She gave Meg a look of great gravity. "You must marry Lord Rathmore. There is nothing else to do."

"No!" Meg leaped to her feet. "I'm tired of people telling me what I must do. All my life, other people have made the decisions for me. Well, this time, *I'm* making the decision. And I say I'm not ready for marriage."

"But you are ruined. Do you have any idea what would happen to you if word of this got out? The mortification that would be suffered by your entire family, especially your grandfather? You would be completely ostracized, and not even your connection to the duke could save you." She gasped. "Good heavens, does the duke know?"

Meg shook her head. "I convinced Algie not to tell him. I'm worried the news might bring on another attack."

"And so it might. Yet another thing that lays fully at your door, my girl."

Melancholy weighed on her. "I know."

Penelope sighed. "I cannot fathom that this has even happened. Do you know, you seemed so taken with Lord Rathmore at my wedding, I deliberately left you free to socialize with him. And I continued to do so because I thought perhaps you wanted to marry the man but knew that his reputation would give your grandfather pause about granting his permission." She gave Meg a brittle smile. "I thought that you cared for Lord Rathmore."

"I do care for him."

"Then why have you cast his honor back in his face?" Penelope cried, throwing her hands up.

"Oh, dear, I never thought of it like that. The whole situation has gotten rather complicated."

Penelope leaned forward. "Tell me, Meg. Perhaps I can help."

Those words, uttered in such a maternal tone, stirred emotions that Meg hadn't felt since her mother died.

"Oh, Penelope," she said, sinking down on the sofa again. "It's such a coil!"

Penelope laid her hand over Meg's. "Tell me what's troubling you, Meg, because this is a very serious situation in which you find yourself."

"I didn't realize *how* serious until just now."

"Yes, I can see you didn't realize how what you've done will hurt the people you love."

"I never meant to hurt anyone," Meg whispered. "I only wanted to protect myself."

"The best thing you can do is to accept Lord Rathmore's proposal."

"The house party will prove his innocence. Then we won't have to wed."

Penelope stared at her, aghast. "My dear girl, that's not the way it works at all. Rathmore has ruined you. Even though it's not common knowledge, what's done is done." She leaned forward to emphasize her point, blushing as she addressed the intimate topic. "Men expect their brides to be innocent, Meg. A woman's purity is the most important thing she can bring to a marriage. Without it, the union starts with distrust. You have given your innocence to Lord Rathmore, and now your value as a potential wife has substantially lessened."

"I'm not some piece of livestock!" Meg exclaimed, her face reddening at Penelope's bluntness. "The man I marry has to want more than that."

"You may not like it, but the English aristocracy has much in common with livestock when it comes to marriage. One must marry suitably and bring to the union a genealogy that has value to one's husband. One must also try whenever possible to marry above oneself and advance one's family line into the higher echelons of society."

"What if one wants to marry for love?" Meg asked sarcastically.

Penelope gave her a pitying look. "Not everyone can marry for love, and the granddaughter of a duke is no exception. Apparently you and Lord Rathmore are compatible in . . . certain aspects of marriage. Chances are you will be very happy wed to him."

"I won't be forced into marriage," Meg said. "I want more than to advance my genealogy higher up the social ladder."

Penelope's face darkened. "You haven't heard a word that I've said, have you?"

"I'm sorry, Penelope, but I'm an American. Perhaps we look at things differently than the English do."

"Of that I have no doubt." Penelope stood, smoothing her skirt with her hands. "You do realize that if we were not related, I would be forced to cut you now that I know you have been disgraced?"

Meg paled. "It's a good thing that we're related, then."

"A very good thing." Penelope paused. "You know, Meg, you're very adamant about remaining unwed. Is it really marriage that repels you? Or is it something else, something you're afraid to even admit to yourself? What is it that you really want?"

Meg opened her mouth, but then she realized that she had no answer.

"Think about it. Now if you excuse me, I have some plans to finalize for the house party." Penelope turned and left the room.

Meg watched her go, feeling more lost than she ever had in her life.

Was she wrong to want more than a tame union of bloodlines? To want respect and partnership? To be able to meet her mate on equal terms as a person in her own right?

From the English standpoint, apparently it was

very wrong. Penelope was angry with her, as was Algie. And Rathmore?

She sighed. Rathmore was persistent. And hard to resist.

She loved him. She knew that she loved him; it was not a secret she hid from herself like a heroine in a novel. Penelope was wrong. She wasn't deceiving herself. She was just being realistic.

Rathmore liked her. He desired her. But love? No.

And it would take a man who loved her to appreciate the person she was trying to become. She could accept nothing less.

Chapter 20

~~~◦◦◦~~~

The house party thrown by the Earl and Countess of Knightsbridge was the most talked about event in Devon. All the patronesses of the Friday night assemblies put their heads together and discussed the first house party thrown by Lord and Lady Knightsbridge.

Meg dressed for dinner with a feeling of trepidation. The guests had arrived throughout the day and had either retired to their rooms to rest or taken part in other pursuits. She wondered what was going to happen when everyone assembled in the drawing room recognized the significance of the gathering.

There was only one way to find out.

Dressed in white satin, with pearls in her hair and around her throat, Meg looked like a young Diana as she entered the drawing room. At most affairs conversation would be humming along, but in this case the occupants of the room remained eerily silent. They glanced at one another from the corners of their eyes, murmuring to one another behind frantically fluttering fans.

As she made her way to Algie and Penelope, she glanced around the room. Lord and Lady Aggerly were present. No doubt the couple's carriage had dug new ruts in the road from the speed with which they had rushed to attend—especially since Algie had cut them socially at Lady Denniston's ball.

Lord Fenton was also in attendance. She stayed on the opposite side of the room from him. She still hadn't forgotten his strange warning to her at the Friday night assembly.

And there was Mrs. Imogene Warington, the blond-haired woman with the amazingly large bosom whom Rathmore had danced with at the assembly. Though Rathmore had explained to Meg that he had merely been trying to question Mrs. Warington about Ophelia's death, Meg couldn't help but notice that the woman had watched Rathmore the whole time like a starving cat eyeing a bowl of cream.

There were other people there: a thin, older man who had the look of an outdoorsman about him; two society matrons whom she didn't know; a balding, pudgy older man; and a young dark-haired woman with a man who seemed to be her husband.

Penelope introduced her to all of them. The outdoorsman proved to be Sir Charles Wraxton, an old friend and hunting partner of the late Earl of Rathmore. The two society matrons were Lady Tilton and the widowed Lady Alston, who was the longtime amour of Sir Charles. The balding man was Lord Tilton, and the young woman with her husband was Lady Nussburton, daughter of Lord and Lady Tilton.

There were some guests from the original house party who weren't present, such as Miss Eugenia Minor, the elderly aunt of Lord Fenton who had acted as chaperone for his sister at the time. Miss Minor had caught a chill two years before and passed away in her sleep. The others who were missing were the late earl and Desmond St. James.

And, of course, Ophelia.

The clock struck four, and the guests looked up expectantly as a gong sounded throughout the house, indicating that dinner was served. As they gathered themselves together to proceed down to dinner, the door to the drawing room opened, and the last guest was announced.

"The Earl of Rathmore!"

A collective gasp sounded throughout the room as Rathmore strode into the drawing room. He paused in the doorway, looking dangerously handsome in his black evening clothes, and moved his gaze slowly from one person to the next. His flat, black-eyed stare unnerved even Meg, though the look he gave her was considerably warmer than the one he bestowed on the guests. Then with a nod to the assembled company, he moved forward to greet his host and hostess.

"I say, what's going on here?" Lord Aggerly demanded. "What's Rathmore doing here?"

Algie stared the man down. "Perhaps you have forgotten that Lord Rathmore is a particular friend of mine, Aggerly."

Aggerly flushed and backed away.

"I'd like to know the answer to that as well," Lord Tilton demanded. "Havey-cavey, the whole situation."

Rathmore glanced around the room. "You are all here to help solve a mystery," he said with a small smile. "Before this party is over, we will have discovered who *really* killed Ophelia Haversham."

"It's all a hum!" Sir Charles declared, his thin face flushed with anger. "We all know who it was."

Rathmore gave Sir Charles one of his long, unblinking stares. "Do we, now?" he murmured.

Sir Charles grew redder and looked away, muttering to himself.

"I don't like the looks of it," Lady Tilton declared. "Edward, do summon our coach. We're leaving."

"But you can't leave," Penelope said in dulcet tones. "We need everyone's help to unveil the true killer."

"We're leaving, too," Lady Nussburton said, following the actions of her mother. "How dare you summon us under false pretenses?"

"Should have known it was too good to be true," Mrs. Warington said with a disappointed pout in Rathmore's direction. "I'll be calling up my carriage, of course."

Lady Aggerly stood. "We're leaving, too. Come along, Robert. It's not to be borne!"

"Do something," Algie hissed to Rathmore.

Lord Fenton rose from his seat on the sofa. "My dear lords and ladies," he said with a charming smile, "pray at least stay for dinner."

"Lord Fenton," Lady Alston said, her notoriously soft voice barely audible in the room, "it seems to me that you most of all should be offended at this heinous drama."

"How so?" Fenton asked. "Because it was my sister who was the innocent victim in all of this? I can't say that I blame Rathmore for wanting to shed himself of the shadows that have lingered over him these past six years. In fact, this little tableau is clever in the extreme. How better to clear his reputation than to convince the very people who were present at the original party that he is innocent?"

"So you believe him innocent, do you?" Sir Charles demanded.

Fenton smiled. "I never said that."

"Enough of this," Meg said. "Lord Fenton, you are not helping matters."

"And why should I?" he asked. "It was my sister who died, and while much of it was her own doing, she was still unfairly cut down in the flower of her youth. I have forgiven Rathmore, for I am certain the whole thing was an accident. But I cannot allow him to completely absolve himself of blame."

"I didn't kill Ophelia," Rathmore said. "And no one is leaving this house until we discover who did."

"Are you accusing one of *us*?" Lord Tilton demanded. "The cheek! We don't have to listen to this another minute. Come, Lucretia."

Lord and Lady Tilton headed up the line of guests who began to make their way toward the door. Meg looked helplessly at Rathmore, whose grim expression broke her heart.

Algie looked astonished. "Can't say anyone's ever walked out on a Knightsbridge party."

"Stop them, Algernon!" Penelope whispered.

Algie spread his hands. "How? Can't trip them and tie them to the chairs."

Just before the first of the guests could exit the room, the door opened and the butler intoned, "The Duke of Raynewood and the dowager Countess of Millington!"

"Grandfather!" Meg exclaimed.

The duke appeared in the doorway and eyed the exiting guests with haughty disdain. "Good evening."

The Tiltons halted, uncertainty flickering across their faces.

"Dinner is served," the duke noted as the dinner gong sounded again. "I assume that's where you were all going?"

Lady Tilton pasted a huge smile on her face. "Why yes, Your Grace." Murmurs of assent came from the rest of the guests.

"I thought so. Now, I'd like to greet my hosts and my granddaughter and Lord Rathmore. In private, if you will."

The guests filed out, all talk of leaving forgotten. When the last of them had cleared the door, the duke shut it behind them and turned to face the people left in the room. "Now would someone kindly explain to me what the devil is going on here?"

The duke glared down his aristocratic nose at the four of them, black eyes glittering with arrogance, skin flushed with good health. He looked, Meg thought, simply *marvelous*. She flew to him and threw herself into his arms. "Grandfather, I'm so happy to see you!"

The duke patted her back awkwardly. "There, there, child."

"Grandmother," Algie said, coming forward to kiss Lady Agatha's cheek. "It's lovely to see you. Wonderful timing, actually. How ever did you come to be here?"

"An excellent question," Rathmore said, his tone loaded with innuendo. He looked pointedly at Algie.

"What?" Algie said. "You don't think *I* summoned them?"

"And what if he did?" the duke demanded. "Is there something wrong with that, Rathmore?"

Rathmore stiffened at the autocratic tone of the

duke's voice. "Not at all, Your Grace."

"He didn't summon them," Penelope said. "I did."

"You?" Meg turned to face Penelope.

"We needed the duke's help. And he needed to know what was happening."

"Bloody right, I needed to know what was happening." The duke turned a stern face to Meg. "You, miss, have much to explain."

Meg paled.

"Pen, how could you?" Algie groaned.

"How could I . . . what?" Penelope replied. "How could I write to the duke and tell him that Lord Rathmore has declared his intention of offering for Meg? That we have staged this elaborate drama to prove Lord Rathmore's innocence in order to make his suit more amenable to Meg's grandfather?"

Meg, Rathmore, and Algie stared at Penelope in amazement.

"Yes," Algie said finally, his voice barely a whisper. "Of course. I just wish you had told me you had sent for him."

Penelope gave Algie a meaningful look. "I wish you had told me some things as well."

Algie reddened. "Yes, well . . ."

The duke fixed his fierce gaze on Rathmore. "I trust we will speak after this business is done."

Rathmore nodded. "Yes, Your Grace."

Meg stood rooted to the spot. Penelope had summoned her grandfather, who seemed in favor of Rathmore's suit! And while the duke apparently knew nothing of her disgrace, his intervention meant that Rathmore's offer would be taken seriously.

Part of her was thrilled, and the other part of her felt as if the walls were closing in on her.

"Tomorrow I shall begin interviewing the guests," the duke declared. "I'll get to the bottom of this business, to be sure."

"You, Grandfather?" Meg asked. "Do you think that's wise? You must think of your health."

"Wise or not, this lot won't tell a thing to Knightsbridge or Rathmore. But they'll talk to me, by God, or I'll ruin each and every one of them socially." He patted her hand. "Have no fear, Margaret. We'll prove the boy's innocence."

Meg blinked in amazement that anyone could refer to Rathmore as a boy, but she wisely said nothing. If the duke was willing to stand behind Rathmore, it would go a long way toward influencing the *ton* to forget the dreadful rumors.

And once Rathmore's reputation was restored, she could refuse his suit once and for all without fear of damning him and Emily to a lifetime of ostracism.

Again she felt a twinge of dismay at the thought of sending Rathmore on his way, but the fear inside her would not allow her to do otherwise. She couldn't take the chance of marrying a man who didn't understand her. Didn't love her.

"Well then," Penelope said. "Shall we go in to

dinner? I'm certain our guests are waiting."

"They'd better be, if they know what's good for them," the duke grumbled. He offered his arm to Meg.

Rathmore bowed to Lady Agatha. "May I have the pleasure of escorting you to dinner, my lady?"

Lady Agatha laughed. "You may, you handsome scoundrel. Be glad I'm not twenty years younger."

"Ten," Rathmore countered.

Lady Agatha laughed again and placed her hand on his arm. "Flatterer."

Algie offered his arm to his wife, and the party made their way to dinner.

Dinner was a strange affair, oddly silent with bursts of overly hearty conversation from the unnerved guests. It was no surprise to anyone that there was no lingering in the drawing room afterward for cards and musical entertainment. Everyone went up to bed rather early, unsettled by the events of the day.

Meg had every intention of retiring, but she had been thinking about Emily and wondering how the little girl was feeling after her illness. Before she undressed for the evening, she made her way down to Emily's room to check on her.

She cracked open the girl's bedroom door. Emily lay sleeping soundly, her chest rising and falling with the soft breathing of slumber. A movement in the darkness drew Meg's attention, and she noticed

Pudding raise his head from where he lay curled up in Emily's arms.

Meg smiled. "Guard her well, Pudding," she whispered, then quietly backed out of the room and closed the door behind her. She turned to go back to her own room and cried out as a shadow detached itself from the wall.

"Hush," Rathmore said, laying a finger across her lips. "I have no desire to meet Knightsbridge for a dawn appointment."

Meg pushed his hand away, her heart pounding. "You scared me to death! What are you doing lurking in the hallway?"

"I was going to check on my ward, but I saw someone had gotten there before me." His lips thinned. "I was about to charge into the room when you came out. I had no idea who was in there."

"Then we've both had a fright today," she said.

"Indeed."

An uncomfortable silence fell. The hallway seemed very dark all of a sudden, and very isolated. Quiet had descended over the sleeping household, and Meg was suddenly aware that she was very much alone with Rathmore.

Dangerous.

"Well, my lord, I must return to my room," she said with forced cheer. "I do hope you sleep well."

"Wait a minute," he said, taking her arm. "This is the first private moment we've had where we'll not be interrupted."

"As it has been pointed out to me, my lord, private moments with you are not allowed."

"Will you *stop* calling me 'my lord' like that?" he snapped.

"It's your proper title."

"You used to call me Justin."

She shook her head slowly. "I'm trying to do what's right. And it's not right to address you by your given name."

"You are the veriest hypocrite," he growled in a sudden burst of temper. "You make love with me and then refuse my offer of marriage, but now you're hiding behind the proprieties?"

"I'm not *hiding*! I just don't want to make things worse."

"What can be worse than this? I've dishonored you, and you refuse to wed me. Penelope knows what happened and has summoned the duke. Knightsbridge has challenged me to a duel—"

"He rescinded it!"

"—and on top of everything else, one of the people in this house is most probably a murderer."

"Will you stop preaching about honor?" Meg hissed. "Do you think *honor* has anything to do with why I should wed you?"

"At the moment, it's a most compelling reason."

"Not to me." She pointed to herself. "I'm American. Stop expecting me to act like a typical English girl!"

"Believe me, Meg, there is nothing typical about you."

From the way he said it, Meg could tell he didn't mean it as a compliment.

"If I were English," she said, "then I would no doubt be thrilled to accept your offer of marriage. But we do things differently in America. Marriage is about love and common interests, not about rules and honor."

"We have common interests. Emily, for one."

She shook her head. "You don't understand. In England, marriage is about breeding. It's a game of matchmaking where money counts and people compete for which bloodlines will best enhance their own."

"There's nothing wrong with that. The English peerage has been following that guideline for hundreds of years."

"But I don't want to be an English wife!" With effort, she lowered her voice. "I've watched the married couples in England be unfaithful to each other. Use each other. I've seen the way English lords leave their wives to rusticate in the country while they whore their way through London, and I tell you, Justin, *I will not be left ever again!*" Her voice broke.

Rathmore reached out to take her by the shoulders. "Meg," he murmured, "I could never leave you anywhere. I need you too much."

She sniffled. Tears welled up as emotions she had hidden for so long raged up and made themselves felt.

"I need you," he repeated.

"For Emily," she whispered.

"No. For me." He touched a hand to her chin, urging her to look at him. "I need you for me, Meg. I need your smile and your laughter. You make people feel good. They love to be around you."

"Then why has everyone always left?"

"I'm not going anywhere." He pulled her into his arms, holding her tenderly. "Is this what you've been trying to do, prepare yourself for being left behind again?"

"Perhaps." She snuggled into his embrace, taking comfort just for one moment. "I just wanted to have something in my life for me, like everyone else has. I wanted to have some purpose, some talent."

"You do have talent. And I'm not just referring to your artwork." He dipped his head closer to her ear. "Meg, don't you realize what your true gift is? It's not painting or singing or gardening or any of those pastimes. Your talent lies with people, Meg. You have a knack for seeing a person's innermost desires and helping that person fulfill them."

"I do?" She glanced up at him, rocked to her soul that such a notion could be true.

"Of course you do. Look how you brought about the reconciliation of your brother and grandfather. I heard they were barely speaking when your brother first came to England."

"True."

"And look what you've done for me," he

pointed out. "And for Emily. We can talk now, where before we always argued."

"That was just a simple matter of communication."

"But don't you see, Meg? That's what you're good at, getting people to communicate. Why if you were a man, you'd make an excellent diplomat."

"Perhaps."

"Don't be afraid." He took her face in his hands. "Marry me, Meg."

"I'm not afraid." She pulled free of him. "I just want more than honor as a reason to wed."

"What more do you want? My honor is all I have to offer."

"I know," she whispered sadly.

"Why do you continue to be so stubborn? Have you given a thought to the fact that you might be carrying my heir?"

"The chances of that are unlikely."

"But there is a chance." He regarded her with bleak disappointment. "I've tried everything I can think of to convince you to do the right thing. I just don't understand why you're being so childish."

"Childish! It seems to me it would be more childish to marry without thinking the matter through rather than waiting as I have chosen to do. I will marry when *I* choose, Justin, and not before."

"I believe you," he said. "Unfortunately, your willfulness is hurting the people you love."

"You exaggerate," she scoffed, yet she was deathly afraid it was true.

"You're like a little girl who's afraid of shadows," he said, pity heavy in his voice. "Light a candle, Meg. Face your responsibilities. See what's *really* happening around you. And then tell me that you're doing the right thing."

He turned away and left her standing in the dark, with only her fears to comfort her.

Was she acting like a child?

She couldn't get the idea out of her head. Was she really refusing to marry because she was afraid of getting hurt? Of being left alone?

She had thought she wanted a hobby to retain her individuality in the face of marriage. Yet was that truly the reason? Perhaps she wanted something else. Comfort, maybe.

Something to turn to when the inevitable happened, and she was left behind again.

A soft sob escaped her lips as she forced herself to consider Rathmore's words. How was she hurting the people she loved by trying to remain firm in her decision to marry for more than social consequence?

That alone wasn't hurting anyone . . . but the situation had changed when she and Rathmore made love.

That's what was causing the trouble, she realized. Algie was angry with her. Penelope was disappointed and had even said that only their family connection prevented her from cutting Meg completely. Rathmore was hurt that she kept tossing his honorable intentions back in his face.

And it went on and on. Rathmore and Algie's

friendship was on the brink of destruction over the incident. Penelope was furious with Algie for keeping the scandal a secret. And now Penelope had involved the duke, who knew nothing about their lovemaking and was helping Rathmore only because he believed Meg wanted to marry him.

All she had to do was agree to marry Rathmore, and everyone would be happy again.

And yet if the marriage didn't work, if he left her as she expected him to do, it would devastate her.

Not that he would ever leave her permanently, oh no. But the English peerage had a distressing tendency to live lives separate from their spouses. That wasn't a marriage, it was a living arrangement. And she wanted more.

She loved Rathmore. She knew it, had known it for a long time. And while she wanted nothing more than to become his wife, she didn't dare. What if he tired of her? Banished her to the country while he pursued his fashionable life in London?

Then again, what if he didn't?

The thought was new and cut through the childish fears that gripped her. Having constantly been left behind with her mother as her brother went on his sea voyages, Meg had always longed for him to return, for him to stay home for good. She didn't want to be longing for Rathmore to come home to her.

Was she being selfish? Face your responsibilities, he had said. See what's really happening around you.

She had willingly given her innocence to Rathmore because she had wanted to be with him. While she didn't regret the act, she did regret the consequences.

Algie had walked in on them, which put a serious rift in his friendship with Rathmore. He had seemed mollified by Rathmore's willingness to wed her, however.

And Algie was upset with *her* both for succumbing to Rathmore's charms and for refusing Rathmore's offer. He had agreed to the house party only because he hoped the duke might be able to convince her to wed Rathmore once his reputation had been restored. As he was a properly raised Englishman, Meg could only surmise that Algie was horrified by her actions, and mortification washed over her as she considered the situation from his point of view.

How would she feel if a young girl she cared about took it into her head to commit social suicide by giving herself to a man outside wedlock and then refusing to wed him?

Angry. Frustrated. Helpless.

Meg began to feel ashamed. How could she have done that to poor Algie?

And Penelope. She winced as she remembered their conversation. Penelope was so disappointed in her. Meg had been truly shaken by the knowledge that only the family connection kept Penelope from shunning her. No doubt her behavior was shocking and dishonorable to Penelope, too.

Meg didn't think she had ever seen the newlyweds argue, but now Penelope was put out with Al gie for keeping the scandal a secret from his ow wife. Another relationship damaged.

The situation was grave indeed, which was wh Penelope had summoned the duke. Out of all o them, only Penelope had realized that they woul need the duke's influence to get out of this scanda broth with their reputations intact.

Especially Rathmore.

Here was a man whose honor was in question b most of society, yet she had found him to be honor able almost to a fault. He was more upset by thei lapse than she was, and he had offered for her agai and again, coming back after each rejection. H wanted to do the right thing. He had offered her hi name and his protection, however dented and tar nished they were, and she had thrown both back i his face.

Good Lord, how must that have affected him He was so proud and so determined to restore hi good name. He wanted the best of futures fo Emily, and yet Meg had carelessly taken what littl social credibility he had left and nearly ruined i with her continued refusal of what was really a ver honorable offer.

And all because she was afraid of being left be hind?

Good heavens, she *had* been acting like a child Her fears had twisted the situation into a terribl knot, pitting all the people she loved against eac other. How could she possibly make it right?

The answer was simple. All she had to do was say yes.

She loved Rathmore, didn't she? And even if he didn't love her, he *liked* her, and he even liked her paintings! Being liked by one's husband might even be more important than having him besotted with her. After all, beauty faded, and when they were doddering ancients, she'd rather have him laugh at her jokes than mourn the loss of her looks.

Besides, she already knew that theirs would be a passionate union. Perhaps she had enough love for the both of them.

And then there was Emily. She really didn't mind being a mother to the girl, having already formed a bond with her. And if her social position helped to dispel the shadow of dishonor around Rathmore, so much the better!

Why had she been so afraid of this? It was everything she wanted. All she had to do was reach out and touch it.

Then a scream rent the night, jerking Meg from her thoughts with frightening force. Terror shot through her.

The scream had come from Emily's room.

Chapter 21

❦

Doors opened all the way down the hall. Voices babbled in confusion.

Meg burst into Emily's room.

The child sat up in bed, clutching Pudding and shaking with terror.

"What happened?" Meg demanded. "Are you hurt?"

"N-no," the girl answered. "It was that dream. That *horrible, awful* dream!"

Meg sat on the edge of the bed. "The same nightmare?"

Emily nodded.

"What the devil happened?" Algie appeared in the doorway with Sir Charles just behind him.

"Did someone scream?" Lady Nussburton popped into view, her hand at her throat.

"Emily had a nightmare," Meg explained.

"Is that all?" Algie sighed with relief. "I was afraid someone was hurt."

"Or killed," Sir Charles added.

Lady Nussburton gasped. "Really, Sir Charles!"

"Nothing to worry about," Algie reassured her. "Just Emily having a bad dream."

"How reassuring." Lady Nussburton folded her arms across her chest. "Now *who* is Emily?"

"Rathmore's ward," Algie replied.

And then Rathmore was there, pushing through the crowd in the doorway.

"Emily," he said, making it into the room, "are you all right?"

"Cousin Justin!" she cried and held out her arms to him.

Meg rose, and Rathmore took her place on the edge of the bed and wrapped the girl in his arms.

Meg went to the door as Rathmore murmured reassurances to his ward. "Urge everyone to return to their rooms," she said quietly to Algie. "Let them have some privacy."

"Of course," Algie said. "Just the thing."

As Algie ushered the guests from the room Meg turned back to Rathmore and Emily. She busied herself lighting the candles and chasing the shadows from the chamber.

"What happened in the dream, poppet?" Rathmore asked, stroking her hair.

"It's always the same," Emily sniffled. "Horrible!"

Meg opened her mouth to speak, then hesitated,

but Emily had seen the movement. Both she and Rathmore looked at Meg.

"Yes, Meg?" Rathmore asked.

"I only wanted to say that very often talking about your fears can make them go away."

"Really?" His brows rose in mocking reminder of their earlier conversation.

"Yes, really." She cleared her throat and focused on Emily. "Perhaps if you tell us about the dream, it won't be so scary anymore."

"I . . . I don't know."

"It's all right, Emily," Rathmore said. "You don't have to talk about it if you don't want to."

Emily hesitated. "Maybe I should," she said finally. "I'm tired of the dreams, Cousin Justin. I hate being scared to go to sleep."

"All right then." Rathmore signaled to Meg, who came closer. "Tell us about them."

"The dream starts out fine," Emily said, staring off into the distance as if watching something neither of them could see. "I'm home at Rathmore Hall, and I'm walking through all the hallways. I see all the servants, and they all smile at me. And Papa is there, and Grandpapa." She smiled. "I like that part of the dream."

"Go on," Rathmore said, stroking her hair. "You're awake now, so there's no reason to be frightened."

Emily nodded. "I keep wandering through the halls until I come to one that's dark. Everything in this hallway looks funny. The doors are all different shapes and the paintings on the walls are scary-looking. Then the dragon comes."

"A dragon!" Meg remarked. "They can be fearsome."

"This one is gold and he roars with the voice of a man. He's yelling so loudly that I have to cover my ears. And the lady is frightened, too."

Rathmore grew suddenly alert. "What lady?"

"The pretty one with the brown hair. She wears a big emerald ring and even though she's frightened, she yells back at the dragon."

"What does she say?"

"Something about justice."

"Justice?" Rathmore glanced at Meg, who was equally puzzled.

"And the lady tries to give the dragon a star, but he hits her hand, and the star flies through the air. Then the dragon roars really loudly and shoves the lady off the stairs. She keeps falling and falling and her head starts spinning around—" Emily stopped with a sob. "And then the dragon comes down the hall toward me, and I think he's going to throw me down the stairs too, but he doesn't see me, he keeps going past me."

"That *is* a terrifying dream," Rathmore said, his tone thoughtful. "Shall I have one of the maids sleep in here with you tonight?"

Emily thought about it for a moment, then slowly shook her head. "No, I've got Pudding with me. I'll be all right."

"You're certain?"

Emily nodded.

"All right then," Rathmore said. "If you want me, I'm just down the hall."

He stood, and as Emily settled back into her bed, he signaled to Meg that he wanted to talk to her outside in the hallway.

Meg took a moment to tuck the covers in around the child. "Pudding will bite any dragons that come near you," she said with a smile. "Sleep well."

"Good night," Emily whispered.

Rathmore and Meg left the room and paused just outside Emily's door.

"I think Emily saw Ophelia's murder," he said without preamble.

"What!"

He nodded. "I'm almost sure of it. Ophelia had dark hair, and the betrothal ring that Desmond gave her was a gaudy emerald. She never took it off."

"Obviously the dragon must be the murderer," Meg mused. "It sounds like there was some kind of argument and Ophelia got pushed down the stairs."

Rathmore nodded. "And that part about her head spinning around? Her neck was broken."

Meg wrinkled her nose. "Oh, dear."

"But what about justice? And the star? None of that makes sense."

"It's a dream, Justin. Sometimes our imagination takes over in our dreams." Meg snapped her fingers. "Justice? Or *Justin*?"

"You think she was talking about me?"

"Possibly. I heard that your cousin was jealous of you, that Ophelia pursued you."

He looked uncomfortable. "Yes, but I never touched her."

"But Desmond wasn't sure of that. Good heavens, Justin, could *Desmond* be the killer?"

"I don't like to think so, but it's possible. Ophelia was very persistent in her attentions, and maybe she pushed him too far. Maybe they were arguing about me, and it was an accident. I just don't know."

Meg laid her hand on his sleeve. "We'll find out. Together."

He glanced down at her hand, then back to her face. Something in her expression gave him hope. "Meg?"

She knew what he was asking. Taking a deep breath, she said, "Yes, Justin. I'll marry you."

Joy lit his features, and he lifted her up, swinging her in a circle in the hallway while she tried to stifle her giggles. Then he kissed her, devouring her mouth with a hunger that sent her head spinning.

She meant to push him away, to tell him other things. Like they needed her grandfather's permission first. But as her hands came up to flatten on his chest, she found herself pulling him closer instead of pushing him away. Somehow her fingers tangled in his hair and her body pressed into his. His kiss was all heat and hunger, and she ardently responded.

He finally moved his mouth to her throat. "What

made you change your mind?" he murmured against her ear.

"You did." Her eyes slid closed as shivers of desire trickled down her spine. "You were right. I was afraid."

"Don't ever be afraid of me." He raised his head, looked deep into her eyes. "Don't you know I would never leave you? I love you, Meg."

She gaped. "You what?"

"I love you." He caressed her cheek and gave her a wicked smile. "I love your outspoken ways and your American courage. I love the way you make me so angry I can barely speak, and yet get me so aroused it's all I can do not to make love to you."

"Oh, Justin." She threw herself back into his arms. "I love you, too."

"You do?" Amazement crossed his features, to be replaced by great satisfaction. "Did I mention how intelligent you are?"

Meg laughed and hugged him tighter. "I just hope we can get Grandfather to approve the match."

"I think he will." Rathmore stroked a finger down her cheek. "He adores you and will do anything to make you happy."

"I'll speak to him in the morning. He once told me he would let me choose my own husband, as long as that husband has a title or wealth equal to mine."

"I have both."

"I know." She grinned up at him. "You're every

matchmaking mama's dream of the perfect husband."

"Except for the bad reputation."

Her smile faded. "Don't worry about that, Justin. We *will* prove your innocence."

"I hope so." He pulled her into his arms. "For your sake and for Emily's."

"And for our children."

He smiled down at her. "I like the sound of that." He stroked a hand through her hair, his gaze tender as it rested on her face. "I promise never to leave you in the country."

Meg smiled. "I'll hold you to that. And if you forget, I'll follow you to London and remind you. I'm an independent woman, don't forget."

"As if I could." He studied her face, caressed her cheek. Then he gave her a wicked grin. "I shall pay my addresses to your grandfather tomorrow about our wedding, but in the meantime . . ." He bent down and whispered in her ear a suggestion so sinful that she was genuinely shocked.

"Justin! We couldn't!"

"I've already compromised you." Teasingly, he nibbled at her neck. "I might as well do it again."

"I should tell you no."

"You should," he agreed. "But you won't. Because I'm the Devil Earl, and I'm kidnapping you to my bed." With that, he swept her into his arms and carried her down the hall, her giggles muffled against his shoulder.

Deep in the darkness, a shadow stirred.

* * *

Justin followed through with every wicked suggestion he had whispered to her, and then some. And just before dawn, he shook her awake gently.

Meg stretched, purring as the sheets tangled around her naked limbs. She turned on to her back and opened her eyes to see Justin leaning above her, his jaw dark with his morning beard, his brown eyes tender.

"Good morning," he said, pressing a kiss to her lips.

She curled her arm around his neck. "It's not morning yet."

"Good. Then we have some of the night left." He grinned and tugged the sheet down, baring her soft white breasts to his gaze.

"I should go back to my room," she whispered, then gasped as his mouth found her nipple. Her fingers clenched in his hair.

"Do you really want to?" He swirled his tongue around one nipple, then shifted to pay equal attention to its twin.

"I want to stay here with you." She arched her back, letting her legs fall open for the questing hand he slid beneath the sheet. "But we can't. It's almost morning."

"Then I'd better hurry." He peeled back the sheet completely, then went back to stroking the softness between her legs. "Look at that," he murmured. "You're ready for me already."

"I feel like I'm always ready for you." Her pas-

sionate declaration ended on a gasp as he slid inside her.

"Nice and easy," he whispered, starting a slow
and steady rhythm.

"Yes . . . anything." Her eyes closed as the fric-
tion excited her. "Please . . . please, Justin."

"I will please you."

She wrapped her legs around his waist, pulling
him deeper inside her. He groaned and quickened
his thrusts. She could feel the instant his climax
came upon him . . . for he felt even bigger, even
harder, inside her. And that was all it took to send
her senses spinning in ecstasy, his hoarse groan of
release music against her skin as he followed her to
completion.

Much later, she said, "I have to go."

"I'll go with you." He pulled himself into a sitting position with effort. "In a moment."

"I really do need to go. Grandfather doesn't
know about the other time, and I'd like to keep it
that way." She rolled from the bed.

Quietly they both dressed, and then Rathmore
made sure the hallway was clear before they
headed back down toward Meg's room, which was
just past Emily's. They paused outside Meg's door
for a last lingering kiss. "It seems like forever until I
can have you in my arms again," he murmured.

She wrapped her arms around his neck and
smiled seductively. "You could always come inside
with me."

"As much as I would like to—"

A furious barking shattered the peace of the night.

"What the hell . . . ?" Rathmore pulled out of her arms. "That came from Emily's room."

Then a scream rent the air, and Rathmore raced toward his ward's bedroom, Meg at his heels.

The terrified girl huddled in the corner of the bed, a snarling Pudding cradled in her arms. And a man stood over her bed, a pillow in his hands. He uttered a loud curse as the door opened.

Rathmore charged into the room and tackled the dark shadow.

The instant the two men rolled out of her path, Emily darted from the bed and ran to Meg in the hall.

Rathmore continued to wrestle with the man who meant Emily harm, but the fellow was quick. He managed to leap to his feet while Rathmore was still down and ran for the door.

Meg got a good look at his face. "Lord Fenton!"

"Out of my way!" Fenton bellowed, shoving them aside.

Emily's face paled. "That's the voice from my dream, Meg!"

"Dear God." Meg held Emily close. Lord Fenton had murdered his own sister? "Stay here," she said, then took off after Fenton.

"Meg, no!" Rathmore cried from behind her, but she paid no heed. Perhaps she could slow him down, delay him. Get the servants to stop him, even.

"Stop, Lord Fenton!" she shouted, increasing her speed.

The villain paused at the top of the stairs, then spun suddenly and charged at her. He caught her with both hands around her arms. "My dear Miss Stanton-Lynch. Didn't I warn you about keeping company with Lord Rathmore?"

"What were you doing in Emily's room?"

A secretive smile played about his lips. "You know exactly what I was doing. I heard the girl talking to you and Rathmore before. I know what she saw."

Meg's stomach lurched. "You were going to kill her?"

He leaned in until they were practically nose to nose. "No witnesses," he intoned, then flung her toward the stairs.

Meg screamed as she took flight. The ornate staircase of Knightsbridge Chase was one of the house's most beautiful features—and made completely of marble. Her hip hit one of the stairs with a painful thud, but she managed to grab the handrail before she went all the way down. Pulling herself to her feet, she teetered precariously on the step. Then Fenton reached over and grabbed her by the front of her skirt, yanking her off balance again. She twirled her hands helplessly in the air, but she was completely dependent on him to keep from falling.

"She wanted Justin, you know," he told her. "I got her Desmond. I got her a title and wealth, but all she wanted was a handsome lover in her bed."

"Don't do it, Fenton!" Rathmore demanded,

reaching them at last. Emily trotted up behind him
Pudding in her arms.

"Stay back." Fenton gave Meg a shake, and she
let out a squeak of distress. "If you come anywhere
near me, I'll let go."

"Why did you do it, Fenton?" Rathmore asked.
Behind him, the various guests had emerged from
their rooms to watch the drama unfolding before
them. "Why did you kill Ophelia?"

A collective gasp came from the crowd, but
Rathmore never took his eyes from Fenton.

Fenton glanced at the group of peers and gave
them a cherubic smile. "It was an accident," he
said. "We quarreled. She wanted to be Justin's
lover, and I wanted her to be true to Desmond, at
least until she had borne him an heir. She wanted
both. She thought to bribe me and gave me a dia-
mond stickpin, but I wouldn't accept it."

"The star," Emily whispered.

Unsteadily Meg stretched for the handrail.

"Why did you kill her?" Rathmore asked.

"I told you, it was an accident!" Fenton snarled.
"When she told me she wanted to be your lover
even if she lost Desmond, we argued. She screeched
at me, and I pushed her, and she fell down the
stairs. And then she was dead."

The duke pushed his way to the front of the
crowd. "Fenton!" he barked. "Release my granddaughter at once!"

"I don't think you want me to do that," Fenton
said. "Unless you want her to fall."

Rathmore caught Meg's eye. She nodded and stretched those last few inches to clasp the railing tightly.

"So, Fenton, you've played the grieving brother all these years and watched me take the blame for something *you* did."

Fenton chuckled. "I *was* grieving. If my light-skirt of a sister hadn't been so eager to get into your bed, we would have been rich. She would have been a rich widow now, and perhaps would have even borne Desmond an heir."

"So you were grieving for the money."

Fenton gave a little chuckle. "Certainly not for Ophelia."

"You're ruined, Fenton," the duke said.

"How do you expect to escape?" Rathmore asked. "You can't hold Meg there all day. And if you let go of her, I'll hunt you to the ends of the earth."

"Such a quandary," Fenton mocked. "If your lady lies broken at the bottom of the steps, I can guarantee that you'll not be thinking about following me."

"You've caused me enough grief, Fenton. I don't intend to let you cause any more."

"Brave words," Fenton taunted.

Suddenly Emily cried, "Pudding, attack!" and released the little dog. Growling, Pudding charged at Fenton, whose expression comically changed to one of alarm.

Pudding leaped—

Fenton held up his hands to ward off the attack.

Rathmore jumped after Meg and caught her skirt in his hand to pull her to safety.

Pudding's momentum shoved Fenton down the stairs, and the little dog landed near the top of the staircase, only slipping down a step or two.

Fenton tumbled straight down, landing hard at the bottom with a shout of pain, his leg at an awkward angle.

As Knightsbridge and Lord Tilton went down to see to the howling Lord Fenton, Rathmore helped Meg to the top of the stairs, then took her in his arms, hugging her tightly. "I thought I had lost you."

The unsubtle clearing of a throat made Rathmore look up. The Duke of Raynewood was staring at him.

"May I assume that you have something to say to me, young man?"

Rathmore reluctantly released Meg. "I do, Your Grace."

"I thought so." The duke looked at Meg. "Is this what you want, my dear?"

"Oh, yes, Grandfather!" Meg kissed the old man on the cheek.

"Very well." The duke turned his gaze back on Rathmore. "I shall meet with you later this morning at eleven o'clock in Knightsbridge's study. Don't be late."

"I won't, Your Grace." He grinned down at Meg. "I have every intention of making this woman my wife as expediently as possible."

"Finally," Meg said with a grin.

"Forever," Rathmore said.

"It's about time," Emily grumbled, then went to fetch Pudding.

Epilogue

Rathmore Hall, Devon
One year later

"**F**ascinating."
          "Quite . . . colorful."
"Yes, interesting."

Rathmore smiled as he listened to his guests' comments about Meg's paintings. They had decided to have a dinner party at their London home to show off Meg's recent works. In the months since their wedding, she had taken to her art like a zealot, pausing only to spend time with Emily or to make love with him. They'd hardly attended any social functions at all.

Not that he was complaining.

He studied one of the works displayed on the wall of the drawing room, a clashing harmony of reds and yellows and greens with smears of deep blue shadowing the brighter colors. He remembered watching her paint it.

Naked.

After they had made love on their wedding night. It was still his favorite of her works.

"Can't say as I understand it." Meg's brother, Garrett, Marquess of Kelton, came to stand beside Rathmore and perused the painting. "It doesn't look like anything. It's just . . . somehow . . . Meg."

Rathmore nodded. "Exactly."

Garrett grinned and feigned disappointment. "Well, seeing as she's your wife, you're the lucky fellow who gets to hang these paintings in your home. Darn."

Rathmore raised his brows at his brother-in-law. "Actually, I do believe Meg gifted Lucinda with one of them this morning. For the baby."

Garrett winced. "Young William will go blind."

Rathmore roared with laughter.

Hearing his booming laugh from where she stood across the room with her sister-in-law Lucinda and Emily, Meg couldn't help but smile. As the months had gone by, Justin had laughed more frequently than ever. Gone was the Devil Earl and his brooding temper. In his place was a handsome, charming man who smiled easily and devoted himself to his family.

Lucinda glanced over at the two men and then smiled at Meg. "You chose well, Meg. He'll make a wonderful father."

Meg grinned back and laid one hand on her still flat belly, the other on Emily's shoulder. "He already is."

She caught Rathmore's eye across the room and smiled at him. He smiled back, his dark eyes warm with love and desire. Then a wicked look came over his face.

"Ladies and gentlemen," he called out. "I would like to salute the talented artist of the works you see displayed here tonight—my wife, Lady Rathmore."

The thunderous applause brought a blush to Meg's cheeks, even as her heart swelled with pleasure at the pride on her husband's face.

It looked as if she had won, after all.

Discover Contemporary Romances at Their Sizzling Hot Best from Avon Books

THE DIXIE BELLE'S
GUIDE TO LOVE   by Luanne Jones
0-380-81934-1/$5.99 US/$7.99 Can

TAKE ME, I'M YOURS   by Elizabeth Bevarly
0-380-81960-0/$5.99 US/$7.99 Can

MY ONE AND ONLY   by MacKenzie Taylor
0-380-81937-6/$5.99 US/$7.99 Can

TANGLED UP IN LOVE   by Hailey North
0-380-82069-2/$5.99 US/$7.99 Can

MAN AT WORK   by Elaine Fox
0-380-81784-5/$5.99 US/$7.99 Can

WHEN NIGHT FALLS   by Cait London
0-06-000180-1/$5.99 US/$7.99 Can

BREAKING ALL THE RULES   by Sue Civil-Brown
0-06-050231-2/$5.99 US/$7.99 Can

GETTING HER MAN   by Michele Alber
0-380-82053-6/$5.99 US/$7.99 Can

I'VE GOT YOU, BABE   by Karen Kendal
0-06-050232-0/$5.99 US/$7.99 Can

RISKY BUSINESS   by Suzanne Macpherson
0-380-82103-6/$5.99 US/$7.99 Can

Have you ever dreamed of writing a romance?

*And have you ever wanted
to get a romance published?*

Perhaps you have always wondered how to
become an Avon romance writer?
We are now seeking the best and brightest undiscovered
voices. We invite you to send us your query letter to
avonromance@harpercollins.com

What do you need to do?

Please send no more than two pages telling us
about your book. We'd like to know its setting—is it
contemporary or historical—and a bit about the hero,
heroine, and what happens to them.

Then, if it is right for Avon we'll ask to see part of the
manuscript. Remember, it's important that you have
material to send, in case we want to see your story quickly.

Of course, there are no guarantees of publication,
but you never know unless you try!

*We know there is new talent just waiting
to be found! Don't hesitate . . . send us
your query letter today.*

*The Editors
Avon Romance*